A KNIGHT FOR
THE RUNAWAY NUN

Carol Townend

MILLS & BOON

First published in Great Britain 2023
by Mills & Boon, an imprint of HarperCollins*Publishers* Ltd,
1 London Bridge Street, London, SE1 9GF

www.harpercollins.co.uk

HarperCollins*Publishers*, Macken House, 39/40 Mayor Street Upper, Dublin 1, D01 C9W8, Ireland

A Knight for the Runaway Nun © 2023 Carol Townend

ISBN: 978-0-263-30524-1

06/23

This book is produced from independently certified FSC™ paper to ensure responsible forest management.
For more information visit: www.harpercollins.co.uk/green.

Printed and Bound in the UK using 100% Renewable Electricity at CPI Group (UK) Ltd, Croydon, CR0 4YY

Carol Townend was born in England and went
to a convent school in the wilds of Yorkshire.
Captivated by the medieval period, Carol read
History at London University. She loves to travel,
drawing inspiration for her novels from places
as diverse as Winchester in England, Istanbul in
Turkey and Troyes in France. A writer of both
fiction and non-fiction, Carol lives in London
with her husband and daughter. Visit her website
at caroltownend.co.uk.

To my daughter Katie, with love.

Chapter One

The Chapter House, Saint Claire's Convent,
Avignon—1342

Lady Bernadette, a small figure in a grey novice's habit and white wimple, hurried in. She had her sewing basket with her, for the light that morning was perfect, and she was determined to make the most of it. The Chapter House was not usually used for sewing, but in this instance, Bernadette knew she would be safe from reproof. Mother Margerie had asked her to embroider an altar cloth for the new Pope and was eager for her to finish it.

Lady Bernadette chose a seat in one of the stalls and put her work basket beside her. Her needle was soon flashing. Deftly, she filled in the petals on the final rose. A distant door slammed. Her needle stilled. Hope flaring, she held her breath and listened. She was expecting a letter from home. Her sister Lady Allis was a diligent correspondent, but it had been a while since Bernadette had heard from her, a letter was overdue. Doubtless, it was a sin for Bernadette to long for her sister's letters, particularly when she would shortly be turning her back on the world outside, but she couldn't help it. She missed her family and loved hearing what everyone was doing.

Regrettably, all Bernadette could hear was quiet. There were no scurrying footsteps, no one calling her name. With a sigh, she squashed her disappointment and bent over the altar cloth. She should be thankful for small mercies. These days, Mother Margerie was allowing her to sew. It hadn't always been like this. When Bernadette had first come to Saint Claire's, Mother Margerie had scowled at her from dawn to dusk. Since their order was largely silent, a scowl went a long way.

Mother Margerie, the head of their order, was a formidable woman and Bernadette's time as a novice was supposed to be testing. Rightly so. Bernadette held back a grimace. She had known what to expect. She had not arrived at Saint Claire's all starry-eyed. Novices were only permitted to take full vows after they had proved that their vocation was true. She had known that the most menial of tasks would come her way.

Back then, she had been so determined to take the veil that she had looked forward to them, even though, as the daughter of a count, she knew more about managing servants than undertaking the work of a servant herself. No, the tasks themselves hadn't bothered her. It had been salutary discovering how hard it was to hoe a vegetable garden, how exhausting it could be to scrub a kitchen floor when the flagstones were covered in grease. What had bothered her was the hunger.

At mealtimes when the nuns gathered in the Refectory, Mother Margerie had gone as far as to deny Bernadette more than one helping of bread. Bread, for pity's sake. The staff of life. And all because Bernadette's father had delayed sending her dowry to the convent.

Once her dowry finally arrived, Mother Margerie's attitude transformed overnight. It had not been a moment too soon, for by then Bernadette—already slim—was as thin as a reed. Thankfully, that was in the past. Nowadays, when Bernadette took her place on the novices' bench in the Refectory, the breadbasket was pushed her way. Honey cakes sometimes appeared.

Best of all, when she admitted that she was a fair needlewoman, she had been asked to make some habits. Having passed that test, finer work had come her way and eventually, she had been shown this length of gold samite and several colourful embroidery silks. Would she care to embroider an altar cloth? It was to be given to the recently installed Pope as a gift, for use in his private chapel. She was left in no doubt that it was an honour to be given such a task.

Bernadette examined the last rose. A few moments'

work and it would be finished. Overall, the cloth had turned out well. Bernadette smiled. Pride might be a sin, but she couldn't help being delighted. Even Mother Margerie should be pleased.

The smell of baking wafted through the Chapter House door and Bernadette breathed in the mouth-watering scent of almond cakes. Her stomach rumbled. She would reward herself with a visit to the kitchen. Sister Catharine was taking her turn at baking today and Sister Catharine liked it when Bernadette sampled—and praised—the quality of her cakes.

By a quirk of fate, Sister Catharine's brother was married to Bernadette's sister Allis, which meant that Sister Catharine and Bernadette spent much time talking—or rather, whispering—about Allis and her husband Leon. It wasn't the same as going home and seeing everyone. But it was the next best thing.

Fastening off, Bernadette cut the thread and folded the precious cloth. Tomorrow, she would choose a lining for it. The gold samite would be best. If Mother Margerie approved, naturally.

Leaning back in the stall with the altar cloth on her lap, Bernadette frowned at the Chapter House door. Her Profession Day was fast approaching. She ought to be pleased that her days as a novice were coming to an end and that she would shortly become a nun. Yet her stomach felt hollow, it felt as empty as it had done when she'd been denied those extra portions of bread. All she could think about was home. Castle Galard.

What was happening at home?

Why hadn't Allis written? Was she enjoying married life?

Were Papa and Sybille well?

Shaking off her disquiet, Bernadette put the embroidered cloth safely in her work basket and pushed to her feet. Those almond cakes were calling. She was hungry, that was all. Just a little hungry. She would feel better when she'd eaten.

Sir Hugo Albret stared blankly at Lord Michel Galard, Count of Arles, his liege lord. He had surely misheard. 'I beg your pardon, my lord?'

Hugo was standing at ease in front of the Count's desk in the estate office. Behind the Count, shelves were crammed. Scrolls and parchments were piled up next to an impressive row of leather-bound books. The Count was a clever man, and Hugo had learned to temper his reactions to Lord Michel's impulses, however unfathomable they might seem. They invariably had purpose.

This time, Hugo would swear he had misheard. He couldn't have heard correctly. Couldn't. 'You're giving me a squire, my lord?'

Squires were expensive. Exorbitantly so. If Hugo had a squire, the boy would need serviceable weapons and decent clothing over and above the clothing Lord Michel supplied to each member of his household. Most costly of all, a squire would need a horse.

Hugo's pay as captain of the Castle Guard barely covered his own needs, let alone the needs of a squire. Even if he wanted a squire, he couldn't afford one.

Lord Michel leaned his elbow on the table and stroked his beard. Seeing his smile, Hugo felt himself relax. He had come to Galard when he was eight, which meant he had been here for sixteen years. Under Lord Michel's tutelage Hugo had won his spurs and become a knight. Lord Michel understood him as well as he would understand his own son if he had one. He knew Hugo liked working on his own.

'You are jesting, my lord.'

Slowly the Count shook his head. 'I've never been more serious. In truth, I should have thought of this years ago. You've worked hard at Galard. I trust you and I'd like you to stay. Think of it as a reward for your years of service.'

'You are saying you will stand the expense, my lord?'

'Naturally. You have certainly earned it.'

'My lord, you are generosity itself, however I would rather not—'

A faint frown crossed Lord Michel's face. 'What's the problem? Are you thinking of returning to your brother's estate in Nérac? If so, let me reassure you. You will still need a squire.'

Hugo's stomach clenched. 'I won't be returning home.' He might have been considering leaving, but Nérac was the last place he'd go.

The Count's brown eyes searched his. 'You and your brother are no longer in touch? I assumed—'

'I have not heard from my brother in years.'

The Count let out a long sigh. 'My apologies, Hugo, I had no idea.' He straightened and his voice became brisk. 'Well, that settles it, since Galard is your home, you will accept the squire. I will stand the expense. In addition, your pay is to be increased. Think of it as a promotion.'

Hugo blinked. This was generosity indeed. It was probably the Count's way of ensuring that Hugo, as a younger son with no land and consequently no revenues to fall back on, had some hope of a half-decent future. Hugo was blessed in his overlord. It went some way towards making up for other areas of his life, where he often felt as though he'd been cursed rather than blessed. 'Thank you, my lord. I shall do my best to bring honour to your house.'

The Count nodded. 'I know you will.' His expression was apologetic. 'I regret not doing this years ago. When Sir Leon suggested you be promoted in this way, I saw at once that he was right.'

Hugo froze. 'This was Sir Leon's idea?'

'Indeed, it was,' the Count said, oblivious of the unexpected spurt of resentment his remark evoked in Hugo. Hugo clenched his fists and mastered himself. He liked Sir Leon. He really did. Only a fool would allow envy at another's good fortune to cloud his thoughts.

'I must remember to thank him,' he managed to say.

Until recently, Sir Leonidàs of Tarascon had been a landless knight like Hugo. Unlike Hugo, however, Sir Leon had not been born to the nobility. Despite many disadvantages, Sir Leon's qualities as a leader had enabled him to form a mercenary band of such repute that he had had the good fortune to catch the eye of Lady Allisende, Lord Michel's elder daughter. Something which Hugo, whose lineage was equal to that of his liege lord, hadn't achieved in all his years at Galard.

Sir Leon and Lady Allis were now married, and Lord Michel had done everything in his power to ensure that Sir Leon felt welcome in Castle Galard. Sir Leon had his own office and was being trained in estate management. The entire castle had been enlisted to help, even Lady Allis who was teaching him to untangle the estate accounts.

Everyone knew that Sir Leon and Lady Allis were blissfully happy. Hugo didn't begrudge them their happiness, but every now and then he would remember the kiss that he and Lady Allis had shared behind the stable all those years ago and he would wonder. If that kiss had held even a drop of passion, he might be standing in Sir Leon's place.

He held in a sigh. He must be realistic. It would never have worked. The kiss had felt all wrong.

Allis was beautiful. Tall and slender, with blonde hair and blue eyes. Hugo had always liked her. He had kissed her on impulse. There had been affection in the kiss, but no heat. He knew Allis too well, he supposed. Having spent most of his life at Galard, she was the sister he had never had.

Fortunately, they both had felt the same way. Not once since that incident behind the stable had Hugo considered kissing her again. Even though as the years passed, it became obvious that Allis needed to marry if her father was going to keep his lands in the family. Allis, as the elder daughter, needed a strong husband.

Unfortunately for Lord Michel, Allis had refused every suitor her father paraded before her. Then Sir Leon arrived, and overnight Castle Galard was a different place. Sir Leon, with his troop of well-ordered men, had been ideal.

Of late, Hugo had found himself wondering whether it was time to forge a new life for himself elsewhere. He had done it as a boy, he could do so again. What held him back was the Galard family. Hugo respected Lord Michel. Lady Sybille, the Count's second wife, was a dear. Lady Allis was his friend, and Hugo missed her younger sister more than he had thought possible. He often caught himself wishing Lady Bernadette hadn't cooped herself up in that ghastly convent. It would be hard, if not impossible, to replace one member of the Galard family, never mind all of them.

'Regarding your squire,' the Count said, breaking into Hugo's thoughts. 'What do you say to Olivier of Poitiers?'

'Olivier? He has a natural talent with horses, my lord. And he rides with confidence.' Like Hugo, Olivier had been sent by his family to foster at Galard. He was progressing well. Hugo smiled ruefully. 'Olivier also has a woeful tendency towards practical jokes.'

'Hmm. If you don't care to take him on, you may choose someone else.' The Count drummed his fingers on the desk. 'Sir Leon brought several promising men with him, how about one of them? Stefe, perhaps? There's no need to decide immediately. Think on it.'

'That won't be necessary, my lord. Olivier of Poitiers will suit me very well. Thank you.'

'Excellent. You may inform him when you're ready.' The Count drew a scroll towards him, read it through and reached for his seal.

'Will that be all, my lord?'

'Not quite.' Lord Michel dropped green wax on to the scroll and pressed his seal into it. 'Allis has written to Bernadette, and I have added a few remarks of my own. Her Profession Day will very soon be upon us.'

'It's a month away,' Hugo said. He was half surprised he knew.

Lord Michel grunted. 'Set out before noon with this, will you? That Mother Superior is an absolute tyrant. She is only malleable now because she has got her claws on Bernadette's dowry. I am certain that once Bernadette has taken Final Vows, the convent drawbridge will be raised, so to speak. Communication with my daughter will sadly become impossible.'

'Very good, my lord.'

Taking the scroll, Hugo bowed out of the office. He strode directly to the stable, filled with a curious mix of relief and remorse. He wanted to see Bernadette. It had been well over a year since he had escorted her to the convent, and he'd felt guilty about it ever since. At the time, Hugo had been entirely focused on Allis and her determination to escape an unwanted marriage.

When Allis first announced that she intended to take refuge in Saint Claire's Convent to escape an unwanted marriage, Hugo had laughed out loud. Allis? In a convent? He had swiftly sobered when Allis asked Bernadette to go with her. It had been a desperate, dangerous request for the simple reason that Bernadette's fascination with church services bordered on the obsessive. However, Bernadette's presence had provided Allis with a legitimate reason for seeking sanctuary in the convent. Allis had excused herself by saying that Bernadette needed to experience the harshness of convent life before she accepted it was not for her.

Events had not turned out precisely as Allis had hoped. True, Allis had escaped her unwanted marriage, but Bernadette had stayed on at Saint Claire's. Her heart really seemed set on taking the veil.

In a month's time. *Mon Dieu*, what a travesty.

Hugo would never forgive himself for taking her there. As he threw the saddle on Clovis, it occurred to him that he could ride to the convent in style, with a squire at his elbow. He grimaced. No, it would take too long. Olivier would be ridiculously excited. He would need praise and explanation, which would slow Hugo down. He would have to waste yet more time with idle chatter when Lord Michel wanted Allis's letter to be delivered speedily. In any case, Hugo wanted to give Bernadette his full attention. It might be the last time he saw her.

Hugo led Clovis into the bailey. As he mounted, Olivier rounded the corner of an outbuilding with two comrades. Giving the boy a brief smile, Hugo mounted and spurred forward. Clovis clattered over the drawbridge and Hugo directed him on to the road to Avignon. It would be so good to see Bernadette again.

Bernadette succeeded in her mission to extract more of the gold samite from Mother Margerie. After a frugal noonday meal which left her hungry—no almond cakes appeared—she took the work basket and went directly to the visitor's lodge. Since the lodge was only used occasionally, usually by families of ladies destined for the convent, the main chamber was often empty. The table there was long enough to lay out the entire altar cloth so she could measure it for the lining.

Ensuring the table was clean, Bernadette spread out the cloth and reached into her work basket. And there, lying on top of the shears, was temptation in the form of a small sackcloth bundle. Bernadette's nose twitched and she let out a happy sigh. She didn't have to unwrap the bundle to know what it contained. She could smell the almonds.

'Sister Catharine,' she murmured happily. 'You are a demon, a beautiful, beautiful demon.'

Having eaten the cake, Bernadette set to work. She was tacking the lining in place when the door opened, and Mother Margerie came in. 'I've not yet seen the entire front of the cloth,' Mother Margerie said, in her usual abrasive tone. 'Be so good as to turn it so I may examine it.'

'Of course.' Bernadette folded back the lining to display her handiwork. She found herself holding her breath while Mother Margerie bent over the table.

Mother Margerie poked at a rose and straightened. 'This has turned out far better than I dared hope,' she said. 'Novice, you are without question the best seamstress here. This gift to His Holiness will enhance the convent's prestige.'

'I am glad you approve,' Bernadette said.

Hard eyes held hers. 'By the by, Novice, a messenger has arrived from Castle Galard. He bears a letter from your sister, and he insists on delivering it personally. I have agreed he may do so this time. Please take heed though, once you have taken full vows all such correspondence must cease. There will be no more letters and certainly no more envoys from your father's castle to disturb the tranquillity of our order.'

Bernadette felt a flash of anger mixed uncomfortably with excitement. At last, a letter from Allis! She lowered her gaze. 'I understand. Mother Margerie, I am grateful for your understanding.'

'Run along,' Mother Margerie said. 'Your father's man is hanging about in the courtyard and I would like him to leave as soon as possible. Your work will be perfectly safe here.' She paused, eyes narrowing. 'And before you go, you might care to know that I will be having words with Sister Catharine.'

Bernadette's heart sank. 'You will?'

'Certainly. She should not be encouraging greed. Novice Bernadette, you have crumbs on your chin.'

Chapter Two

Excited though she was, Bernadette did her best to walk with slow dignity to the courtyard. Having wiped the betraying crumbs from her mouth, of course. At last, a letter from Allis! Would Allis's husband Leon be bringing it? If so, Bernadette must find a way to alert Sister Catharine to the news that her brother had come to Saint Claire's. Convent rules notwithstanding, Sister Catharine would love to see him.

The courtyard was cramped and narrow, hemmed in by walls on three sides. An enormous oak door in one of the walls led directly into an alley in the town. It was the only way in and out of the convent, and it was overlooked by the portress's lodge. An elderly nun, Sister Teresa, usually sat in the lodge. Her responsibility was to keep watch and, should it be necessary, ring the alarm bell.

Bernadette stepped through the arch and stopped short. Her sister's husband Leon had not brought the letter. Hugo had. Lord, save her. There he stood, unruly blond hair lighting up the dull courtyard as he leaned nonchalantly against the rump of his chestnut horse, Clovis. Clovis was tethered to a ring in the wall.

'Oh, it's you,' Bernadette said. Belatedly conscious of how rude that sounded, she felt herself flush. Of all people, it would have to be Hugo. Sir Hugo, she reminded herself. They were no longer children. She was a novice and he a knight. The captain of her father's guard, no less.

Hugo had been smiling as she entered the courtyard. With a pang she watched his smile fade. He had always had a lovely smile. Wiping his face clear of expression, he straightened and came towards her. 'Who were you expecting?'

Bernadette craned her neck to look up at him, heart thudding. When she was younger, she had been sweet on Hugo. She found that combination of fair hair and dark brown eyes irresistible. It was disturbing to discover she was still susceptible to his looks. Shouldn't her time in the convent have changed her view of him? Unfortunately, Hugo was as good looking as ever. Since being clothed as a novice Bernadette had only seen him once, at her sister's wedding. He had been handsome then. A ridiculous twinge of longing went through her. Hugo would always be handsome.

Swallowing hard, she held out her hand, whether to ward him off or to accept Allis's letter she wasn't sure. Hugo was so tall and with Bernadette being short, he towered over her. Not for the first time, she wished she had her sister's height.

'My letter, if you please, sir.'

Hugo reached into his tunic for the letter and passed it to her with an ironic bow. 'My lady.'

'Thank you.' Breaking her father's green seal, Bernadette turned away for Hugo was watching her and it made her uneasy. She ran her gaze swiftly over the contents. Papa had scrawled a few lines at the bottom. Allis began.

Dearest Bernadette

I pray this letter finds you in good health. I am writing with news that is not yet common knowledge, and I must beg for your discretion. I am conscious that you will shortly be taking the veil and understand that once your Profession Day is over and you have taken full vows, any communication from the family will be frowned upon. With all my heart I wish you were not taking this step, but it is your life and your decision. I hope you understand that while we have not always seen eye to eye, you are my dear and most beloved sister. I love you. I always will.

Tears prickled at the back of Bernadette's eyes. Blinking rapidly, she raced through the next few sentences.

Dearest, only three people know what I am about to reveal. Leon, Papa and Sybille.

If it were not for your absence from Galard Castle, I would be the happiest of women for I believe I am with child. It is early days of course, far too early for a general announcement, but I wanted you to know because I suspect that Mother Margerie will not budge on her inter-pretation of the convent Rule. Professed nuns should not receive letters from the outside world. Mother Margerie made allowances for our fam-ily before, but that was because she wanted your dowry. She has that now, which means that when you make your full vows the convent gates will be closed to us. She truly is a harpy.

Forgive me if my news comes as a shock, but I wanted you to know. I beg you not to worry on my behalf. I am well aware of the dangers of child-birth, and I would remind you that I do not share your fears. I have attended many births, I know what to expect, and I have no intention of dying.

Bernadette's hand began to shake, and the words Allis had written swirled and blurred. She heard a sob and to her horror realised she was moaning under her breath. 'No, no, no.'

Hugo was at her side in an instant. '*Mon ange*—my angel—whatever is the matter?'

The gentleness in his voice was Bernadette's undoing. As was his old nickname for her, the one he used to tease her with. A tear escaped and ran down her cheek. 'Nothing. My apologies, sir.'

'Nothing? Angel, you never cry, something must be very wrong.' Hugo's voice warmed; concern became playful. 'Someone who is about to take the veil should surely not be lying.'

'That sounds like something Allis would say.' Bernadette let out another choking sound, more laugh than sob, thank goodness. And much as she wanted to explain, she could not. For Allis's letter said, very clearly, that only four people knew she was with child. This was a confidence she must not break.

Conflicting emotions swirled inside her. Terror—Allis might die in childbirth, just as Mama had done when Bernadette had been born. Bernadette might never see her sister again. Delight—Allis and Leon longed for children. Bernadette was pleased for them and for Papa too. Papa had been desperate for grandchildren to ensure that their line would live on at Galard. Papa was sure to be thrilled.

A rebellious idea slipped into awareness so quietly, its power knocked her back. *I need to go home.* She wanted to see Allis and if she went home, she could talk to her before she took her vows. She could not do that here, not with Mother Margerie overhearing their every word.

Hugo touched her cheek. 'Angel, you are as white as

whey and you're shaking. I cannot think Allis would knowingly upset you. What is it?'

Hugo wasn't going to give up. Bernadette knew him of old and he never did. Besides, his closeness was a dear and familiar comfort. She found herself fighting the impulse to lean into him. She wanted a hug. Until she had confirmed her decision to take the veil, Hugo had hugged her a lot. She missed it. Conscious that such closeness was inappropriate, she stepped away. 'Please, sir, allow me to finish the letter.'

Mercifully, Hugo held his peace as Bernadette read the letter from the beginning. This time she succeeded in finishing it. Papa didn't have much to add, save that he regretted Bernadette's decision to take Final Vows. Papa also told her that he had long ago decided that her life was her own to dispose of as she would. He hoped she was in good health, and that Mother Margerie was allowing her enough nourishment. He closed by saying that he and the immediate family had been granted permission to attend her Profession Day and that if she ever needed help in the future, convent Rule or not, the family would be there for her. She read the closing phrases over and over.

The family will be there for you. Always.

Bernadette knew the family would come to witness her taking Final Vows. They would see her, and she would see them, but only from a distance. It really would be impossible to have a proper conversation.

Allis's letter curled back into a scroll, and she looked up. Hugo's head was tipped enquiringly towards her. 'Angel?'

Smiling despite her anxiety, Bernadette shot a swift glance through the arch that led into the heart of the convent. She half expected to find Mother Margerie lurking in the cloister shadows, eavesdropping. Thank the saints no one was there. Sister Teresa was still in the lodge, and she wasn't listening either. She was busy at prayer, her head bent over her rosary.

'Hugo, you really shouldn't call me Angel. Not any longer.'

He shrugged. 'I don't see why not. It's not blasphemous, surely? You are an angel. Always have been. You wouldn't have stayed here otherwise.'

I need to see Allis properly. I must. I could go home, just for a few days—a sennight, perhaps.

It was a terrible idea. Heretical. Bernadette smothered a laugh. Well, it wasn't truly heretical, although Mother Margerie would doubtless condemn it as such. She glanced through the arch a second time. No one. Wondering how long they had before another nun chanced upon them, she checked to ensure that Sister Teresa was hunched over her rosary in the portress's lodge and lowered her voice. 'Hugo, I need to ask you a favour.'

Hugo gave her an encouraging bow. 'Ask away, my lady.'

I must see Allis. She hauled in a breath. 'Take me home, please. Today.'

Hugo's face lit up. 'You're leaving?'

Her heart turned over. When Hugo was happy, it almost hurt to look at him. He was so beautiful. 'You're pleased.'

'Damned right I am. I've never forgiven myself for bringing you here in the first place.'

'Hugo, please. I came, willingly I might add, as a companion for Allis when she was hiding from Papa. You were not to know I would decide to stay.'

'I should have done. You've always loved Church ritual. At Galard you practically lived in the chapel. When I brought you here, I assumed you would see that being a nun was not for you.' A lock of sun-bleached hair fell over his eyes. Impatiently, he shoved it back. 'I've never forgiven myself for leaving you behind.'

Arrested by the idea that Hugo hadn't wanted to leave her here, she studied his expression. His was a face she knew well enough to see that he meant what he was saying. Her pulse quickened. Excitement. He was going to agree to take her home. She could see it in his eyes.

'You'll take me then? Today?'

'Of course.' Hugo glanced through the arch and grimaced. 'I'll even face the harpy for you. Would you like me to tell her?'

The harpy. A huff of laughter escaped her to hear Hugo using Allis's name for Mother Margerie. 'You've been talking to Allis.'

Hugo didn't bother denying it, he stepped purposefully towards the arch. Hastily, Bernadette snatched at his sleeve. 'No. Please, we say nothing. Not to Mother Margerie, at any rate.'

His eyebrows shot up. 'Oh?'

Sometimes Hugo's gaze was just too penetrating. She avoided it by looking at the ground. 'I am not certain what to tell her,' she admitted. 'And if she senses doubt in me, she'll find a way to stop me going.'

'Of course she will. She wants to keep your dowry.'

Bernadette scuffed the ground with the toe of her slipper before meeting his gaze. 'Hugo, I cannot go home for long. My Profession Day is only a month away.'

He pulled a face. 'I know.'

'I'd like to see home again, just the once. I need to be with Allis. And Papa.' Her voice weakened before strengthening again. 'I shall explain to Sister Teresa. She can tell Mother Margerie.'

Frowning, Hugo folded his arms across his chest. 'You are certain you will want to come back?'

'Yes!' The word burst out forcefully although it felt like a lie. How strange. Quashing her misgivings, which suddenly were legion, she strode to the portress's lodge and rapped on the door. 'Sister Teresa, forgive me for interrupting your meditation. I need to speak to you.'

Sister Teresa wound her rosary about her fingers and calmly set her hands in her lap. 'Novice Bernadette?'

Sister Teresa was a wise woman. She knew that sometimes the rule of silence was there to be broken. She listened attentively to Bernadette's somewhat garbled account of going back to Galard Castle for a final visit and muttered something about it being human nature for novices to have second thoughts before they took the veil.

Bernadette bade her farewell and went back to Hugo, who already had Clovis's reins in hand. Her heart felt lighter than it had done in months, and she felt absolutely no inclination to examine why that might be. There wasn't time.

Hugo jerked his head towards the arch. 'You're leaving all your belongings behind?'

Bernadette nodded. 'There's nothing of importance in my cell.' What she really meant was that she didn't wish to run the risk of encountering Mother Margerie.

Sister Teresa came out of the lodge with the keys to the great oak door and, after much knocking back of heavy bolts and turning of keys, Bernadette found herself in the narrow side street with Hugo and Clovis. When the convent door closed with a dull thud behind her, she let out a huge sigh. *Dieu merci.* Thank God.

* * *

The alley was busier than it had been when Hugo had entered the convent courtyard. Townsfolk were squeezing past, moving doggedly in both directions. No sooner had they set out than Bernadette was knocked against the wall by a burly porter with a heavy-looking chest on his shoulder.

The porter swore. 'Mind your back,' he growled and pressed on.

Hugo didn't think. He brought Clovis to a stand, grasped Bernadette by the waist and boosted her into the saddle. She had always been a tiny thing. Only when she let out a squeak did Hugo remember that the days had long passed when he could handle her in so familiar a manner. He ought not to be touching her. And he certainly ought not to enjoy it. The contact, brief though it was, had told him much. His angel had filled out a little since he had seen her at her sister's wedding. She felt soft and womanly. And he really ought not to be thinking this way. 'My apologies, my lady, but you are safer up there.'

Bernadette nodded absently. Thankfully, he didn't appear to have upset her. She was gazing about, warm brown eyes bewildered.

'What's the matter?' he asked.

'It's not usually as busy as this. Is there a festival?'

Hugo stared. 'You are free to wander about the town?' That sounded dangerous. Avignon wasn't simply the home of the Pope and his entourage. Aside from the Cardinals' palaces, it was a lively city. It teemed with shops, alehouses, bathhouses, and places that an innocent like Bernadette probably had no idea existed.

'Hardly.' Bernadette gripped the front of the saddle as Hugo led Clovis down the alley. 'But the convent has a vegetable garden, it is close to the Pope's vineyard. I help there sometimes—hoeing, digging up turnips.'

Hugo's jaw dropped. 'The nuns make you dig up turnips?' He would be the first to admit he was no expert on what it took to be a nun, though he had a vague understanding that humility was important. Even so, the idea that the daughter of Lord Michel Galard, Count of Arles, had been working in a vegetable garden was beyond belief.

A boy pulling a handcart inched past, and Bernadette's soft laugh reached him over the rumble of the wheels. 'I like the vegetable garden,' she said. 'I go there occasionally with another novice. There is a view of the river, and you can see France on the other side.'

Hugo thought he understood. 'You like to get away.' He noticed she was clinging so tightly to the front of the saddle her knuckles were white.

'It wasn't easy at the beginning. Mother Margerie liked to test me. She tests all the novices.' She frowned. 'Hugo, would you mind handing me the reins? I am perfectly capable of directing Clovis for myself.'

'Sorry, Angel, I know you are, but it is simply too busy. Your father would never forgive me if Clovis bolted with you on his back.'

She gave him a look. 'Hugo, please. Clovis would never bolt. I watched countless mêlées at Galard and Clovis never faltered. Despite shouts and screams, despite drums and the clash of arms, he holds steady. You trained him so well, he is the steadiest animal in Christendom. And suddenly he can't walk down an alley in Avignon?'

'Sorry, Angel, my answer stands. I lead Clovis.'

'Very well.' She stared ahead. 'By the way, we ought to turn around, we're going the wrong way. The city gate is behind us.'

'We're not going to the city gate,' Hugo told her. 'Not yet, anyway.'

She fixed him with wide, dark-lashed eyes. 'Where are we going?'

He grinned. 'To The Crossed Keys.'

The Crossed Keys was a tavern favoured by Lord Michel's men whenever they were in Avignon.

'Hugo, Tansy is no longer at The Crossed Keys, Papa took her home a while back.' Tansy was Bernadette's pony.

'I know, but I am not about to walk home like a lackey while you sit in queenly splendour on Clovis.'

She laughed, a bright, joyous sound Hugo hadn't

heard in far too long. Somewhere deep inside, a knot he had not known he had been carrying loosened. 'Hugo, you're mad. If you walk us home, it will take days. Weeks.'

'My point exactly. They keep a good stable at The Crossed Keys. The grooms will be sure to have something suitable for a lady. I don't think you would like the alternative.'

'The alternative?'

'Riding before me. Tempted as I am, it wouldn't be appropriate.'

She flushed and looked swiftly away. 'No, I don't suppose it would.'

For an instant Hugo thought he saw a flash of longing. Longing? What was wrong with him? This was Lady Bernadette, the childhood friend who had made it plain more times than he could count that she was going to become a nun. She might be nervous about making her Final Vows, but that didn't give him leave to start thinking about how much he would enjoy riding home with her on his lap. Or riding home with her sitting pillion behind him for that matter.

'Hugo?'

'Mmm?'

She bit her lip. 'I am afraid you will have to ride home with me on Clovis.'

His heart thudded. 'Oh?'

She wiggled the foot nearest to him. 'I am wearing slippers.'

Sure enough, her slippers were far too flimsy to ride in, she ought to be wearing boots. Hugo did his best to suppress a smile. 'That settles it, you definitely can't control a horse in those; your feet might get caught in the stirrups. It would be far too dangerous.'

She looked away, still biting her lip, which flushed a distracting and rather lovely pink. 'I was embroidering when you arrived, you see. I had no thought of riding home.'

'Very well.' The lane opened out into a small square. Leading Clovis out of the way of the traffic, Hugo brought him to a halt and watched for her reaction. 'You really are happy to share that saddle with me?'

Her cheeks flushed. Irritatingly, for once he could not read her. 'Of course. Thank you, Hugo.' She hung her head. 'I am sorry to be such a nuisance.'

Words deserted him. Angel was many things— pretty, sweet-natured, loving. Bafflingly, her time in the convent had turned her into temptation itself. Those newly rounded curves that the ghastly grey habit failed miserably to conceal. The way her bottom lip flooded with colour when she bit it. 'Angel, you are many things,' he said drily. 'But a nuisance? You have never been a nuisance.'

And there it was again, that charming flush. *Mon Dieu*, but this was going to be an interesting ride.

Chapter Three

Hugo was simply being polite. As a child, Bernadette must often have been a nuisance, but he had never treated her badly. She had known her fascination with the Church had often perplexed him, but he'd never mocked her for it. Not once.

Hugo was naturally warm and courteous and there was nothing wrong in that. Growing up, Bernadette had responded to his warmth. He had been a friendly boy and it seemed he had turned into a friendly man. He was extraordinarily easy-going. He had to be, she supposed. Learning to get on with his foster family had been vital for a child who had been sent far away from his home in Gascony to learn the knightly arts. Hugo made a point of being pleasant to everyone. Even Hortense—the gloomiest maidservant in Galard Castle—had occasionally responded to his charm.

Bernadette's heart had ached for him, though she had never quite understood quite why. She had found herself questioning whether he felt obliged to be kind because her father had accepted him and, eventually, knighted him. At other times, she'd wonder. Did nature or necessity shape his behaviour?

She had quickly realised that what she felt for Hugo transcended friendship. She had understood that much even though she had been too young to define what, exactly, she did feel. It had taken years to work out why she would catch herself wishing that Hugo would shout at her. She, who hated strife more than anything.

She had wanted to know what he was really like under all that kindness. She had wanted to see him, to truly see him. She had wanted passion.

She had been too innocent to see it. Understanding had begun to dawn the day Bernadette had chanced upon Hugo and Allis behind the stables. They had been standing close. Before she realised what she was seeing, they leaned together. And kissed.

It had been a brief kiss and it should not have filled Bernadette's veins with ice. For weeks afterwards she had felt as though she was holding her breath, waiting for the day when she would stumble across them kissing again. Fearing the moment when they would announce their betrothal. It had never happened. Papa had had other suitors in mind for his elder daughter. Bernadette's mouth softened. Her wilful sister had refused those suitors, before falling in love with Sir Leon and marrying him. Bernadette had ejected the kiss in the stable from her mind ages ago.

Or she thought she had. That she was still thinking

about it today was simply a reminder that Hugo had always viewed Allis in a different way.

The kiss no longer mattered. It was irrelevant. Hugo and Bernadette were both changed. He was now a knight, captain of the Castle Guard. She was preparing to take Final Vows. She was only thinking about it today because seeing Hugo reminded her of the past. Of the days she ached for him to look at her in the same way he looked at Allis. How foolish she had been. Setting aside her future as a nun, Bernadette, small, dark and nondescript, could never compare with her tall, fair sister. Allis was stunning. A beauty.

'Angel, you are miles away,' Hugo said, bringing Bernadette back to the present with a jolt. 'What are you thinking about?'

'Nothing of importance.'

'You may choose how we ride,' he said, eyes gleaming with what she recognised was amusement. 'You will have to ride the whole way astride. Tell me, my lady, do you wish to ride before me or behind?'

As she looked at him, her breath seized. The convent courtyard and the cramped lane on the other side were shaded by high walls, sunlight rarely reached them. This square was bathed in light. Sun streamed over everything—the builders loading a hoist with roof tiles, a cardinal hurrying by with a small retinue of monks—everything was bathed in a golden glow. Including Hugo. *Especially Hugo.*

The light seemed to centre on him, gilding that

tousled hair. She could even see the coppery strands threaded in with the gold—fascinating flashes of fire that betrayed his Merovingian ancestry. Hugo had always been well favoured, of course, but the months in the convent had dulled her memory of him. How could she have forgotten that nose? How distinguished it was. His profile was like that of a Roman emperor.

'Angel?'

She gave him a lopsided smile. Why Hugo named her Angel when she was short and dark had always felt like the most bitter of ironies. He enjoyed teasing her though she'd never sensed malice in him. Yet surely, with his blond hair and those fathomless brown eyes, not to mention that distinctive nose and mobile mouth, it was he who resembled an angel rather than her. 'I'll never understand why you call me that.'

He gave her a smile that she felt in her toes. 'I call you Angel because it suits you.'

'Only you would say that.' She huffed out a breath. 'We all know I'm far from angelic.'

He reached up and his hand covered hers. It was a strong hand, calloused from swordplay and marred by the odd scar. Bernadette knew that hand. It was warm and comforting. It was the hand of a knight. It was the hand of her childhood playmate. The hand of an old friend. 'Don't do that,' he said fiercely.

Startled, she drew back. 'I beg your pardon?'

'Do not belittle yourself. You did it as a child. I

assumed that now you had found your vocation you would have grown out of it.'

Bernadette gazed helplessly at him before lowering her gaze. She didn't know what to say. Heavens, when Hugo touched her, she didn't know a blessed thing. Except—alas for her soul—she liked his touch. The slightest contact made her feel more alive than she'd felt in months. Since coming to the convent, she had been dead inside.

No. *No!* She didn't think that. She did not. 'Hugo, you are a bad influence.'

Hugo snorted and to her intense regret removed his hand from hers and shoved it through his hair. Which had the inevitable effect of tousling it even more. Unfortunately, for some reason it made him even more attractive.

'Lady Bernadette,' he said, using his patient voice. She hated that voice. 'If you have not changed your mind about going home, you need to decide. Do you ride before me or behind?'

'I'll ride in front, if you please,' she said, cheeks heating.

Sharing a horse with the man you had idolised was never going to be easy. Particularly if you wanted that man to believe you thought of him in purely friendly terms. Particularly if you intended to take the veil. Which she did, she most definitely did, despite the occasional wayward thought. Even if looking at Hugo—so tall and handsome and at this moment entirely at her disposal—was making her question her intentions as never before.

'Thank you, Hugo.'

Bernadette was not sure she had made the most appropriate decision, but if she faced forward, he would not be able to see her face. He would not be able to watch her reaction to his closeness. And today her reactions, she was ashamed to admit, were all over the place. Hugo confused her. Later, if she found riding in front irksome, she could always ask to change places. They would be bound to stop to give Clovis a rest. Aye, that would be fine, they could easily swap over if riding this way became unbearable.

The road to Galard Castle was thick with traffic. There were horses and carts, knights and pilgrims, goatherds and goats.

A few miles outside Avignon the traffic thinned, and Hugo was soon desperate to urge Clovis into a trot. Bernadette was quite the delightful armful, and the best way to keep her secure was to pull her tightly against him and hold her in place with one hand while he controlled the reins with the other.

Unfortunately, riding in such a manner provoked all sorts of ideas, most of which were appallingly out of place. Sensual thoughts such as how it would feel to lift that short novice's veil and press a kiss to the nape of her neck. It would not do. If she knew what he was thinking she would be distressed and unsettled.

Hugo allowed himself to be distracted by the faint fragrance of rosemary and surreptitiously lowered his head. Aye, that was definitely rosemary. The scent evoked a forgotten memory and his lips curved. Bernadette loved herbs. Before entering the nunnery, she had enjoyed making scented soaps for the ladies of the castle. Thyme, lemon balm, bay. For a woman set on being a nun she had many sensuous interests.

The dominant one, Hugo reminded himself, easing back in the saddle and away from her soft, delicious shape, had always been Church ritual. For as long as he had known her, Bernadette had been interested in religion. Which was why he must, he really must, stop counting the many ways in which it was a pleasure to see her again. He ached to press closer. He would resist. In a sennight she would be back in that convent, she would retreat from the world. It did not feel right, it never had, but it was her wish.

He scowled at her veil. It rippled as they rode, just under his nose. Tantalising him into another deep inhalation, so he could breathe in that scent. Rosemary. Sweet and sharp, just like her. 'My lady?'

She twisted to look at him and Hugo found himself glancing at her mouth. He was busy repressing a most inconvenient impulse to move closer when he was startled to see her gaze stray towards his mouth. His heart missed its beat.

Bon Dieu. Good God. For a moment it looked as

though she was thinking about kissing him. That could not be. Not Bernadette. Unless…

'Angel?'

'Hmm?'

They continued past a clump of gorse, flaring yellow at the side of the road. 'It is not too late, you know.'

'Too late? What do you mean?'

'If you've changed your mind about taking your vows, your family will be delighted. No one save that harpy will hold it against you.'

She went rigid. 'I haven't changed my mind. I merely wish to see Allis before I make my profession.'

Hugo grunted. Was she weakening? Much as he wished her to change her mind, he could not be sure. Something her sister had written had disturbed her. He had no idea what it might be. All he knew was that the more Angel insisted she was taking the veil, the more certain he became that she might be persuaded otherwise.

Smiling, he leaned closer. Bernadette was proud, just like her father. And her sister. Wondering what it would take for her to admit she had made a mistake, Hugo decided he would do all in his power to help her realise.

Clovis plodded steadily on and Hugo let his mind drift. He found himself thinking about Bernadette's hair, of all things. He'd heard that nuns cut off their hair, but he was not sure whether that was true and if so, whether it applied to novices. Bernadette used to have gorgeous brown hair. It was long and lustrous and had a rebellious wave that ensured it was always fighting free of its ribbons.

'Angel, did they cut off your hair?'

She whipped round, frowning. 'I beg your pardon?'

He shrugged. 'I was just wondering. I had heard they did that to nuns.' He could hardly admit that he wanted to lift her veil and find out. He could plant that kiss on the back of her neck while he was about it.

'You are impudent, Sir Hugo.'

Sir Hugo. *Mon Dieu*, that had really won her over. He was an idiot, he was not going to change her mind overnight. He must take it step by step. Clovis trudged steadily on. At this rate their journey was going to take until dawn tomorrow. It was going to be purgatory. Keep it formal, he told himself. 'My lady, I would like to try a trot. Since you don't have stirrups, it is likely to be uncomfortable. You must say at once if you find it unbearable.'

'Very well.'

Hugo urged Clovis into a trot, and she clung to the front of the saddle. She had always been a good horse-woman and that would not have changed. Almost at once though, she practically bounced out of the saddle. Letting out a little squeak, she clutched his thigh.

'Hugo, no!'

That ghastly formality had vanished, but she was not looking him in the eye, not even angrily. 'It is unbearable without stirrups, and with you sitting so far back, terrifying.'

Without thought, he wound his arm about her and realigned their bodies. To his shame, the moment their bodies touched, he breathed a sigh of relief. He swallowed. 'Are you happy to try a canter like this? I will not let you fall.'

Gripping the front of saddle with one hand and his thigh with the other, she faced forward. 'I trust you.'

Hoping that was true, for if he had any say in it this woman was not going to become a nun, Hugo kicked Clovis into a canter.

Bernadette was silent as they approached Galard Castle. Hugo felt her body stiffen as the glossy waters of the moat came into view. By leaning slightly to one side, he was able to watch her gaze skim over the margin of weed, before lifting to the tall curtain wall and the keep towering over it. Her father's green standard was flying at each corner of the tower, bold as ever. She sighed and sagged a little.

'It is just the same.'

Recognising no response was needed, Hugo grunted and guided Clovis across the drawbridge. They entered the bailey where, unsurprisingly, their arrival provoked a small riot. A cry went up and half a dozen grinning stable boys pelted towards them. A babble erupted.

'Lady Bernadette has come home!'

'Are you here for good, my lady?'

'Welcome back!'

'We missed you, my lady.'

Bernadette smiled at the lads. 'I am here for a visit, that is all.'

The smiles faded.

Hugo allowed her statement to pass without comment, he had spotted his new squire in the mill. 'Olivier, stop gawking and do something useful. Please inform Lord Michel and Lady Sybille that Lady Bernadette has come to visit. At once.'

'Yes, sir.' Olivier departed at a run.

Hugo lifted Bernadette from Clovis's back, steadying her as she found her feet. 'Angel, you had best brace yourself. As the boys have just proved, your visit is bound to cause a stir.'

She was smiling as she looked around, nodding greetings at everyone. Then she glanced towards the steps of the keep and her smile vanished. Hortense, the maidservant who had once served her mother was coming down the steps with one of the younger maids. Hugo couldn't help but groan. 'I would have thought even that misery would have had the tact to greet you after your family.'

Bernadette dug him in the ribs. 'Hush, for pity's sake. Hortense isn't that bad.'

Hugo would have said more but Bernadette's scowl prevented it. As Clovis was led away, Hortense marched towards them, a woman on a mission. 'Novice Bernadette, why on earth are you here?' Her tone was biting. She glowered at Hugo and her gaze flickered to his departing horse. Hugo saw her work it out. She put her hands on her hips. 'Please tell me you did not share a horse with Sir Hugo.'

'Good day, Hortense,' Bernadette said quietly. 'I trust you are in good health?'

Hortense's chin lifted. 'I was until Olivier started shouting in the great hall. I assumed it was another of his foolish pranks. How wrong I was.'

Fortunately, just then Lord Michel and Lady Sybille appeared at the top of the steps. Hugo looked down his nose at Hortense and made his voice dry. 'Hortense, your words of wisdom and welcome will have to wait. The Count wishes to greet his daughter.'

Bernadette's face lit up, she slipped past Hortense and ran towards her father.

Hugo watched, chest tight, as Lord Michel opened his arms in the middle of the bailey and gave Bernadette a fierce hug. Lady Sybille kissed her soundly on both cheeks and the three of them started talking at once.

'Papa, it's wonderful to see you.'

'I'm delighted to see you too, if somewhat surprised,' Lord Michel answered, tipping his head to one side. 'Although, given what Allis told you, perhaps your arrival is not so strange.'

Hugo pricked up his ears. Bernadette had mentioned wanting to see her sister, but she had never explained why. He stepped forward. 'Lady Allis is not ill, my lord?'

'Far from it, Hugo,' his lord assured him. 'Far from it.' Winding his arm around his younger daughter's shoulders, he turned her towards the keep. 'Allis is in the solar, sewing.'

Bernadette's mouth fell open. 'Allis? Sewing?'

Lady Sybille laughed. 'She will be glad to see you in more ways than one. Making clothes is not her forte. She has got herself in such a tangle. She will not allow me to help, but I'm sure she will welcome your advice.'

Hugo went in with them, vaguely conscious of Hortense and the other maidservant, Violette, trailing behind him. Lord Michel was so taken up with Bernadette that they had gone up the steps and entered the great hall before he acknowledged Hugo.

'Hugo!' Lord Michel released Bernadette and clapped him on the shoulder. 'A thousand thanks for bringing her home. How on earth did you manage it?'

'I did little, my lord. Once your daughter read the letter there was no stopping her.'

'Papa, you do understand that this visit will be my farewell to Galard?' Bernadette said quietly. 'I cannot stay long. My Profession Day is a month way.'

Some of the light died in Lord Michel's eyes. None the less, he smiled, took Bernadette's hand, and laid it on his arm. 'Yes, yes, we know about that. We have been dreading it for months.'

Bernadette stared at her father, obviously dismayed. 'Not dreading, Papa, surely?'

'Dreading, I assure you.' Briefly Lord Michel caught Hugo's eye before turning back to his daughter. 'So, for your part, my dear Bernadette, try to understand that I shall do everything in my power to prevent you returning to Saint Claire's. You do not belong in that place.'

Other women might have quailed at the determination in Lord Michel's voice. Not Bernadette. She merely smiled her gentle smile and permitted her father to lead her towards the stairwell that wound up to the solar and the family bedchambers.

Lord Michel glanced back. 'Sir Hugo?'

'My lord?'

Lord Michel waved vaguely at a maidservant who was hastily setting out a basin of water and hand cloths on a side table. 'If you would care to take refreshments with us in the solar before supper, you would be very welcome.'

Hugo bowed. 'Thank you, my lord.'

Chapter Four

Lord Michel waved Bernadette up the stairs. 'After you, my dear.'

Nodding her thanks, Bernadette gathered her grey skirts in one hand. She climbed swiftly, eagerly, round each turn until she reached the small landing outside the solar. In the main, the solar was used by the family and, occasionally, by the ladies of the household when they needed quiet to talk or light and space to sew. Bernadette could hear her stepmother following at a more sedate pace, murmuring softly to her father who, presumably, was bringing up the rear.

Allis, sewing? It scarcely seemed possible. Allis was an appalling seamstress. Bernadette had never understood why her sister was so bad at sewing when she was an expert at healing and all that went with it, including stitching the goriest of wounds. But making a garment? Hopeless. Allis loathed making clothes. Had marriage to Sir Leon changed her so much?

The solar door was ajar. Bernadette pushed it open.

Her sister was sitting at a trestle table with her maid-servant Estelle, frowning darkly at a length of blue damask that was wrinkled by much handling. Several pairs of shears and more crumpled material lay messily on the table, suggesting that her sister had been working on more than one garment and had been defeated by them all.

'Bernadette!' Allis lost her frown and dropped the cloth. Her stool toppled as she flew into Bernadette's arms. 'How wonderful to see you!'

'It is good to see you too.' Bernadette repressed a flash of guilt. 'I shouldn't really be here, but when I read your letter, I had to come.' Warily, she eyed Allis's stomach and tried not to think about the dangers of childbirth. 'You are as slender as ever. I pray you are well?'

'Never better,' Allis said, casting a dark look at the blue damask. She lowered her voice. 'It may not show much, but my shape is already changing. My gowns need altering. I had hopes of making new ones, but as you can see, the results are shameful.'

Bernadette shot a glance at Estelle and spoke softly. 'I take it Estelle knows?'

Allis smiled wryly. 'Aye. The instant I brought out the cloth, Estelle guessed.'

Estelle caught Bernadette's eye and dipped into a curtsy. 'Welcome back, my lady.' Bending, she righted Allis's fallen stool.

'Thank you, Estelle.' Bernadette went to the table,

conscious of a spark of excitement. She loved designing clothes and sewing, and since entering the convent the only time she had been given decent cloth had been when Mother Margerie wanted a new habit for herself or, more recently, when she had been asked to make the altar cloth for the new Pope. Mother Margerie used silk for her habits. The fabrics used by the other nuns and the novices were coarse and scratchy in comparison, nothing like the materials displayed here. Worse, the nuns' habits were ill-designed, being little more than shapeless sacks. No art was required to make them.

Bernadette fingered the blue damask. Save for the creases, it was beautiful cloth. 'This blue is intended to make a kirtle, I take it?'

With a nod, Allis looked sadly at it. 'Bernadette, you might not credit it, but I remembered what you said about tacking before stitching so that's what I did. Only when I tried it on, it felt tight. If it's tight now, imagine what it will feel like in a couple of months, never mind when my confinement is due.'

A bolt of green linen caught Bernadette's eye. 'What are you planning to make with that?' she asked.

'I am uncertain.' Allis looked pensively at it. 'It would suit you.'

'Me?' Bernadette stared.

Allis shrugged. 'I bought it an age ago, before I understood that you were set on becoming a hermit.'

Bernadette raised an eyebrow. 'Hermits live on their

own, Allis. I am joining a community, it's not the same thing.'

Her stepmother and father came in as Bernadette dragged up a stool. She reached for the blue damask. 'This kirtle can easily be let out by inserting another panel. It will give the skirt an attractive flare.' Spotting a spare strip of damask, she extracted it from the pile. 'This is perfect unless you were planning to use it for something else?'

'Help yourself.' Allis laughed. 'Making clothes is a wifely skill I shall never grasp. I was so angry at my ineptitude; I was about to give up and hand everything over to Sybille and Estelle.'

Despite her worry over Allis's pregnancy, Bernadette felt happier than she had done in months. It was wonderful to be home. She continued to sort. Pieces of a surcoat were muddled up with the kirtle, and much besides. Having tidied the various garments into piles she handed the surcoat to Estelle.

'What shall I do? I am eager to help,' Sybille said, joining them at the table.

'How about this?' Bernadette held up a clumsily tacked linen chemise.

Opening it out, Sybille raised an eyebrow at the irregular stitching and nodded. Which left Bernadette with the blue kirtle.

As Bernadette, Estelle and Sybille stitched, Bernadette learned what had been happening after she had visited Galard for her sister's wedding.

'Most of Leon's troop have joined Papa's Guard,' Allis said. 'They are happy to have somewhere to call home. Oh, and as you may guess, Sir Philippe has not been seen since before our marriage.'

Bernadette repressed a shudder. Sir Philippe had been Allis's least favourite suitor. He was an uncouth bully and Bernadette had never been more thankful to hear that Papa had seen Sir Leon's qualities and had permitted Allis to marry him.

'Hugo has been given a squire,' Allis added. 'Did he tell you?'

Bernadette looked up. 'No. Who is it?'

'Olivier. Papa is providing him with a horse, and he is increasing Hugo's pay. It is a promotion of sorts.'

'That's good to hear,' Bernadette murmured. And indeed it was—being pleased for Hugo was far better than dwelling on the fear for her sister that had brought her home. Luckily, sewing was fully absorbing, so she could work on Allis's new wardrobe without paying too much attention to why the new clothes were needed in the first place.

Allis was a strong woman, in body as in mind. She was not going to die in childbed as Mama had done. She was not.

Hugo entered the solar to find the ladies seated industriously around the trestle chatting nineteen to the dozen. The Count of Arles sat in splendid isolation on a cushioned settle, wine cup in hand. Rising, he greeted Hugo with that helpless look that one man gave another when the women in his life were discussing matters over which he held no sway. In this case, it was obviously fashion. Bernadette's eyes were shining, she was in her element. Her sister was holding forth on castle gossip. Catching the names Eglantine and Claude, Hugo understood Allis to be regaling Bernadette with the shocking, although not entirely unexpected news, that Allis's former betrothed Sir Claude of Carpentras had shocked everyone by marrying his mistress, a simple village maiden from Galard. Except that the girl had hardly been a maiden, given that she had already borne Sir Claude a daughter.

Bernadette's brown eyes were round with astonishment. 'How has Claude's father taken it?' she was asking.

'Lord Robert is furious. He and Claude are no longer speaking.'

Bernadette stared at the blue fabric she was working on, before looking back at her sister. 'Lord Robert's anger won't last,' she said slowly. 'I think that marriage to Eglantine might be the making of Claude.'

Allis grinned. 'My thoughts exactly. Claude has never had to fight for anything before. This disagreement with his father could be exactly what he needs.'

Lord Michel caught Hugo's eye and waved him towards a side table. 'Wine is in the green jug, and ale in the blue. Help yourself, lad. You've earned it.'

Hugo nodded his thanks and poured a cup of wine.

He wouldn't dream of taking offence at Lord Michel's use of the word 'lad'. His liege lord was something of a father figure and he had begun calling Hugo 'lad' when he'd first come from Nérac. He continued to use the term occasionally, and always with affection. Hugo took a seat next to Lord Michel.

Eyes on Bernadette, Lord Michel scratched his beard. 'It is a puzzle to see her here, a wonderful puzzle,' he said, softly. 'Admit it, Hugo. You must have said something?'

'No, my lord. It was truly your letter. I simply helped.'

'I can't see the Mother Superior agreeing to this visit. What the devil did you say to the woman?'

'As to that, my lord, we didn't speak to Mother Margerie.' Hugo grimaced. 'Lady Bernadette was so anxious to get away, we left a message for her with the nun at the portress's lodge.'

Lord Michel muffled a snort of laughter. 'I would give a fistful of silver to have seen Mother Margerie's face when she realised Bernadette had gone. She is bound to think my daughter is uncertain about taking her vows.' He scratched his beard again. 'Lord, I pray she changes her mind. The thought of her wasting her life in a convent is utterly abhorrent.'

'Amen to that, my lord.'

Lord Michel leaned in conspiratorially. 'She has a soft spot for you.'

Hugo blinked. It was the first he had heard of it.

'My lord, you must be mistaken. It's true we played together in our youth, but Ang—Lady Bernadette, that is—was quick to outgrow childish games. Once she decided to take the veil, she barely spoke to me.'

The Count waved dismissively. 'Bernadette does not wear her heart on her sleeve, but she is fond of you. Listen, lad, while she is here, I would like you to do everything you possibly can to ensure that she stays. You will be well rewarded if you succeed.'

As Hugo sipped the wine, his gaze strayed to the ladies. Bernadette had a pretty profile, just looking at it was oddly warming. She was concentrating on her stitching, dark eyelashes fanned across her cheeks. It was certainly fortuitous that the ladies had been sewing when they arrived, Bernadette loved it above all things.

He felt his brow crease. But what the devil did Lord Michel think to achieve by asking him to do everything he could to ensure she stayed at Galard Castle?

A violent rush of emotion that he was unable to identify had him clenching his wine cup. His chest hurt. Lord Michel was not speaking of marriage. Hugo had no land and consequently no income other than that granted to him by Lord Michel as one of his trusted retainers.

It went without saying that Bernadette would make someone the perfect wife. She was loving, gentle. Disturbingly attractive. No, no, no. What was he thinking? An alliance between Hugo and the Galard family would be as unequal as the marriage between Sir Claude of Carpentras and his Eglantine.

It wasn't a question of bloodlines. Hugo's forebears, like Bernadette's, claimed descent from the Merovingian kings. In that sense, they were equals. Unfortunately, in this world, bloodlines weren't everything. If Hugo married Bernadette, he would for ever be the foster son who had charmed his lord's younger daughter in order to rise through the ranks. Hugo wanted to make his way in the world on his own merits.

The Count sat beside Hugo, a small smile playing about his mouth as he listened to his ladies. He was oblivious of the desires he had let loose in Hugo's brain. Yes, desires. Shamefully, that was the correct word.

Bernadette had always had a place in Hugo's heart and that would never change. However, it was unsettling to realise that his feelings for her were not as straightforward as they had been. Something had altered. And it seemed to have happened today, the instant he had set eyes on her. Initially, when Bernadette had walked into that gloomy convent courtyard all he had felt was relief. He had been thankful to see for himself that she was well.

Hugo didn't want Lord Michel to notice him staring at her, but he sent another surreptitious glance towards the worktable. Bernadette was frowning at a section of blue fabric, mouth pursed as though preparing for a kiss. She had the most kissable mouth.

Why was he thinking these thoughts today? He did not want to kiss her. To taste. It was wrong. Wrong, wrong, wrong. She was a nun in all but name.

Knowing it was wrong had not prevented Hugo from enjoying holding her. Every step of the ride back he had been unable to stop himself imagining what she might taste like. He yearned to draw her fully into his arms and discover for himself whether her cheeks were as soft as they looked. Her lips…

Lord, what was wrong with him? Hugo's feelings for Bernadette might be altering, but she would be appalled if she knew the earthy nature of his thoughts. She was a novice, for pity's sake. These shameful impulses must be overcome.

Lord Michel didn't want his younger daughter to take the veil. Hugo could not blame him for that, he was reluctant to bid her farewell himself, but if Bernadette had a true vocation even Lord Michel must see that he ought not to overrule her. She deserved support from her family, particularly from her father. Lord Michel was strong and decisive. He was used to getting his own way. It wasn't going to be easy for him to allow Bernadette to follow her heart.

Hugo swallowed a sigh along with his next mouthful of wine and forced a smile. 'My lord, Lady Bernadette told me she has every intention of taking full vows.'

'You refuse to dissuade her?' the Count said, lips tightening.

'I'm sorry, my lord, I do. If Lady Bernadette has a vocation, she should be allowed to join the sisterhood.' Guilt lay like a lump of lead in Hugo's gut. The soul of generosity, Lord Michel had promoted him and had agreed to sponsor his squire. He probably assumed he had every right to believe Hugo would jump to do his bidding. Hugo set his wine cup on a side table and looked the Count directly in the eye. 'I apologise if my answer disappoints you, but I feel strongly about this.'

The Count gave him a searching look. 'So I see.'

'My lord,' Hugo continued awkwardly, 'you might care to know that I have said nothing to Olivier regarding taking him on as my squire. If you wish to change your mind on that score, I will understand.'

The Count made a dismissive gesture. 'I am not going to change my mind about Olivier. What do you take me for? What we decided this morning stands, whether you agree with me on other matters or no.'

'Thank you, my lord.'

'For heaven's sake, man, pour yourself another drink,' Lord Michel said, testily. 'And while you are about it, fetch me another.'

'Of course, my lord.' Hugo smiled his relief, took the Count's wine cup and got to his feet.

When he returned to the settle, the Count's eyes were speculative. 'You never cease to surprise me, lad. You are correct, of course. The decision is Bernadette's and only Bernadette's.' He leaned in. 'However, I see no harm in testing her vocation. They do that at the convent, I believe. I also believe that you might be just the man to help her see sense.'

Hugo laughed out loud. 'You are incorrigible, my lord.'

The chapel bell pealed, and Bernadette looked up from the kirtle with a start.

'Is that Evensong already?'

'I believe so,' Sybille said.

Bernadette wove the needle carefully into the seam, folded the blue damask and rose.

'I must go. I missed Office earlier.' Flushing with sudden embarrassment, her hands went to her head to adjust her veil and wimple. 'Goodness, what must I look like? I was so excited to be home I quite forgot to tidy myself.'

Sybille laughed. 'My dear, there's no need to stand on ceremony with family. However, if you would care to refresh yourself, I have had water sent up to your bedchamber.'

Bernadette's throat tightened. 'I still have a bedchamber?'

'Of course.'

'Thank you, Sybille.'

'I also took the liberty of asking Violette to act as your maidservant. I thought you would welcome a change from Hortense.'

Bernadette found herself blinking back tears. Sybille was her stepmother rather than her birth mother and Bernadette knew that when Papa had married her, he had hoped for more children, particularly a son. It hadn't happened. Notwithstanding the lack of more children, her father and Sybille were happy together. One did not have to look far for the reason. Sybille was a darling. She loved everyone and it was impossible not to love her right back.

Reaching across the table, Bernadette squeezed her stepmother's hand. 'Thank you, Sybille. For everything.'

'Surely you can miss chapel this once?' Allis asked. 'No one at the convent will know if you skip the occasional service.'

Bernadette sent her a regretful smile. 'I would know.'

Sybille gave a gentle cough. 'My dear, you must do as you think best. I trust you are not fasting at present?'

'I am not fasting.'

'Excellent. We shall look forward to seeing you at supper. If you prefer not to eat in the hall, I can have trays brought up here.'

'Heavens, Sybille, there is no need for that. I am content to eat in the hall. It will be a novelty to be able to converse during supper.'

Allis pulled a face. 'I remember, every meal at Saint Claire's is taken in silence. I hated that.'

'Not complete silence,' Bernadette reminded her.

'We have readings from scripture and announcements and—'

'Mother Margerie rationing every mouthful.' Allis shuddered.

'You get used to it after a while.' Bernadette gestured at the unfinished kirtle. 'Allis, do not worry about your clothes. If Sybille is happy to leave everything out on the table, we can set to work again straight after breakfast.'

Sybille agreed there was no need for the sewing to be tidied away and Bernadette left the solar.

Bernadette's bedchamber was exactly as it had been on the day she had left for the convent. There was the large, canopied bed, piled with pillows. The air smelled of beeswax. There was her old travelling chest, with the wood polished to a high shine. The only difference was that someone had placed a jug of daisies on it.

Walking toward the cupboard she used to store her treasures in, she pulled out a small box. Opening it, she found herself staring bemusedly at a lock of her mother's fair hair; at a small wooden angel, carved for her by Hugo; at scraps of parchment with childish drawings—patterns for clothes. There was a sketch of Allis. Another of the layout of the herb garden. And her old missal. Taking out the missal, Bernadette closed the box and put it back in the cupboard.

In a sense it was as though she had left this chamber moments ago. The empty grate in the fireplace was the only sign that her chamber hadn't been occupied in over a year.

So much was the same. So much was different. Bernadette was staring through the window to the courtyard below when the peal of a bell called her back to the present.

Chapel!

Hastily dragging off her veil and wimple, she splashed her face and neck with water, dragged her fingers through her hair and braided it. As she replaced her wimple and veil, she found herself wondering where Hugo had gone. She had noticed that both he and her father had left the solar a while back. No doubt they had been bored to tears with chatter and fashion.

She smiled. Before Hugo and Papa had gone, she had heard them laughing together. It had been an age since she'd heard men laughing in easy camaraderie, and it had given her quite a jolt. It was odd the things one missed without realising it. It was certainly a relief to see that her father remained on easy terms with Hugo. After Allis had married Leon, Bernadette had feared that Hugo might be overlooked. Papa must still think well of him to agree to sponsor Hugo's squire.

Her hasty toilette complete, she snatched up her missal and left the bedchamber at a run. Down the twisting stairs, along the back of the hall, and through the cool stone-flagged corridor to the family chapel at the end.

As she reached the chapel, the door swung open. Hortense stood there, hands folded at her waist. She had changed her gown and was clad in black from head to toe and for one ghastly moment, it was like looking at Mother Margerie. The resemblance was so uncanny Bernadette's heart jumped into her mouth. Confusingly, it made her feel she had stumbled back in time and was a small girl again. Hortense pursed her mouth and looked down at her. Her expression was every bit as disapproving as Mother Margerie's had been before Bernadette's dowry was delivered to the convent.

'Didn't you hear the bell?' Hortense demanded. 'You're late.' She stepped aside with an impatient gesture and indicated that Bernadette should enter the chapel. 'Furthermore, you missed Office earlier.'

Standing her ground, Bernadette gave her a cool look. 'I was busy, Hortense. I was with my family.'

Hortense put her fists on her hips. 'You put family before calling? When you are on the verge of becoming a nun?'

A faint draught whispered down the corridor. A footfall. Bernadette ignored it. She would not allow Hortense to bully her, and the sooner Hortense realised it the better.

'Hortense,' she said, gently. 'It is not your place to

chastise me. I am no longer a child. You stopped being my nurse some years ago.'

'That is irrelevant. While you are here, I am still your maidservant,' Hortense declared. 'I know my duty. When you fail in yours, I am bound to recall you to your senses.'

'As to that, Hortense, you are no longer my maidservant.' Bernadette felt a wave of nausea. She hated conflict and she knew Hortense would dislike hearing that Violette was taking her place. She had to tell her. Hortense must understand that Bernadette was not the same person who had entered Saint Claire's. She had grown up, and no one, not even her mama's maidservant, was going to force their will on her.

Hortense's eyes narrowed. 'How so?'

'My stepmother suggested that while I am here, Violette should be my maidservant. I have agreed.'

Hortense's cheeks mottled. 'Violette is your maidservant? You are lying.' Her gaze flickered past Bernadette to someone behind her.

Turning, Bernadette felt herself relax. Hugo. He was staring at Hortense as though he couldn't believe his ears. 'Hortense?' Hugo's voice, though quiet, held menace. 'I surely misheard you. You cannot be accusing Lady Bernadette of lying.'

'Can I not?' Hortense blustered. 'I thought I'd taught her well. Her place is in there.' She jabbed a finger towards the spot in the chapel where Bernadette's mother rested. 'It's her duty to pray for her mother's soul. Lady Genevieve was the kindest, most perfect woman. If Novice Bernadette prayed for her every day, it wouldn't expunge her guilt.'

'Guilt?' Hugo drew his head back. 'What the blazes are you talking about?'

Bernadette swallowed. 'Hortense blames me for my mother's death.'

Hugo stepped swiftly between Bernadette and Hortense, forcing Hortense away from the chapel and further into the corridor. 'That's preposterous. Don't listen to her, my lady. Such words are pure poison.'

Bernadette was touched by Hugo's support. He looked so angry. Gently, she laid her hand on his sleeve, ignoring the hiss of disapproval from Hortense. 'I realise that. Thank you for coming to my rescue. It is not necessary, but I appreciate the gesture.'

Nodding, Hugo cleared his throat. 'My pleasure.' He looked coldly at Hortense. 'Lady Bernadette wishes to pray. In peace. You are not required. I shall stand guard to ensure her safety.'

Hortense glared at Bernadette. 'Your stepmother will hear of this. You have changed, Novice, and not for the better. You are falling into sin.' She rounded on Hugo. 'As for you, sir, I used to think well of you. No more. You are a disgrace.' Nostrils flaring, she marched away from them, down to the end of the corridor and out of sight.

Bernadette put her hand to her forehead. 'That woman...'

'What happened to her? She has become a viper.'

'She has certainly got worse,' Bernadette agreed. 'Thank goodness you stopped arguing with her. We would have been here all day otherwise.'

'Oh?'

'She likes to have the last word, you must have noticed.'

Hugo laughed. 'I shall watch out for that. Good Lord, I never realised she was such a bully.'

Bernadette shrugged. 'I am told she served my mother faithfully.'

'By whom? Hortense herself, I suppose.'

Bernadette nodded.

'Well, she is not showing much loyalty to you,' Hugo said. 'Angel, I doubt she has your interests at heart. It is amazing you put up with her for as long as you did.'

Bernadette's gaze strayed to the white marble flagstone near the altar. Her mother's resting place. 'It was not easy, but Hortense adored Maman. She would tell me stories about her. While I was growing up, she was constantly reminding me how devastated she was by her death. She maintains that because Maman died when I was born, I am to blame for her death.'

'What! Angel, that is outrageous. Hortense has been using your guilt—your ill-founded guilt, I must stress—to manipulate you. I wish I had realised sooner.'

'Hortense was not always like this,' Bernadette said,

slowly, thinking it through. 'As a child I was curious about my mother. I wished I had known her. I believe Allis has a few shadowy memories, but I had nothing. Hortense would indulge me by answering my questions.' She sighed. 'Over the years that changed. She began to suggest I went to the chapel to pray that Maman rested in peace.' She stared at her mother's ledger stone and her voice broke. 'Hugo, what if history repeats itself with Allis?'

'What do you mean?'

'Allis might die in childbed.'

Frowning, Hugo studied the tight set of her mouth and shook his head. 'Angel, Allis is a strong woman.'

Bernadette's eyes filled with tears. 'According to Hortense, my mother was a strong woman. The birth went well at the beginning. I was born and then… There was a lot of blood. A never-ending river of red, Hortense told me. Hugo, the same thing happened to a woman who had taken refuge in the convent. She died just like my mother. It happens often. Childbirth is dangerous.'

Swearing under his breath, Hugo folded her hand in his. 'I had no notion you had such a strong fear of childbirth. Hortense had no right to fill an impressionable, sensitive child's head with such images. How old were you when she began tormenting you in this way?'

'Tormenting? Hugo, Hortense did not intend—'

'Did she not? I disagree. She must have seen

how upset you were, yet she deliberately made matters worse. She has given you a terror of childbirth. Granted, not all women survive childbed, but most do.'

Huge brown eyes held his. 'Hugo, many women die in childbed.'

'And many do not.' Hugo swore under his breath. Angel's features were so drawn and anxious, she looked like a stranger. Hortense had much to answer for. The ghastly images she had planted in Bernadette's mind seemed to have flowered into a blind, unreasoning terror of pregnancy and all that went with it. Fear had taken Angel to a place where rational argument was meaningless. If he was to help her, he must lighten the mood.

'Hortense is a misery. She hated it when you had fun. There was that time in the barn when we were playing hide and seek. She routed you out and chased you into the chapel. Come to think of it, it happened quite regularly. Another time we were fishing.'

Bernadette gave him a watery smile. 'I remember. I had landed a trout—my first. I was so excited.'

'She sent you to the chapel. Always the chapel.' Hugo shook his head. 'It never ceased to amaze me why you obeyed so meekly.'

'I thought it my duty. I believed her when she insisted that praying for Maman would ensure her soul rested in peace. I thought it would expiate my sin.' Hugo's eyes held hers, dark and intent, and for a moment Bernadette couldn't breathe. It was as though they could see into each other's hearts.

She let out a soft sigh. 'Hugo, you must not feel badly for me. I soon discovered I liked being sent to the chapel. It was so quiet.' She held up her missal. 'I could read through the psalms in peace. I could think. Hortense never disturbed me when I was at prayer.'

He grunted. 'The chapel became your hiding place.'

'More than that, much more. It was my refuge. My sanctuary.'

'The world is the poorer without you in it. And Hortense is to blame. I see that now.'

'Hugo?' Startled by this blunt conclusion, Bernadette stared.

He lifted his shoulders. 'Forget it. I spoke out of turn. I am glad you have found your calling.'

'Thank you,' she said, even as she was wondering why Hugo's acceptance of her vocation should be so dispiriting.

'You still wish to pray?'

'Aye.'

'Very well.' With a slight bow, he stepped back. 'I shall stand guard lest the viper returns.'

'Hugo.'

'She is a viper, and you would do well to remember it. Every time she tries to drive you into the chapel, ask this—is she doing it for your benefit or hers?'

Bernadette huffed. 'Sometimes, Hugo, you are too quick to condemn.'

'Am I?'

'Yes! Have some compassion. Hortense was my link to my mother, and she remains so today. She is never happier than when she talks about her. How does she benefit by my leaving to join the convent in Avignon?'

'She gains prestige. The knowledge that it was she who encouraged your desire to turn your back on the world.'

Bernadette felt a flash of anger and quickly suppressed it. Hugo didn't notice, he was in full flow.

'Angel, that woman punished you when you were an innocent child, and she is still punishing you. She enjoyed being Lady Genevieve's maidservant. It brought her status. And thanks to her sour nature, she lost that status when your mother died. When Lady Sybille married your father, I understand she brought her handmaid with her. Lady Sybille didn't need another maidservant.'

'Hugo, Papa married Sybille long before you left Gascony. How on earth did you find that out?'

Hugo avoided her gaze, and his cheeks darkened. 'I asked around.'

Bernadette blinked. 'When did you ask? Today?'

'No, years ago. Angel, it is common knowledge.' He gave her a gentle, heart-wrenchingly affectionate shove. 'Go on. Go and pray.' His voice strengthened. 'Go whenever you want. Do whatever you want. Just as long as you ignore Hortense. That woman is a viper.'

Chapter Five

Three days later, Bernadette was on her own in the solar, distracting herself by putting the finishing touches to the blue kirtle she was making for Allis. She had not seen Allis that morning, though Violette was due to join her any time now.

She shook out the kirtle, examining it with a critical eye. The lining sat well, and the silver braid running along the edges was very pretty. She felt a sense of real accomplishment. Making gowns for Allis, sewing for someone she loved was, Bernadette realised, altogether different from making things with duty in mind. The kirtle had turned out perfectly. Allis would look well in it. Beautiful. Mind, Allis would look beautiful in a sack. Pregnancy—and Leon's love, Bernadette acknowledged with a pang she was reluctant to examine—suited her. Her sister positively glowed.

Bernadette was glad she'd witnessed Allis's well-being and only wished it had allayed her fears over

Allis facing the rigours of childbirth. Unfortunately, it had not. Her anxieties remained, although seeing Allis so happy certainly helped. As did designing patterns for the rest of the sewing. Bernadette hated being idle and there was solace in taking practical action. Sybille and Violette had followed her instructions diligently. Just sitting with them here, casually chatting as she sewed had been a joy.

A chill stole over her. Being here, sewing in the comfort of her family was certainly casting a different light on her vocation. Bernadette was dreading going back to the convent. She felt sick whenever she thought about it, so much so that she'd put off thinking about it entirely. She could do so no longer. When she had been clothed as a novice, she had made a solemn promise to herself and to God, that she would do her best to honour her calling.

I must go back.

Hearing footfall in the stairwell, she cocked her head. It couldn't be Violette, the tread was far too heavy. And surely that slight chink was a spur. Her breath stopped. Hugo. It must be Hugo. She really wanted it to be Hugo.

The latch lifted and there he was grinning at her. 'Good morning, Angel.'

'Good morning, sir,' she said, placing a slight emphasis on the 'sir', even as she caught herself wondering why she found his teasing insolence so attractive.

He came to the table and looked down at her, grin fading. 'You are very formal today.'

'I think it best. I shall be leaving soon.'

Hugo's dark eyes held hers and after a moment he bent, pulled out the stool next to hers and sat. He was far too large for the stool and his elbow brushed hers. His knee. The contact was plainly accidental, yet it loosed a host of butterflies in her stomach. To hide her discomfiture, Bernadette busied herself folding Allis's kirtle.

'That is why I wanted to speak to you,' he said. 'Were you planning on leaving in the next few days?'

The butterflies vanished and her skin chilled. Slowly, she placed the kirtle on the table. It was ridiculous how ill the thought of returning to Saint Claire's made her feel. Final Vows were irrevocable. She would have to make her oath before God and all the sisters. Was this more than nerves? It certainly felt like it. She bit her lip. 'Why are you asking?'

'One of your father's allies has trouble at his borders and your father has invited me to lead a patrol. We would be going north and it would take a few days. Before I commit myself, I wanted to know your mind. If you are returning to the convent, I would like to offer myself as your escort.'

'That is very kind,' she murmured. 'I should be going back, and I would prefer your escort above all others. However, if you escort me, who will lead the patrol?'

'Sir Leon is happy to go.'

Bernadette's brow creased as she stared into Hugo's dark, long-lashed eyes. *I must go back.* She willed herself to say the words, but they would not come. Suddenly she could barely think. Her mind had been invaded by the most irrelevant of thoughts. Hugo was the kindest, most thoughtful man on earth. A true friend. Why had it taken her so long to see it?

'Hugo?'

His face softened, and she knew without being told that he was pleased she had dispensed with formality. 'Mmm?'

'Do you think it is odd we have had no word from the convent?'

'Not really.' His eyes took on a hard glint. 'The harpy has no need to haul you back, you are already in her claws. She has your dowry. She is confident you will be taking your vows.'

Bernadette's mouth dried. 'Hugo, I do not want to go.' There, she'd said it. Her fingers curled into the blue kirtle, creasing the fabric. Heavens, her eyes were burning. Blinking fast, she held back the tears.

Hugo went still. Then, bless him, he simply placed his hand on hers and gently straightened her fingers, smoothing out the blue cloth.

'No?'

She stared at his hand and the words flew out of her mouth. 'No. Definitely no. I cannot go back. I cannot become a nun.' They were awful, dishonourable words. Words that made a mockery of her novice's vows and her efforts to win Mother Margerie's approval. They fell like stones into a deep well of silence. She glanced warily at Hugo. 'If you dare say "I told you so", I swear I shall kill you.'

Hugo simply looked at her before saying, 'Angel, it's your decision. It's always been your decision.'

Her eyes misted. It was hard to break eye contact. For a moment, there was something in Hugo's expression she had not seen before. He was relieved she'd changed her mind, but it was more than that. Briefly, she caught a glimpse of something else. Something unidentifiable. A spark. It was there one moment and gone the next.

Becoming aware of his thumb moving comfortingly over the back of her hand, she pulled free. She was not going to notice how good that felt, it would be wrong. Absurd. Hugo was simply being kind and she was nothing but a dreamer. There was no point longing for the impossible.

She lurched into speech. 'I know it does not make sense. I fought so hard to stay at Saint Claire's. There were hardships, but I understood my vocation would be tested and I expected them.' She gave a tight laugh. 'At the beginning I even enjoyed it. The challenge of proving I had a true calling was irresistible.'

'It's understandable. You had never been tested before and there is satisfaction in proving yourself.'

Bernadette stared blindly at Allis's kirtle and struggled to sort through the muddle in her mind. 'The worst of it is, I have no idea whether my reluctance to take Final Vows is because I'm temperamentally unsuited for convent life, or whether it's down to something else.'

A something else, she recognised with an alarming jolt, that took the form, the very attractive form, of the knight sitting next to her. The knight who had long been in love with her beautiful sister.

'It seemed so right at the beginning,' she added. Having no doubts had been easy. This—being beset by them—was misery indeed.

He shrugged. 'Perhaps you have changed.'

She rubbed her brow. In fairness, Hugo was not wholly to blame for her reluctance to make her profession. There was more to it than that. Her family, for one thing. She hadn't realised how much she loved them. How much joy she would feel simply by being with them again. Not to mention that Galard was far more involving than Saint Claire's. 'I cannot have changed that much. I was so certain.' She hesitated. 'Life at Saint Claire's certainly changed, particularly after my dowry arrived.'

Hugo's mouth thinned. 'That Mother Superior is as manipulative as Hortense.'

Bernadette drew in a deep breath. 'Mother Margerie is a complicated woman.'

'Angel, you are too kind. She is a harpy. Judging by

your appearance at your sister's wedding, they never fed you. You looked positively skeletal.'

Bernadette shook her head at him. 'Hugo, I despair. Do you have to be quite so blunt?'

'At the wedding, you were naught but skin and bone.' He looked her up and down and his mouth relaxed. And was it her imagination or did his gaze linger on her breasts? 'Thank God you've filled out. You look charming.'

His voice rang with sincerity. Bernadette's cheeks warmed and to her astonishment she had to repress the impulse to cross her arms over her breasts.

'Charming?' She plucked at her threadbare habit and choked back a laugh. 'In this? Hugo, for pity's sake stop it. It is pointless flirting with me.' She was very fond of him. She had been sweet on him when she was younger, but she did not love him, except as a friend. A dear and old friend.

There were many types of love, after all. The love between sisters, such as the love she felt for Allis was one; the love between friends, such as that which existed between her and Hugo was another. The other sort of love, the passionate love the poets spoke of was something she had yet to experience.

He leaned in, hand on his heart, and a peculiar agony shot through her. 'Pointless, you say? Angel, are you sure about that?'

Disturbed by a burst of longing for Hugo to want to flirt with her, Bernadette bit her lip and racked her brains to remember what they had been talking about. Oh, yes, her dowry. She kept her voice light. 'You, sir, are a menace. But you are correct in one respect. Once my dowry was added to the convent coffers life did become easier. Nowadays I only work in the vegetable garden if I choose to do so.'

'In my opinion, a lady shouldn't be working in the vegetable garden,' Hugo said, curtly.

'I quite like it.'

Hugo gave her a look which told her he thought she had lost her mind. 'You? Digging up turnips? God save us. And the turnips for that matter.'

She stiffened. 'Tread carefully, sir, I've become quite the expert with a hoe.'

He laughed and held up his hands in a gesture of defeat she recognised from their childhood. 'Pax. Pax. I am sure you are a fiend with a hoe.'

'You had better believe it. Seriously, Hugo, life transformed once my dowry was delivered. I was also permitted to sew.'

Hugo ran his gaze over the garments on the table. 'That is a blessing. I know how you love it.'

'Aye, the convent needlework was enjoyable but coming home has been a revelation. The pleasure of sewing in a dismal chamber off the cloisters can't possibly compare to sewing in the company of women I love. And sinful though it might be to enjoy praise, it is good to be genuinely appreciated. Mother Margerie is sparing with praise.'

'That woman is sparing with everything.'

Bernadette couldn't argue with him there. 'Allis on the other hand,' she continued, 'well, her joyful appreciation gave this work wings. Today, with the exception of that green bolt of cloth which Allis apparently has no desire to use, her new wardrobe is complete. Allis herself, needless to say, hasn't set a stitch. Not one. She has talked and laughed and generally kept us all entertained.'

Hugo's dark eyes softened. As usual, she sensed he understood far more than she was saying. 'In conclusion, Angel, you have realised you are not made to be a nun.'

'I have.' She grimaced. 'Hugo, this isn't going to be easy. Papa wants me to stay—'

'I want you to stay,' he interrupted softly.

'You do?' Despite herself, her heart swelled.

'Of course, everyone does.' He pulled a face. 'Everyone save Mother Margerie.'

Bernadette put her hand on his arm. 'Hugo, I ought to tell Papa before I tell anyone else.'

'That would be wise.' He hesitated. 'Would you like me to come with you? Your father will doubtless wish to write to the harpy himself. He will want your dowry back. I can convey his letter to the convent and secure your dowry while I'm about it. When that is done, I am sure Lord Michel will breathe a sigh of relief.'

'Thank you, Hugo, your support is welcome, but you need to know that I shall be coming with you.'

'What? No.' Untidy fair hair flopped over his eyes as he shook his head. Impatiently, he pushed it back. 'Angel, leave this to me, for pity's sake. If you get within an inch of that woman, she will try to coerce you. She will—'

She gripped his arm. 'Hugo, listen. I must go. Not to do so would be a terrible act of cowardice. I need to inform her to her face. It was my decision to enter the novitiate, and it is mine to leave it.'

'It would be easier to write to the woman.'

'It would be easier, but it would be wrong. Hugo, I am coming with you. This is my responsibility.'

They were still arguing when they walked into the main estate office and found Lord Michel at his desk.

'Hugo, it is my decision, not yours,' Bernadette said. As the door latch clicked behind them, she scowled. 'You have no right to dictate to me, none whatsoever.' She broke off abruptly. Her father was watching them, mouth twitching.

Slowly, he stroked his beard. 'Such heat, Bernadette,' he said, mildly. 'What's amiss?'

Somewhat awkwardly, Bernadette explained her change of heart.

'So you see, Papa, embarrassing as it is to admit I have made such a grave mistake, I wanted you to be the first to know that I will not be making Final Vows.' She stared fixedly at an inkpot. 'I would like to apologise for not seeing it sooner. I cannot explain it, but—'

Her father's chair scraped the floor as he stood to take her hands. His eyes were shining and his smile radiated relief and happiness. 'My dear, there is no need to explain. Nor is there need for apologies. I am just thankful you have come to your senses. Saint Claire's...' her father gave an expressive shudder '...is my idea of hell. I could not for the life of me understand what you were about.' His eyes twinkled. 'I confess that sometimes I find the ease with which women change their minds a trial. In this case, I am delighted. So, please, no more apologies.'

'Thank you, Papa.'

Her father kissed her forehead and glanced knowingly at Hugo. 'I am not quite the first to know, am I?'

'Papa?'

'Why is Hugo here? I take it you took him into your confidence.'

'Yes, Papa.' Heat rose in Bernadette's cheeks, though why she was blushing she had no idea. Her father's gaze shifted between her and Hugo and his expression warned her that he was probably reading far too much into Hugo's support.

Hugo stepped forward. 'My lord, it occurred to me that you would be writing to the Mother Superior about Lady Bernadette's decision.'

'Aye. I shall also send a purse as an offering. The convent gave both my daughters board and lodging

for some while, it is only fair. Are you offering to deliver the letter, Hugo?'

'I would be delighted to do so, my lord. And with
your agreement I can bring back Lady Bernadette's
dowry. I would take a large escort, so it would be perfectly secure. The only difficulty is that I will not be
able to lead the patrol to the north.'

Her father grunted. 'No matter, Leon can take the
patrol. My thanks, Hugo, you seem to have thought
of everything. I suggest you do not mention the purse
until you have the dowry.'

Shooting Hugo a dark look, for he seemed to have
conveniently forgotten that Bernadette too intended
to go to Saint Claire's, she nudged him aside.

'Papa, Hugo has neglected to tell you that I shall be
accompanying the escort to Saint Claire's.'

'You will, will you?' Her father turned back to Hugo
and an amused smile flickered into life. 'So that is
what you were bickering about when you came in.'

Bernadette spoke through gritted teeth. 'Papa, Hugo
does not understand, but you will. You have always
stressed the importance of being responsible for one's
actions.' Her father nodded agreement and she continued. 'It was my decision to enter the novitiate. Mine
and mine alone. Therefore, I must speak to Mother
Margerie. I must tell her to her face that I cannot take
my vows. Papa, by all means give Hugo your letter. I,
however, will deliver it.'

A line appeared on her father's brow. 'You are happy to have Hugo lead your escort?'

'Of course.'

'Very well.'

Bernadette had not realised she had been holding her breath, but she released it on a long sigh. Relief. 'Thank you, Papa.'

Bernadette and Hugo's reception at Saint Claire's was less than gracious. At noon the next day, shortly after the bell had rung for Sext, they found themselves in the convent courtyard. They had not been permitted further inside. Hugo's new squire Olivier had not even got that far, he was stationed in the alley on the other side of the convent wall. Meanwhile, their escort was waiting in the nearby square. Olivier's task was to inform the men when Bernadette's dowry was secure, and they were ready to leave.

'Is it not possible to wait in the guest chamber?' Bernadette had asked. She was still clad in her novice's habit. Until she had spoken with Mother Margerie, it seemed wrong to wear anything else.

Sister Julia—far fiercer than Sister Teresa—was acting as gatekeeper that day. She had given Bernadette a cool look. 'My apologies, Novice. Mother Margerie's instructions were clear, she will meet you here.'

Sister Julia's tone had been anything but apologetic. Bernadette shrugged at Hugo. They waited. And waited. Unfortunately, the longer they waited, the drier Bernadette's mouth became. Her stomach clumped into one huge knot.

Hugo touched the back of her hand. 'Relax, Angel. The harpy is doing this on purpose.'

'I know,' Bernadette muttered. 'I knew this was going to be dreadful when Olivier wasn't allowed to enter.'

Bernadette's foot began to tap and to her surprise, she realised that the knot in her stomach wasn't fear, it was anger. 'Mother Margerie had better honour us with her presence soon,' she muttered. 'We have been well over half an hour. Sext does not last that long.'

'Angel, the woman has guessed you have changed your mind. It is the last thing she wants, and she thinks to make you nervous. Prepare to be intimidated.'

Bernadette stood very straight. She was generally even tempered, anger was not an emotion she dealt with often, but in this case, it was invigorating. She took a deep breath. She felt powerful. Strong. 'I am fine, Hugo.'

A shadow filled the archway leading to the cloisters. Mother Margerie. She was wearing the silk habit Bernadette had sewn for her. The black of the habit made a stark contrast with her white wimple. It made her look like a magpie. Magpies, Bernadette thought, stifling an unexpected urge to giggle, weren't half as intimidating as harpies. As Mother Margerie stepped forward, black skirts rustling, Bernadette sent her a haughty look, one designed to remind the woman that she was the daughter of a count.

Irritably, Mother Margerie flicked her hand at Hugo as though brushing away a fly. 'Novice, dismiss your lackey. He has no place here.'

'No.' It was the first time Bernadette had contradicted the Mother Superior and it came out with quiet force. Mother Margerie's eyes narrowed. Bracing herself for an outburst, Bernadette added, 'The lackey, as you call him, happens to be captain of my father's guard. His name is Sir Hugo Albret of Nérac.'

Hugo stood unmoving at her shoulder, not deigning to acknowledge the introduction. Silent and strong and, *Dieu merci*, letting her do the talking. Bernadette had been dreading that he would interrupt, and with her flow broken she feared she might not emerge from this with her head held high. She pushed on.

'Mother, I have come to inform you that I will not be joining the Order. Recently, I have had doubts concerning the strength of my calling. Over the weeks these doubts have strengthened to certainty. I cannot become a nun.'

Mother Margerie came closer and looked down at Bernadette from her superior height. 'You took your novice's vows happily enough.'

'That is true. I have always taken comfort from prayer. I enjoy reading the psalms. And Saint Claire's was undoubtedly a haven when I needed it most, for which I am grateful. I have learned much in my time here and must thank you for that. Regrettably, it is not enough to justify giving my life to the convent.'

'You would be giving your life to the Almighty, not the convent,' Mother Margerie bit out.

Bernadette kept her voice calm. Steady. Certain. 'I do not know what God plans for me, that is for me to discover. But I am clear on this, I was not meant to become a nun.'

Mother Margerie stared, an expression on her face that Bernadette had never seen before. She looked utterly bewildered. 'But you were so sure. So certain. You understood the nature of the tasks imposed upon you to test your calling better than any other novice.'

A muscle flickered at the side of her eye and her voice became hard. 'Novice Bernadette, such doubts are common before Final Vows. You are a nun in all but name, and I pray that you reconsider. You are a boon to this convent.' She plucked at her black silk skirts. 'You sew so well. God would not have given you such skills if He didn't intend that you remain here.'

'I can use my talents elsewhere,' Bernadette said. 'I am sorry, Mother, I cannot become a nun.'

'That is your final word?'

'It is.' Bernadette turned to the man at her side and held out her hand. 'Sir Hugo, if you would be so good as to hand me my father's letter.'

Hugo passed it over and Bernadette offered it to Mother Margerie. 'Mother, this is from my father. As you will see, he endorses my decision. He asks that you hand my dowry to Sir Hugo. We will take it with us when we leave.'

Mother Margerie went rigid. She did not deign to look at the letter. 'Your dowry stays.'

Slowly, Bernadette shook her head. 'Papa will not allow that.'

'He will have to. I took my pains with you, Novice. You cannot simply take your dowry and walk away.'

Hugo cleared his throat. 'I must remind you, Mother, you are speaking to Lady Bernadette Galard of Arles.'

Mother Margerie swept on as though Hugo hadn't spoken. 'Your dowry, Novice, is forfeit. Payment for the trouble you have caused. I invested much in you.'

Hugo opened his mouth and Bernadette held up her hand to stop him. To no avail. 'And what pray did you invest?' he demanded. 'Not food, certainly. As I recall, Lady Bernadette was little more than a wraith when she attended Lady Allisende's wedding. It is plain Lady Bernadette gave far more than she received.'

'What would you know of such things?'

'I know her. Lady Bernadette always gives more than she receives. What about her work in the vegetable garden? The vestments and altar cloths she embroidered?'

Mother Margerie looked incredulously between Bernadette and Hugo. 'You have been gossiping, I see.'

'Friends talk to one another, Mother Margerie,' Bernadette said. 'Sir Hugo is an old friend.'

Hugo was raking Mother Margerie with his eyes, from the top of her snowy wimple to the hem of her black habit. 'Aye, it has been my privilege to know Lady Bernadette for many years, and as you yourself acknowledge she has many skills. Why, I would wager she made that gown you're wearing.' His eyes filled with scorn and, ignoring the gasp of indignation, he reached out to finger the stuff of the skirt. 'Silk, I see. How does that fit with your vow of poverty?'

'Take your hands off me, you ignorant churl!' Mother Margerie spluttered in outrage.

'With pleasure. You, *madame*, are…' Hugo stepped back, his sentence unfinished, and Bernadette found herself biting the inside of her cheek to stop herself from smiling.

She held out her father's letter. 'Read it, Mother Margerie, please. We are taking my dowry back.'

'Today,' Hugo added. 'We take it back today.'

'I shall not permit it.' Refusing still to look at the letter, Mother Margerie nodded pointedly at the door that led into the alley. 'If you insist on leaving, you had best go now. The dowry stays.'

Hugo made a noise that was suspiciously like a growl. 'Mother Margerie, mark my words. It will be in your interest and the interest of everyone in the convent, that you do.' Though soft, his voice was so threatening that it sent a chill down Bernadette's spine.

'I shall make this simple,' he continued. 'Lady Bernadette and I are indeed leaving, and we are taking her dowry with us. This can go two ways. You can act like the devout nun you are meant to be and direct me to your treasury. If not, you may care to know that my squire is on the other side of that wall, waiting to carry my orders to the Castle Guard.'

Mother Margerie took a hasty step back. 'The Castle Guard? They are here in Avignon?'

'They are in the nearby square. To a man, they are seasoned warriors. They will not hesitate to use force to gain entry. They will search this convent from cellar to bell tower. They will brook no resistance and no stone will be left unturned. They will find Lady Bernadette's dowry. Resistance may result in unpleasantness. Do you understand?'

Hand shaking, Mother Margerie took the letter.

Chapter Six

'Thank God that's over,' Hugo said fervently. They were riding back to Castle Galard. With Bernadette's dowry.

In the unlikely event of an ambush on their company, the chest containing Bernadette's dowry was strapped to a packhorse and surrounded by his men. It was easy to see why Mother Margerie had fought to keep it. It was weightier than Hugo had expected. A substantial dowry indeed.

'Aye. It is a relief that Mother Margerie saw sense and returned it without further trouble,' Bernadette said, quietly.

'Indeed. I had no wish to employ force in a convent. Your father will be pleased.'

Bernadette nodded. She had been subdued since leaving the convent, Hugo wasn't sure why, though as a former novice, trained to obey her superior without question, she must have found the whole business taxing. She was probably exhausted.

When he caught her sending him a furtive glance, he lifted an eyebrow. 'Angel, you're no longer bound to the convent, which as far as I am concerned is something to rejoice about. When you get home, you can burn that ghastly habit and put on whatever you wish to wear. Yet you look anything but happy. What is troubling you?'

'Nothing.' Breaking eye contact, she trained her gaze on the back of a man riding in the vanguard. Her voice was dull, it did not ring true. 'Thank you for your help, Hugo, I could not have done it without you.'

And there it was. As Hugo stared at her profile, at the frustrated set of her mouth, he realised what the difficulty was. Bernadette had wanted to deal with that woman herself. In that respect, she was remarkably like her sister. Somehow, the shy little girl he had left in the convent had become fiercely independent. She resented having to rely on him.

He put warmth in his voice. 'Think nothing of it. I am always happy to help a beautiful lady like yourself. Besides, you could hardly have carried a dowry such as yours back on your own. It weighs more than Clovis.'

That won him a shy smile and a faint blush. Bernadette really was entrancing when she blushed.

'Don't flirt with me, Hugo Albret.'

'Angel, you are no longer a novice, what is wrong with flirting?' He grinned. 'Think of it as practice.'

'Practice?' She rolled her eyes. 'Why on earth should I practise flirting?'

'Flirting has its uses. For one thing, flirting can be fun.' When a sound of exasperation escaped her, he gave an exaggerated sigh. 'That's right, Angel. Fun. There is nothing wrong with a harmless flirtation. I do hope your sojourn in Saint Claire's hasn't spoiled that for you.'

She shook her head at him. 'Honestly, Hugo, you talk such nonsense. Flirting is mere dalliance.'

'Not at all. With the right woman it can be extremely enjoyable.' And he, Hugo recognised with a jolt, would enjoy flirting with her.

'Dalliance is dangerous.' She spoke curtly and her lips tightened.

Hugo stared. Dangerous? What did she mean? He knew better than to interrupt. If he waited, she would explain herself.

'It can lead to unwanted babies,' she said. 'And if a woman dies in childbed, to death.'

Reaching across, he touched the back of her hand. 'Angel, I was not talking about seduction, that is something else entirely. Believe me, flirting between men and women can be sweet.'

'Sweet,' she repeated, shaking her head. Unconvinced.

'Yes. Sweet.' It came to him that Bernadette had not truly grown up until after she had gone to the convent. Thus, her only experience of observing the interactions between men and women that were a part of castle life were through the eyes of a cossetted and extremely innocent young woman. 'Angel, believe me, dalliance does not invariably result in unwanted children. The important thing is that both parties understand the rules.'

Her eyebrows shot up. 'Rules? Hugo, there were rules in the convent. Do not tell me there are rules regarding flirting.'

He laughed. 'Well, perhaps rules is too strong a word. What I'm saying is that it is important that each person understands how far the other is prepared to go.'

Her eyes held his, dark and unusually intent. 'Do you flirt, Hugo?'

'When the opportunity presents itself, and if the lady is personable, of course. You should try it some time.' He glanced at the packhorse, laden with her dowry. A pang went through him. 'Seriously, Angel, when the local knights and lords hear you are no longer tucked away in the convent, you will need to be able to flirt. You will be mobbed by noblemen suing for your hand.' He saw her shudder and broke off.

'Stop, Hugo, please. I've only just left Saint Claire's. It's far too soon to think about marriage.'

'I doubt your father will push you into it immediately. But word will get about. You may have to think about it sooner than you would like.' He found himself frowning, wondering why the idea of Bernadette marrying another man held so little appeal. No, it was worse than that, the idea of her marrying elsewhere was extremely distasteful. There was a hollow feeling in the pit of his stomach. Why?

It was the first time Hugo had entertained the idea of Bernadette marrying. That wasn't surprising. When she'd entered the convent, she'd been safely out of harm's way. There had been no risk of her marrying, none whatsoever. Overnight, that had changed. She had entered the convent a young girl, and she was leaving it a pretty—an exceedingly pretty—young woman.

The pretty young woman was still staring at the back of a man in the vanguard, so it was easy for him to study her without being observed. She rode well. Just like her sister she preferred to ride astride, there was nothing new in that. There she sat, straight backed, holding Tansy's reins with her usual easy confidence. The short novice's veil fluttering about her head did nothing to disguise her profile. It was the profile of a young woman who was his friend.

Her nose hadn't changed. Her eyes hadn't changed, they were the same rich brown that they'd always been, framed by thick eyelashes. Bernadette had always had long eyelashes. Nowadays, they were positively luxuriant. His gaze lingered on her shape. Her body had changed. New subtle curves made every inch desirable. Extraordinarily so.

Desirable? Half shocked with himself, feeling as

though he had lost his way and wandered into a thorn thicket, he forced his gaze back to her profile. Her skin was clear. Her cheeks were kissable. Kissable Bernadette.

Had she altered so much? As he studied her, it occurred to him that the changes he found must be down to a shift in his viewpoint. Having practically grown up with her at Galard, he had assumed she would always be there. He had taken her—his dearest friend and playmate—for granted. Her decision to stay in the convent had knocked him back. How he had missed her!

The hollow feeling intensified. There was no doubt about it. Once word got about that Lady Bernadette Galard was free to marry, noblemen for miles about would fall over themselves to win her.

'It will be a positive stampede,' he muttered.

'A stampede?' Beautiful, long-lashed brown eyes caught his. 'Hugo, what are you talking about?'

When they rode into the bailey at Galard some time later, they had talked non-stop. About Galard. About Bernadette's family and how much she loved them. The conversation about flirtation and dalliance had not been referred to again. It was probably just as well, Hugo reflected, as a shout from the guardhouse announced their arrival.

Several guards appeared. The sergeant ran up and saluted.

'Sir Hugo, Lord Michel asked to be informed the moment you return,' the man said.

'Papa will want to know you have the dowry,' Bernadette murmured.

The sergeant nodded. 'Just so, my lady. The Count has asked to see both of you in his office.'

The reckoning took place with Bernadette's father sitting at his desk. Wine and ale were brought so that Bernadette and Hugo could refresh themselves. When the accounting was done, Lord Michel closed the dowry chest with a satisfied sigh and locked it. He smiled at Hugo. 'My thanks, sir. You have taken a weight off my mind in more ways than one.'

'Will that be all, my lord?' Hugo asked, replacing his ale cup on the table.

'For now. We shall see you at supper, no doubt.'

'No doubt.'

After Hugo had left, Lord Michel set the dowry chest aside and smiled at his younger daughter. 'Bernadette, my dear, I need to speak to you.'

Bernadette folded her hand on her lap. 'Of course, Papa. What about?'

Her father leaned back in his chair. 'I cannot tell you how relieved I am that you have left Saint Claire's. However, now that you have done so, you must consider your future. What are your intentions?'

'My intentions, Papa?' Bernadette felt a definite frisson of alarm. Her father was frowning at her dowry box. Surely, he was not planning to marry her off already? Hugo had warned her that this might happen. He had told her that suitors would come calling. He had said something about a stampede. 'Papa, I have only just come home.'

Her father grunted. 'You need to prepare yourself; you may not have as much time as you hope for. My dear, the local noblemen have their ears to the ground. Word of your return—with your dowry—will fly about in no time.' He laughed, oblivious of the knot that had formed in Bernadette's stomach. 'You are quite a catch. With our family connections and this dowry, I foresee Galard will soon be under siege.'

'Under siege,' Bernadette whispered, gripping her hands tightly together. 'Oh, no.'

'Oh, yes.' A faint frown crossed her father's face. 'Bernadette, I do hope you are not going to prove difficult. I had a terrible time finding the right man for your sister.' His expression softened. 'And here I was thinking that once we got you out of the convent you would be more amenable.'

'Amenable?' Bernadette pushed to her feet. Her mind was reeling. She was cold with dread. 'Papa, I cannot marry.'

Her father's brow darkened. 'Cannot or will not?'

She thought quickly. She could not tell her father about her dread of childbed. Not only would he not understand, but it simply was not done to discuss intimate matters with one's father. Not to mention that if she did manage to explain why she was so afraid, Papa would be reminded of her mother's horrible death. 'Papa, I am not ready to marry. It is far too soon. Perhaps in time...' Her voice trailed off.

Her father's finger drummed the desk and stilled. He sighed, heavily. 'Bernadette, do sit down. I will not rush you. But you must come to terms with the idea of marriage. Over the coming months, I expect a steady trickle of suitors to arrive. You will greet them courteously. Your dowry needs to be put to good use. A strong dynastic alliance would be ideal.' His mouth quirked into a wry smile. 'Provided you do not choose a complete lackwit, you may take your pick.'

Bernadette sat down with a relieved thump. Her father, though often brusque, was the kindest of men. He had not forced Allis into marriage, and he would not force her. And surely there was hope that her fear of childbirth would fade. She would have to pray for a suitor as kind and understanding as Hugo. Someone who would not rush her. Someone who...

Realising her father was waiting expectantly for her response, she managed a smile. 'Thank you, Papa. I am not against marriage as such. I just need space to come to terms with my change in status.' And at this moment, she thought, that was all she was prepared to say to her father about marriage.

On leaving Bernadette in the office, Hugo had retraced his steps to the stable. He had fulfilled his obligations to Lord Michel and had every reason to be content with a job well done. Yet he felt surprisingly out of sorts. Horribly so. He'd not felt this bad since his brother Aleran, Count of Nérac, had refused to acknowledge his letters and that was years ago. He was alone. He had no one. To be sure, Lord Michel valued him as his captain. His lord had gone out of his way to makė Hugo feel valued. Needed.

It was no longer enough. Unable to put his finger on why that should be, Hugo stalked into the stable. Clovis was in the first stall. A stable boy had removed his saddle and the glossy chestnut sheen on Clovis's coat told him that he had already been well groomed.

No matter. Clovis always enjoyed extra attention. A swallow—as a chick it had nested in the stable roof earlier in the season—shot over his head and flew through the door. Hugo picked up the body brush.

He was almost finished when he heard footsteps. Bernadette was walking towards him. His hand stilled. 'I believe Tansy is in the other stable, my lady,' he said.

'I know.' Her voice was soft. Husky. She walked steadily towards him. 'I wanted to speak with you.'

Even with the door open the stable was shadowy. Bernadette bit her lip and the movement transfixed Hugo to such an extent that all he could think about was how much he wanted to kiss her. He pushed the thought away. She came nearer and Hugo, closing his ears to Clovis's whicker of protest, eased into the corridor and hung the body brush back on its hook. 'My lady?'

She moistened her lips and his interest flared, and just like that his melancholy left him. Melancholy? What melancholy? Angel was standing before him looking deliciously shy. If she were any other woman Hugo would conclude she wanted him to sweep her into her arms and kiss her senseless.

He hesitated. Was he misreading her? He did not think so. With Hugo's position in life so uncertain, he did not have much to offer a lady and his experience was limited. However, he knew that when a woman moistened her lips as Angel was doing, when her cheeks flushed and her eyes darkened, it meant that she was thinking about more, far more, than friendship.

'Angel?'

'Hugo, I have been thinking about what we were discussing earlier.'

'You have?' He had to stop himself from stepping closer. He didn't want her intimidated by his height. Besides, they had covered several topics on their ride, he needed her to be more specific. 'About what, exactly?'

Her colour deepened. Dark rose. It was entrancing. Her gaze flickered briefly to his mouth. 'About flirting.' Shyly her eyes met his before darting away. 'About d…dalliance.'

That did it. Bernadette never stammered. Hugo set

his hands on her waist and gently, holding his breath lest she gave any sign of distress, drew her towards him. They were standing toe to toe, their only point of contact his hands at her waist. She did not demur and he allowed himself to relax a little.

They stood there staring at each other as a swallow flew in and then out again.

'Something has happened,' he said.

'You might say that.'

'Angel?'

'You were in the right when you mentioned that Papa will expect me to marry.'

'I take it he mentioned it after I left the office?'

She nodded. 'He promised not to hurry me, but he wants to be sure my dowry will be put to good use.' Her voice faded. Even in the gloom of the stable, he could see her colour was high. She looked mortified. No, he was wrong about that, she was embarrassed. Hugo drew her an inch closer. He could feel her body heat, which unfortunately made it nigh on impossible not to close the distance entirely and pull her directly against him. Using every ounce of willpower, he held off. Instinct was telling him that this—whatever it was—must come from her.

'Angel?'

She fiddled with the edge of her veil. 'Hugo, if it's not too much of an imposition, I should like you to kiss me.' Their eyes locked and it was the most extraordinary thing, Hugo felt himself swept away by a feeling of rightness, of inevitability.

'I was thinking about our conversation earlier,' she went on in a rush. 'The one about flirting. Plainly Papa wishes me to forge an alliance of some kind that will benefit Galard. Which means I shall have to learn to flirt, so I can get to know my suitors better. I have no wish to marry someone I cannot like, and I can see the sense in holding them at arm's length until I have chosen the best candidate. That strategy worked for Allis, it might work for me too.

'Hugo, I am sorry to ask you, but would you please teach me how to kiss? I dare say one can flirt without having to kiss, but I should like to know what to expect.'

'Someone might come in.'

'I do not care.'

Hugo's mouth dried. He ran his forefinger down her cheek. Or rather, what he could touch of her cheek. Her novice's wimple got in the way somewhat. He arched an eyebrow. 'Angel, it would be my pleasure.' He drew her against him and, smiling, pressed the lightest of kisses to her cheek. Her nose. She angled her head, and he managed another kiss on her cheek. Once again, the wimple impeded further progress. He lifted his head, frowning. 'Blast this thing.' Encouraged by a small gurgle of laughter, he caught her chin in his hand and touched his lips to hers.

Softly. Gently. Light as thistledown. Little more

than a light brushing of lip over lip. It was not enough, Hugo wanted more. He wanted a proper kiss. He wanted to pull her firmly against him, so he could feel the swell of her breasts, but Bernadette had never kissed a man before. He had no wish to startle her. He drew back. 'All right so far?'

'Mmm.' Reaching up, she caught hold of his shoulders and slipped her arms about his neck.

It was most satisfactory. Encouraged by the way her body plastered itself to his, he kissed her again. Through the fabric of her habit, her breasts felt soft and welcoming and in a moment the desire to touch them was an ache deep inside. Ignoring the ache, Hugo restricted himself to light, nibbling kisses.

When she moaned and swayed slightly, he took it further, outlining her mouth with his tongue and finally pushing inside. She tasted faintly of spiced wine. Dimly he recalled she had chosen wine when her dowry was being counted. Mostly she tasted of Bernadette. Of sweetness and light. Of belonging.

'Hugo?' She pulled back, eyes hazy. 'I am doing it right?'

'Perfect,' he muttered. 'Angel, it is heaven to kiss you. You are perfect.'

And that, he realised with a shocking jolt, was the truest thing he had ever said. Recognising that he had ventured on to treacherous ground, particularly given how much he wanted to continue, he cleared his throat and stepped back. 'There. Happy?'

She looked up at him, eyes puzzled. 'It was truly all right?'

He put warmth in his voice. What else could he do? She was the younger daughter of his liege lord and though she enticed him in a way that was uniquely hers, he could take this no further. 'You, Angel, are a tease. You know it was.'

She frowned, pursing her lips to show her displeasure. 'I need another kiss to be certain. And I need more practice.' Before he had time to react, she reached up, put determined hands round the back of his head and pulled him down.

This kiss took longer. It was thorough. Her fingers wove into his hair and the two of them clung to each other as though life itself depended on it. The shadowy stable filled with sighs and gasps. Straw rustled as Bernadette stumbled against him. Surrendering to need, Hugo moulded her body to his. Their tongues teased. Their hands caressed and stroked. Hugo's blood grew hot. Needy. So needy that he found himself pushing his hips forward, for a moment so lost he quite forgot her innocence.

Not that Angel seemed to mind. Maybe she had not noticed. When, briefly, he cupped a breast with his palm, she let out a sound that was part-groan, part-growl and entirely feral. She melted against him, and it was glorious. He came to his senses when he realised he was gathering the fabric of Bernadette's habit, curious to see if her thigh was as soft as her cheek. If this continued any longer, they would be rolling about in the straw.

'Enough, Angel.' He wrenched himself away. 'You do not need lessons, believe me.'

She pouted. Bernadette. If Hugo had not seen it with his own eyes, he would never have believed her capable of doing such a thing. With a jerky nod she moved away and smoothed down her habit. 'Thank you, Hugo. That was most enlightening. And very pleasant.'

His jaw dropped. 'Pleasant?' She had brought him to his knees with desire, and she thought it merely pleasant?

'Very much so, although I do wonder…' Her doubtful expression appeared. 'Hugo, did you enjoy it too?'

'Of course, couldn't you tell? You kiss very sweetly, Angel.'

'Truly?' She was retreating far too quickly. Hugo caught her hand and she stopped and looked at him, the doubt still very much evident. 'Forgive me for asking, Hugo, but was it as good as when you kissed Allis?'

What on earth? 'I never…' His voice trailed off as he remembered. Jésu, he *had* kissed Allis. Behind this very stable. It had felt all wrong and he had never been tempted to repeat it. A movement above caught his eye. Three swallows were sitting on a roof beam, they seemed to be watching them. How long had he and Angel been kissing? Hugo couldn't say. It had felt like an eternity and yet it had been far, far too brief. It was a good thing, he thought ruefully, that they'd only been seen by the swallows. Anyone might have walked in on them. And the repercussions if they had been caught...

Mind racing, he stared blindly up at the roof beam, suddenly uncertain what the repercussions might have been. Lord Michel liked and trusted him. However, for all that he had the Count's favour, Hugo had nothing substantial to offer Bernadette in the way of lands. He would bring nothing to the table in terms of forging the kind of dynastic alliance the Count must surely hope for. But... But...

Bernadette belonged here. She was a hearth and home person, and she adored her family. He was fond of her and she of him, and her response to kissing him indicated that she was a passionate woman. Perhaps his suit might be acceptable.

He looked back at the door. She had gone.

Chapter Seven

Bernadette's head was whirling. Vision misted with tears, hardly knowing where she was going, she raced from the stable. Spotting Hortense out of the corner of her eye, she managed to swerve away before the woman noticed her. She did the same thing when she saw Violette. She wasn't ready to speak to anyone. She needed peace.

Almost without realising it, she found herself at the chapel door. Warily, she lifted the latch and peered inside. Empty. Letting out a sigh of relief, she ran in and fell to her knees before the altar.

That kiss. Or rather those kisses, for there had been too many to number, had overwhelmed her. Bernadette had never been in a whirlpool, of course, but she imagined that kissing Hugo was rather like falling into one. She had been drawn into the maelstrom gradually. The first chaste kisses had given no warning of the intensity that was to follow. The overwhelming inevitability. That surging, terrifying need. The urge to devour and be devoured. It was too much. This was Hugo. Her friend.

Shame washed over her. What was happening to her? She had clung to him with no sense of propriety. What must he think? A tear rolled down her cheek. She dashed it away. He had been so gentle. So dear. He had responded to her strange request without a qualm. Yet far from teaching her how to flirt, the moment his lips touched hers she filled with a rush of heat. There was no way anyone else could evoke such a response. The mere idea of kissing another man in that manner was completely abhorrent.

On fire with embarrassment, she pressed the back of her hands to her cheeks. She could not marry. It was impossible. And yet...

Her breath caught as her thoughts ran wild. Hugo understood. He knew the fear of becoming a wife and mother had haunted her for years. He might not love her, but he was fond of her.

Hugo came from a noble family. Like her, his distant ancestors were Merovingian. She fingered her lips, still warm from his kisses. His touch did not repel her. And neither, she thought with a reminiscent smile, did her touch repel him. She was hardly an expert in flirting, yet Hugo had given every sign he had enjoyed her touch as much as she had enjoyed his.

Could Hugo be the answer to her difficulties? She bit her lip. Was he still in love with Allis? Or had he found someone else now that Allis was married? She did not think so. It was imperative she find out.

Would Hugo consider marrying me? If he did, there would be no need for the castle to be invaded by suitors I could never consider. Hugo would not dream of forcing me into his bed and in time—who knows?—I might overcome my fear of childbirth.

If she had to marry, Hugo would be her safest choice. He did not love her, but he had seen her dowry, he knew it was significant. Significant enough, she thought bleakly, to draw noble suitors from all quarters. Suitors who would not care about her half as much as her dowry. Bernadette was not so naive that she did not know what marriage usually meant for a noblewoman. The moment a girl of her station married, her dowry was no longer hers. All her property belonged to her husband, who had the authority to dispose of it as he wished. His wife's wishes did not come into it. Further, it was a noblewoman's duty to obey her husband in all things.

I could not bear to marry a strange man who has come to court me because of my dowry and family connections. She knew it was the way of her world, yet Hugo would never think of her purely in those terms. They had too much shared history. Too much affection. In his case, she would not mind using her dowry to help him accept her. If he had doubts about marrying her, which seemed probable given his attraction to Allis, they might be dispelled by the thought of it.

He might not need the gold she would bring him, but it might prevent him from dismissing her out of hand.

She was biting her thumbnail when the click of the door latch broke her train of thought. She had been so preoccupied she had not heard the footsteps in the corridor. As the door opened behind her, she stared blindly at the cross above the altar. Her skin heated and her heart thumped. She didn't have to turn to know that Hugo had followed her. He was a kind man. Her soul ached.

'Angel? Are you all right?' he said, voice getting louder as he tramped down the nave.

Hastily wiping her cheeks, Bernadette rose. 'Of course.' He was smiling, brown eyes concerned. As he leaned towards her, that wayward lock of blond hair fell into his eyes and she found herself clenching her fist to prevent herself from tucking it neatly back behind his ear.

'You, sir…' Bernadette gave what she hoped was a creditable smile '…are quite the flirt.'

'Angel, I didn't mean it to go so far. I don't know what came over me.' He looked utterly baffled. And she knew, she just knew, that he was about to apologise.

'Hugo, for pity's sake, I will kill you if you apologise. I liked it. And I want to believe that you did too.'

A brief silence fell while puzzled brown eyes blinked at her. 'Well, of course I liked it. What man would not? But I can see you have been crying.' He caught her hand. 'I need to know why. Did I frighten you? Angel, that is the last thing I wanted.'

'I was not frightened.'

His face cleared and his mouth went up at the edges. 'You liked kissing me and you're embarrassed. Angel, there is no need to be embarrassed. I am your friend.'

'Thank you, that is a great relief.' She gave him a thoughtful look and gestured at the cushioned wall bench. 'May we talk a while?'

'Of course.'

When they were seated, Bernadette smoothed down her habit. Her heart lurched about in her chest as she braced herself to do what no lady should ever do, namely propose marriage to her best friend. She had no idea how he would react. 'I realise Allis's wedding must have upset you.'

His dark eyes went wide. 'Angel, nothing's further from the truth. I'm delighted to see Allis so happy. Delighted she's going to have a baby—'

'You know about that?' Bernadette said, momentarily distracted. 'How can you? She's not told a soul.'

He shook his head at her. 'Bernadette, it's obvious. Anyone who has been up to the solar and seen the feverish activity at the sewing table can work out she is expecting a baby. You are making her new gowns.'

Bernadette had little choice but to nod. Hugo was an observant man and further denials were pointless. 'Hugo, it's too early for an announcement, you must not say anything.'

'My lips are sealed.'

'Thank you.' She found herself thinking that if she had not seen that kiss behind the stable his denial that Allis's marriage to Leon had upset him would have more weight. Like all men, Hugo had his pride, she supposed. She forced a bright smile. 'Is there a special lady in your life?'

Hugo's brows snapped together. 'A special lady?'

'A...a favoured lady. Someone you are fond of and would care to marry.'

'No,' he said, brusquely. 'There is not.'

Bernadette felt a jolt. Hurt. She shoved it aside. There was no reason for her to feel hurt. Hugo didn't love her, she knew that. However, he was fond of her. And she rather thought he trusted her in the same way she trusted him. If Hugo could not stomach the thought of marriage with her, he would say so. They would laugh about it and move on to other topics. This should be easy. Except, with Hugo's brown eyes fixed on hers, it was harder than she had imagined. 'Hugo, I have a proposition to put to you.'

'A proposition?'

Bernadette's mouth dried. Her hands felt clammy. 'Aye.' She cleared her throat and held his gaze as though her life depended on it. 'Hugo, I was wondering whether you might consider marriage. To me.'

The silence was deafening. A puzzled crease appeared between his eyebrows. Briefly, his gaze dropped to her mouth before lifting again. 'Angel?'

She had shocked him; she could see that. It wasn't surprising. Truth be told, she had shocked herself.

'Angel, you are not serious.'

'I assure you, I am.' She swallowed down a lump in her throat and looked sharply away, focusing on her mother's ledger stone, but not truly seeing it. 'Hugo, as you have recognised, I enjoyed what happened in the stables, it has helped me immeasurably.'

'I am always glad to help a lady,' he said in a teasing tone.

Frowning, she threw a dark look his way. 'Hugo, this would be easier if you allowed me to speak.'

His eyebrows shot up. 'Please, continue.'

And then suddenly it was easy. The words poured out. 'Hugo, you have been my friend for as long as I can remember. We get on well, well enough for me to be totally frank with you. Papa wants me to marry. Soon. The idea of Galard being filled with noblemen with whom I have nothing in common is beyond daunting. I could no more flirt with a total stranger than fly. Further, the idea of being bound to an arrogant lord who sees me as a broodmare bringing him a casket of gold is unbearable. I cannot do it. So, please, do me the honour of considering my proposal. I would rather marry you.'

The silence stretched out. Then, 'Angel, you do me much honour, but—'

She could practically see his refusal on his tongue and a sick shiver went down her spine. 'Hugo, please.

At least think about it.' She gave him a desperate smile. 'You have seen my dowry; it would all be yours.'

He made an impatient gesture. 'Angel, it is simply not possible. We cannot marry. If I were to suggest it, your father would fling me out on my ear for my impudence.'

Her eyes widened. 'What are you talking about? Hugo, Papa would never do that. You are one of his most talented knights, he made you captain of the Castle Guard.'

'Bernadette, I cannot marry you.'

Frowning to hide her hurt, she folded her arms across her chest. 'I don't see why not. My bloodlines are as good as yours, we both have Merovingian ancestry. You have lands in Gascony—'

A bitter laugh cut her off. Aghast to be rejected so roundly, she was about to shove to her feet, on the point of fleeing when something in his eyes caught her attention. There was a bleakness there, a world of darkness she had never thought to see in him. 'Hugo, what is it?'

A muscle flickered in his jaw. 'You have been under a misapprehension. I have no lands in Gascony, Angel, I never did.'

'But…but your brother is Aleran Albret, he is the Count of Nérac, you must have lands.'

His sigh was loud in the quiet of the chapel. A tiny smile appeared at the corner of his mouth. 'I might have known you would want chapter and verse. Angel,

I do not have lands. Nérac follows traditional laws of inheritance. The eldest brother takes all.'

Bernadette shook her head. 'I know about that law, but I also know it is not rigid. If your brother wished it, he could give you a small estate.'

The small smile vanished and Hugo's mouth, that mouth that had kissed her with such care in the stable, set in a hard line. 'My brother does not wish it. The last communication I had from him, and that was years ago, made it plain that I can expect nothing. I am on my own, Angel, I always have been. Forgive me if I have upset you. It is the last thing I wanted.'

Rising jerkily, he bowed curtly and strode to the door.

Bernadette stared after him, appalled and shocked to learn about the rift between him and his brother. Questions rushed through her mind. If Hugo had not heard from his brother in years, why was this the first she had heard of it? Why had the rift taken place? And when? She could not begin to imagine which might have caused the Count of Nérac to repudiate his only brother, but his action had plainly cut deep. One thought put the questions to flight. Hugo didn't love her, she was sure of that, but he needed her.

Scrambling to her feet, she hurried after him. All these years Hugo had been her friend and she had never had an inkling about this falling out with his brother. He must have been miserable. Lonely. How dreadful. She had been so wrapped up in childish concerns that she had never noticed. The pain Hugo must have endured. The sadness. He had given no hint of it. He had hidden his sorrow behind a mask of carefreeness. To be rejected by his brother, his only sibling...

If she and Allis came to blows, which did occasionally happen, they invariably made up. But a permanent rift between them...? Such a thing would be impossible. Unbearable. Hugo might not wish to admit it, but he did need her. 'Hugo, wait!'

He stopped. Turned. 'My lady?'

She moved swiftly towards him. If she could persuade him to marry her, he would no longer be alone. 'Hugo.' She reached for his hand, brought it to her lips and kissed it. When she straightened, his eyes were glassy, and his mouth remained tight. Giving him a slight tug, she drew him into the chapel and back to the cushioned wall bench. 'Please, Hugo. I must talk to you.'

Hugo grunted and allowed himself to be seated. A muscle was twitching in his jaw. 'Angel, I had no wish to upset you.'

She clung to his hand. 'Hugo, I am so sorry to hear about your brother.'

He shrugged. 'It was not your fault.'

'No, but it must have been awful. I wish I had known.' Bernadette was not sure how she expected him to respond but she wasn't prepared for another silence.

His dark gaze held hers and she couldn't look away. Then his face softened. 'You are a sweet woman.'

'Hugo, I am not going to beg.' Her cheeks burned. 'But I would like you to listen. I have to marry soon, Papa made that clear. You know me, so you understand that the idea of marrying a stranger holds no appeal whatsoever. You are no stranger. You are my dearest friend.' *And I should have known before now, she thought guiltily, how lonely you were.* 'If you can promise not to spend my dowry on wine, women and song, I believe we can make a good marriage.'

Hugo's fingers had entwined with hers and that tiny smile dawned. 'I could promise that, easily.'

He could promise it? That was not yet an acceptance. Anxious for him to agree, Bernadette returned his smile as though he had. 'Thank God. Hugo, I would like you to take my proposal seriously. If Papa were to allow it, there is nothing I would like more than to be married to you.' They could make it work. It would be a marriage of convenience, but there was no reason why it should not be a success.

Hugo put his finger under her chin. 'If I were to marry you, I would be faithful to you, Angel,' he said. It sounded like a vow. Almost.

'I know.'

'I would cherish you till the end of my days.'

Bernadette's throat closed. The lancing pain caught her unawares, warning her that being cherished was not the same as being loved. Would it be enough? It dawned on her that in her soul, she yearned for love. Still, Hugo needed her and there was nothing wrong in being needed, if it wasn't purely for her dowry. 'I need you to keep all those suitors at bay,' she reminded him.

His eyes glittered. 'Ah, yes. The stampede. Marriage to me would certainly get rid of them.'

His fingers dropped away. Scenting victory, she leaned against his shoulder and his arm slid around her waist. She caught her bottom lip between her teeth. She was longing for another kiss. Wanting to see and feel a hint of the passion she had glimpsed in the stable. But she knew him, and he would not kiss her again until he had agreed to go with her to speak to his father. 'Do you think Papa will agree?'

That long-lashed, dark gaze met hers. 'There is one way to find out, though I warn you, you may not enjoy your father's response.' Hugo drew her to her feet. 'Come on, if you insist, we can ask him. With luck, we shall catch him in the estate office.'

He was gazing down at her when she saw the kiss in his eyes. Carefully, he bent his head and their lips met. She knew instantly that he intended to offer only the briefest of salutes for he made to draw back. Bernadette was not surprised—they were in the chapel, after all—but she was far from pleased. One gentle salute from Hugo had her casting years of training aside. Heedless of where they were, she pressed against him and the light slanting through the chapel windows whirled about them.

When Hugo finally stepped back, they were both breathing hard, and he was wearing an endearing, lop-sided grin. Half-shamed, half-laughing, she pressed her hands to her cheeks. She felt so hot. A response which, she had no doubt, would only happen with Hugo. She could not kiss another man. And she could never marry a stranger.

'Papa had better agree,' she muttered. Hugo's grin faded and in a moment his expression was so cool it gave her a jolt. 'Why, Hugo, you look quite stern.'

'Angel, we must tread carefully. In many ways your father is the most traditional of men. He would be out-raged if he discovered that you proposed to me. So, if you truly want him to agree, let me do the asking.' Hugo gripped her hand and towed her from the chapel.

Hugo felt unusually uncertain of his ground. As he and Bernadette made for the estate office, he was uncomfortably aware that his credentials as a suitor were less than ideal. Lord Michel trusted him, but it was inevitable that his lack of land would be a large mark against him. A landless man had no indepen-dent means of support. Everything Hugo had had been awarded to him by Bernadette's father. His knight-hood, his horse, his squire, his pay…

'Angel, I am only a captain,' he warned. 'Lord Mi-chel would be within his rights to dismiss me out of hand.'

Bernadette looked steadily at him. 'Have a little

faith. Papa knows your worth as well as I. I am relying on you to prevail.'

Mouth dry, Hugo sent her a crooked smile and rapped on the door.

'Enter!'

Hugo stood back to allow Bernadette to precede him into the office. Her father was making a note in the margin of a large leather-bound book. The Count closed the book and looked up. 'There is a problem?' he asked.

'Not a problem, my lord.' Hugo cleared his throat. He had been uneasy when agreeing to approach Lord Michel, but perhaps marriage to Bernadette was not such a bad idea. As she said, they knew each other well. What she did not know was how much Hugo hoped for children. It was another thing he had not told her. Having been alone for so many years, he longed for a family of his own, which meant Bernadette's terror of childbirth was no small problem. Naturally, he would not force her to share his bed, but he hoped she would overcome her fears. Having a family of his own would help fill the void created when Aleran had forbidden him to return home.

Would Bernadette conquer her fears? Hugo had done his best to show her that Hortense had poisoned her mind against bearing children. The woman had laden the poor girl with so much guilt over Lady Genevieve's death that she had run off to the convent at the first opportunity. With luck, Bernadette would begin to see that getting with child was not always a death sentence. Her reaction to his kisses was heartening. Deep down, Hugo knew Bernadette was capable of passion and he felt confident that if they married, he could, in time, win her round.

None of which made asking her father for the hand of his younger daughter easy. He must take this little by little, for if Lord Michel took this badly…

'My lord, Lady Bernadette tells me that you hope she will marry soon.'

'Eventually, yes,' Lord Michel replied. He reached for a scroll. Unrolling it, he used weights to hold it open on the desk and looked up at them. 'There is no rush.'

Hugo nodded. 'I understand. My lord, I would like to add my name to the list of Lady Bernadette's suitors.'

Just then a small hand slipped into his. Lord Michel noticed—how could he not?—for his gaze flickered briefly. His expression betrayed nothing.

Hugo pressed on. 'Lord Michel, you of all men know how I am placed in the world. I do not pretend to have anything in the way of lands and wealth. However, I can promise that should my suit prosper, Lady Bernadette will be cherished all her days. I will be a faithful husband and I will do my utmost to bring honour to my family and yours.'

'Well.' The Count leaned back in his chair. 'You've outflanked me, Hugo. I was not expecting this so soon.' His face still unreadable, he looked pointedly at their clasped hands before lifting an eyebrow at Bernadette. 'I take it you put him up to this?'

'It was Hugo's idea,' she said, the lie so blithe that Hugo blinked. 'But you should know that I endorse it. There is no one I would rather marry than Hugo.'

A flicker of unease curled in Hugo's gut as the Count studied them. 'The two of you have been friends for years,' he murmured. 'There will be no unpleasant shocks on either side in that regard.' Hugo and Bernadette glanced at each other and nodded, and the Count fixed his daughter with his eyes. 'Bernadette, when we spoke earlier, I was mindful that you had only just left the convent and that not long ago you were hell-bent on taking your Final Vows. That was why I promised to give you time before you married. Are you sure about this? It is rather sudden.'

'Papa, I am very sure.'

Lord Michel stroked his beard. 'Your change of heart is a little surprising. Excuse my bluntness, Daughter, but men—even good friends like Hugo— have desires. Do you think you will be able to fulfil them? He will probably want children. Are you ready for that?'

Crimson-cheeked, Bernadette let out a strangled sound and nodded. Her father's bluntness seemed to have struck her dumb.

Clearing his throat, Hugo stepped into the breach.

'There's no need for concern on that score, my lord. I consider us well matched.'

The Count's eyebrows shot up. 'You do, do you? What have you been doing?'

'Papa, please!'

Lord Michel fingered the weight on the scroll, picking it up before tossing it thoughtfully from hand to hand. The office was so quiet, all Hugo could hear was the soft pat, pat, pat of the weight moving from palm to palm. He waited, scarcely able to breathe. He was painfully aware of Bernadette; she didn't seem to be breathing either.

Finally, the Count replaced the paperweight on the scroll. He nodded curtly, his expression so severe that Hugo was certain his name would never be added to the list of suitors. 'Very well. Since Bernadette has endorsed your proposal, I shall accept it,' the Count said gruffly. 'And since we are all decided there is no point hanging around, you will marry within the week.'

Within the week?

Bernadette gasped and sagged against him. Hugo could feel her clinging to his belt. Thoughts suddenly frozen, he slipped his arm about her waist to support her. It was all he could do, he was struggling to absorb what the Count had said.

Accepted. The Count had accepted him for Bernadette. As commendations went, it could not be bettered. Furthermore, with Bernadette as his wife Hugo would never feel alone again. Her family would become his for ever. It was wonderful and terrifying in equal measure. 'Thank you, my lord,' he managed to say, so delighted he could hardly frame the words. 'Thank you. I will do my best to honour Bernadette.'

'I know that, lad.' The Count smiled.

Bernadette straightened. Her eyes were sparkling. 'Thank you, Papa. With all my heart, I thank you.'

Slipping out from under Hugo's arm, she went to the desk. 'Thank you so much.'

Rising, Lord Michel hugged and kissed her. 'Daughter, there is no need to thank me. You could not choose a better man than Hugo.'

'I know, but earlier you mentioned hoping to make a political alliance.'

Arm firmly about Bernadette, Lord Michel grimaced. 'Did I say that?'

'Papa, you know you did.'

Lord Michel gave an airy wave. 'I have plenty of allies. In any case, Hugo here hails from an area where we already have family connections. That may, in future, prove useful.'

Hugo felt a cold shadow fall over him. He had never told the Count about his falling out with his brother. It would be dreadful if he had been welcomed into the family because of his non-existent links with Nérac. He cleared his throat. 'My lord, I must be frank with you. The last time I heard from my brother, he told me I was no longer welcome at Nérac.'

'What?' The Count's gaze sharpened. 'When did this happen? Why was I not told about this?'

'It happened years ago, my lord. I was very young and initially I thought it could be mended.' He shrugged. 'I was wrong.'

Frowning deeply, the Count stroked his beard. 'You are certain there won't be a reconciliation?'

'It is extremely unlikely. I have written several letters. Aleran has never replied.'

'Hugo, you have my sympathies, this must have been deeply unsettling. However, you might like to know that your troubles with your brother do not affect my decision regarding Bernadette. If she is happy to marry you, I will not change my mind. To be honest, I never relished the idea of the place being overrun with suitors. This is much better.'

He transferred his attention to Bernadette. With a disparaging frown, he eyed her novice's habit. 'I am hopeful that this means you will dispense with that rag you are wearing. Like myself, your husband-to-be would, I have no doubt, appreciate seeing you in something a little more becoming. For pity's sake, Bernadette, stop making Allis's clothes and make a start on your bride clothes.'

'Yes, Papa.'

'You have a week, Daughter. One week.'

Chapter Eight

Hugo ushered Bernadette out of the estate office. She was astonished by the flash of happiness that ran through her. She was betrothed to Hugo. She gave him a shaky smile. 'A week,' she murmured. 'It's not long.'

'That's one way of looking at it.' Hugo took her hand and kissed it, very much in the gallant manner. 'I prefer to think that it is far too long.' Having kissed her hand, he pushed the sleeve of her habit up and began kissing his way up her arm. He was obviously delighted. Her dowry, she reminded herself. Hugo was pleased about her dowry because he had no land. Her stomach clenched and her happiness fled. She was not Allis.

'Hugo!' She snatched back her hand and looked swiftly over his shoulder. 'Anyone might see us.'

He propped his shoulder against the wall. 'And this matters?'

'Of course.' She avoided his gaze and began fiddling with her belt. 'People will think that we—' Her voice faded.

'Angel, within the hour the entire castle is bound to hear about our wedding.' He paused thoughtfully. 'Your father's retainers will be delighted. They adore you and they are aware we like each other. The occasional show of affection will hardly cause offence.'

'Affection,' she murmured, in a dull voice. Then she squared her shoulders and looked him in straight in the eye. 'Hugo, there is something I must tell you.'

Sobering, he pushed away from the wall. 'Angel, what is wrong? Don't tell me you are having second thoughts already.'

'No.' She gripped his arm. 'It is not that. Never that. I want to marry you.' Her gaze wavered and her throat worked. 'Hugo, I was not sure Papa would agree, but it never occurred to me he would want us to marry so soon.'

'You feel rushed. Hold on to the thought that you don't have to face that horde of suitors.'

She murmured assent. Another man might not be patient with her qualms. She knew she was safe with him. Footsteps from further down the corridor caught Hugo's attention. Someone was coming. Tucking Bernadette's hand into his arm, he led her away from the office. 'Angel, we cannot talk here, we probably ought to go back to the chapel.'

'I think that would be best.'

* * *

Bernadette said nothing more until Hugo had settled her on to the cushioned wall bench in the chapel. Smiling, he ran his forefinger down her cheek. 'Angel, tell me what is worrying you?'

'Babies,' she said, biting her lip. Hugo found it extremely distracting. It drew his attention to her mouth and made him ache to kiss her. He held off. What had she been saying? Ah, yes. Something about babies. 'Babies?'

She nodded vigorously. 'Papa mentioned children. I expect you want them.'

'Well, yes.' Hugo's mind flew back to his childhood. His falling out with Aleran had happened when he was a boy. In the years since then, he had occasionally dreamed about having a family. He loved it here at Galard, but Lord Michel's family was not his. Fortunate though he had been to rise through the ranks, he wanted his own family. Having a family would make up for everything he had lost at Nérac. He had tried to dismiss such yearnings; with no security it would have been impossible to support one. Yet at a stroke, all that had changed. With luck, he could have that family. A little girl with Bernadette's sweet smile. A boy with her quiet determination. His mouth dried. It was odd how clothing his unborn children with Bernadette's qualities served to deepen that yearning. He could not lie to her. 'I do want children. Very much. Eventually, I hope that you will want them too.'

'Hugo, I am not ready for children.' She was staring at the white marble ledger stone beneath which her mother lay in eternal rest. A sigh left him. Her mother's untimely death cast a long shadow. He could only pray that Bernadette's fears would be quick to fade.

'Very well. I understand.' His heart squeezed. Would a declaration of love help? He could not give it. He would never be able to give it. Love let you down, as the rift between him and his brother proved. Hugo had worshipped Aleran. As a young boy he'd had been confident the feeling was reciprocated. The knowledge that Aleran would always be there for him had sustained him during those confusing early years at Galard. Being sent away from Nérac—and from Aleran in particular—had left him feeling oddly dislocated. Knowing that Aleran was waiting for him at home had kept him going.

And then Aleran's letter had arrived. Hugo was no longer welcome at Nérac. The love he had relied on had let him down.

Love? It melted away like morning mist. It didn't last. Affection, however, most certainly did. Comradeship lasted. Friendship lasted. What Hugo felt for Bernadette was as strong as steel. It would not fail because it was more secure than love could ever be.

Wishing to reassure, he put warmth in his voice. 'Angel, you have moved so quickly from convent to castle, it is not surprising you are unprepared for marriage. I can wait. With one proviso.' She had, he noticed, caught the tasselled fringe of the cushion and was twisting it this way and that.

'Oh?'

Gently, he pulled her hand from the tasselled cushion and kissed her knuckles. 'We shall be sharing a bedchamber from the start. I refuse to have the entire castle speculating about whether or not our marriage is a sham. Agreed?'

'Agreed. Thank you for understanding. Hugo?'

'Hmm?' She was smiling shyly at him, and Hugo let out a quiet sigh of relief.

'I ought to tell Allis and Sybille about our wedding straight away. They'll be hurt if someone else tells them.'

Her sister and stepmother were in the solar, where Sybille was making the most of the daylight by putting finishing touches to a length of white linen for Allis's unborn baby. 'The child will need more linens than you can imagine,' Sybille murmured.

Leaning her chin on her hand, Allis smiled. 'Sybille, I have visited almost all the mothers in the village, I am well aware of the vast volumes that will be needed.'

Winking slyly at Bernadette, Sybille pushed a second length of white cloth towards Allis. 'This might be a good moment to perfect your sewing. This piece is already cut, you simply need to hem it.'

'Hemming.' Allis groaned. 'Must I?'

'Yes, dear,' Sybille said. 'I really think you must.'

Taking up the linen, Allis gave an exaggerated sigh. 'I pity this baby, forced to use linens sewn by me.'

Crushing the instinct to offer help, Bernadette took a seat next to Allis. 'I've news,' she said.

Allis raised an expectant eyebrow. 'Oh?'

'I will not be returning to the convent, and nor shall I be taking my vows. At least,' Bernadette amended, 'not that sort of vow.'

Allis exchanged glances with Sybille. 'What do you mean?'

'Hugo has asked for my hand in marriage and Papa has agreed.'

The strip of white cloth fell to the floor and Bernadette was enveloped in a bruising hug. 'Bernadette! That's wonderful news. Wonderful!'

Slightly taken aback by her sister's enthusiasm, all Bernadette could do was nod. She knew she was blushing.

Sybille leaned in, eyes quietly watchful. 'You are happy, Bernadette?'

'I am,' Bernadette said. 'Nervous, of course, but very happy.'

This statement was greeted with another bruising hug. Allis leapt up and flew to one of the coffers that contained various bolts of cloth for the family and household. Fabric went flying.

'Sybille, where did you put that length of beautiful green cloth? It is just right for Bernadette.'

'Try the other coffer.' Smiling warmly, Sybille held her hand out to Bernadette. 'I wish you the best of marriages, my dear. After all this time at Saint Claire's, it cannot have been an easy decision.'

'Actually, in the end it was.' Bernadette shrugged. 'These last few months I have felt increasingly out of sorts. It was as though I no longer knew who I was.' She laughed awkwardly. 'It will sound strange, but when Hugo appeared with Allis's letter, I realised I had to come home.'

Sybille's expression softened. 'That is love for you.'

'Sybille, I came home because I was worried about Allis. It wasn't long before I realised I had no desire to return.'

'You love Hugo,' Sybille murmured.

Bernadette didn't reply. How could she? The words 'cherish' and 'affection' were ringing a peal though her mind. Hugo was fond of her. He had promised to cherish her. Bernadette might be drawn to her new betrothed, but their relationship was not characterised by the grand passion that Sybille seemed to be imagining. Her stepmother had a romantic heart.

'Found it!' Allis dragged the green linen out of a coffer, brought it triumphantly to the table and put it in front of Bernadette. 'You will accept it, you must. I swear if I see you in that ghastly habit once more, I shall scream.'

'Really, Allis,' Sybille said. 'There is no need to be

so dramatic. I am sure Bernadette's old clothes are in her wardrobe. She will hardly be wearing rags.'

Allis made a tsking sound and waved at Bernadette. 'Look at her, Sybille, look at her properly. She has grown up in the convent. That baggy habit fits, but I doubt very much her old clothes will.'

Bernadette fingered the green linen. It was finely woven and smooth to the touch. 'Thank you, Allis, it is beautiful.' She grinned. 'And Papa did say something about me making my bride clothes.'

'Your bride clothes,' Sybille breathed. She was staring at the green linen with an arrested expression in her eyes. 'Is the wedding date agreed?'

'Papa wishes the ceremony to take place in a week's time.'

'A week!' Sybille put her hand to her throat. 'You mean a month, surely?'

'No, a week,' Bernadette said, and watched the panic form in her stepmother's eyes. She put out her hand as her stepmother scrambled to her feet. 'Sybille, there is no need to worry. I got the impression that Papa wants a quiet ceremony. He will not be sending out heralds. He does not want a fuss.'

Sybille shot Bernadette a look. 'This is your wedding we are talking about, my dear. You are the daughter of Lord Michel Galard, Count of Arles, and it makes no difference whether the ceremony is quiet or not, your bride clothes will do you proud.'

'Sybille, I really don't mi—' Bernadette broke off, Sybille was already halfway to the door.

'I have a length of embroidered silk set aside,' she muttered under her breath. 'Plenty to make the most gorgeous gown. If I make a start at first light, it should be ready for the ceremony.'

'Thank you, Sybille,'

'Now, if you two will excuse me—' Sybille flung a harried smile their way '—I must speak to your father.' The latch clicked and Sybille was gone.

Allis let out a soft laugh. 'I have never seen Sybille quite so distraught. Poor Papa.'

Bernadette bit her lip. 'I had no wish to upset her. Really, Allis, I do not care what I wear.'

'I know that, goose.' Allis squeezed her hand. 'Sybille wants you to look your best. Please, tell me more. I can see from your face you are happy.'

'I am. Very happy.' And if Hugo can only learn to overlook the fact that I am not you, Bernadette thought, she would be even happier.

The week passed in a haze of feverish activity. Much as Bernadette wished for a quiet wedding, it quickly became apparent that her wish was not going to be granted. She was kept so busy she had no time for herself and the worst of it was that she scarcely saw Hugo. She suspected her father was keeping him equally busy and as each day went by without her catching more than a glimpse of her betrothed, the ache inside her grew. She felt out of sorts and unbearably on edge. If they could but speak to each other, she knew she would feel better. It was not to be.

Oddly, in the entire week, Bernadette hardly set a stitch. Slightly bemusedly, one morning she found herself sitting at the dais in the hall with Allis at her side. She was there to accept the congratulations of the household. It should not be hard; she had known most of Papa's knights and retainers all her life and it was clear everyone wished her well. It was heart-warming to hear how much they liked and respected Hugo.

Occasionally, however, one of them said something which made her cringe inside. When the castle cook approached, all smiles, Bernadette tensed. The cook was a heavy-set man who liked to taste every dish that was brought into the hall. He was so used to bellowing orders to his minions in the kitchen that he had a voice like a trumpet, and he rarely moderated his tone. In brief, tact was not his strong point.

'I wish you well on your forthcoming marriage, my lady,' the cook said. 'It warms the heart to think of you marrying Sir Hugo.' He gave her a conspiratorial wink. 'When you were younger, you were inseparable. He was always so attentive.'

Bernadette nodded.

The cook considered her. 'You have grown into a fine young woman.' He waggled his eyebrows, and the knowing light in his eyes heated Bernadette's cheeks and warned her that his next remark was likely to verge on impudence. When another wink came her way, she was sure of it. Exchanging glances with Allis, she braced herself.

'I am certain Sir Hugo has grown into a loving man,' the cook went on. 'He will be more attentive than ever. I am happy for you, my lady, you could not do better.' He leaned in, not bothering to lower his voice. On the contrary, he continued loud as ever. 'Treat Sir Hugo well in the bedchamber and you will want for nothing, if you follow my meaning.'

Bernadette closed her ears to the titters that followed and forced a smile. Was the man about to go into detail about how she might beguile her husband in bed? Fortunately, he spared her this indignity. Bowing his head, the cook turned and lumbered back to the kitchen.

Conscious of Allis watching her, Bernadette blew out a breath. 'Lord, I was dreading what he might say next.'

'It was the same for me,' Allis admitted. 'Weddings seems to give people one hardly knows the right to offer all manner of unwanted advice.'

'It is beyond embarrassing,' Bernadette muttered. Furthermore, it roused her guilt and her doubts. She knew Hugo desired her. As she desired him. Was she wrong to insist they remained chaste for a while? He had promised fidelity which, oddly, she found concerning rather than reassuring. She had no wish for their marriage to sentence him to life as a monk. No one else was approaching the dais, so she held her sister's gaze. 'Is there anyone else I should watch out for?' she asked wryly.

Allis grinned. 'No, with cook out of the way I do not believe you will be fending off any more advice, unwanted or otherwise.' Hesitating, she lowered her voice. 'Unless of course it comes from me.'

Bernadette's eyes rounded. 'You have advice?'

'Only if you need it,' Allis whispered. 'Has Sybille explained what happens in the marriage bed?'

Bernadette stared. It was extraordinary. Her worldly, matter-of-fact sister was blushing. 'Sybille? No, she has not said a word.'

Allis sent her a rueful look. 'I suspected as much. She is probably hoping I will speak to you. Or perhaps she is thinking…well, never mind.' Warmly, she squeezed Bernadette's arm. 'You have been in the convent; you may not be prepared for all this. Still, if you need to talk, about anything, I hope you know you can talk to me. There is nothing to fear behind the bedchamber door.'

'I know that, Allis.'

Allis's eyes widened. 'You do?' Her face relaxed. 'Of course you do. There's nothing to fear. Especially since you're marrying Hugo. He would never hurt you.'

Determined to hide the lurch in her stomach, Bernadette made herself smile. 'I know that too.' Hugo would never hurt her, at least not in the way that Allis was thinking. It was odd though, the idea of a loveless marriage, albeit one which held affection, was becoming less and less appealing with every breath that she took.

'I am glad,' Allis said, whispering behind her hand. 'Because the bond between man and wife is reinforced not only by a meeting of minds, but also by the loving and pleasurable relationship that can develop in bed.'

A shadow fell over them. Violette dipped into a curtsy. 'Excuse me, Lady Bernadette, if you are finished here, your stepmother would like to speak to you in the solar.'

'She wishes to consult me about my gown?' Bernadette asked. Sybille was a perfectionist when it came to making clothes. She always had been. Ever since she was small Bernadette had watched Sybille get carried away with her sewing and embroidery. In fact, Bernadette realised with a jolt, her stepmother's love of needlework probably lay at the root of her own liking for it. She knew Sybille—the embroidery for Bernadette's wedding gown would have to be set just so. Bernadette had already seen Sybille hunting through workboxes for silver and gold thread. Why, she had even unstrung an old string of pearls and seemed determined to sew them on to the bodice.

'No, my lady. She wishes to speak to you about the guest list for your wedding.'

'The guest list?' Bernadette felt her face fall. 'Papa said this was to be a quiet ceremony.'

Allis let out an incredulous laugh. 'Papa said that? Bernadette, you are dreaming if you think Papa will settle for a quiet ceremony. He loves playing the host. I should think every nobleman in the district will be attending.'

'That is not what I agreed to,' Bernadette said, pushing to her feet with a sigh. 'Violette, please inform Sybille I will join her after I've spoken with my father.'

'Yes, my lady.'

As Allis intimated, Papa flatly refused to put a limit on the number of guests he wished to invite to the marriage ceremony and feast. It was an attitude which ensured that Bernadette spent the remaining days before her wedding in a state of dread. The idea that she would be the centre of attention was truly intimidating. Her natural instincts were to hide away, as she had done in the convent. Privately, she had to admit that convent life had not been a lasting solution. Living at Saint Claire's had dulled her mind. She had felt constricted. Trapped. She had had to find another path.

And this path, with Hugo, was much more promising. The idea of her becoming his wife was as exciting as it was nerve-racking. She was frankly terrified, but in her heart, she would not have it any other way. If she must go through the ordeal of a grand wedding and feast to win Hugo for her husband, it would be worth it.

* * *

When Bernadette had retired to her bedchamber on the eve of their wedding, she didn't expect to sleep. Which was why, when dawn broke and she opened her eyes, she was astonished. She had slept the entire night! It had been the deepest, most refreshing sleep she could remember.

Wryly, she rolled over in bed, pushed the bed-hanging aside and frowned thoughtfully at the empty cup on the bedside table. Last night, Allis had pressed it into her hand.

'This tisane will calm your nerves,' Allis had said. 'It is mostly chamomile.'

Mostly chamomile? Bernadette shook her head. Given the level of her anxiety, the tisane must have contained something much stronger than chamomile. Still, whatever it was, it had worked. She had slept and there were no unpleasant after-effects. She felt marvellously refreshed. Her nerves were bound to return. However, because she had slept, she was sure she would cope.

Eyeing the light, she pushed back her bedcover, took up the hand bell and rang for Violette.

There was no time for nerves. Almost before she knew it, Bernadette was processing down the narrow corridor to the family chapel. And processing was the correct word, for the gown that Sybille had made her was no ordinary gown. The fabric—a delicate blue silk—was embroidered with silver and gold flowers. It was so long one could not walk in it, one simply had to process. Despite the old-fashioned, ceremonial nature of the gown, Mother Margerie would have been scandalised had she seen it.

The bodice was cut so low it was practically falling from Bernadette's shoulders and apparently to emphasise this, Sybille had sewn her pearls along the neckline. The blue silk was lightly gathered beneath her breasts and flowed down to form a long train behind her. When Bernadette moved, the train swept the floor with a gentle hushing sound. Her long brown hair was caught back with ribbons, and she was crowned with a chaplet of flowers—daisies, late roses, and delicate sprigs of thyme and rosemary. The gown was so gorgeous it invested her with confidence. For the first time in her life, she felt truly beautiful. She felt like a lady.

Her father was waiting at the entrance to the chapel. As he placed her hand on his arm and they stepped through the door her gaze sought Hugo. He was standing by the altar in a shaft of light with his squire in attendance. He looked magnificent. A tight-fitting cloth of gold jacket emphasised the width of his shoulders and his narrow waist. He was not wearing his sword, instead an ornamental dagger hung from a thin belt. His hair gleamed in the sunlight and his tunic seemed to shine. Her golden knight. Bernadette's eyes misted over. As her father led her towards him, her heart ached with a painful combination of happiness and hope.

The chapel wasn't as full as she had feared, and it helped that as they processed, she glimpsed familiar faces. There was Violette, smiling from ear to ear. Even Hortense was smiling, she looked genuinely happy, despite the tear trickling slowly down one sallow cheek. Bernadette's gaze moved swiftly over the grinning cook and past a handful of stable lads. A contingent of Hugo's guards were present, as were her brother-in-law's men. Finally, at the far end she spotted Sybille with her ladies-in-waiting. Allis stood next to her with Leon and blew her a kiss. Bernadette paused to return it.

And there was the priest, welcoming her with a smile.

'Look after her, lad,' Papa murmured as he placed her hand in Hugo's.

Hugo mumbled a reply, Bernadette did not hear it for the expression on Hugo's face had robbed her of the ability to take note of anything else. His cheeks were a shade paler than usual, and his eyes were stunned. 'You are magnificent, Bernadette,' he whispered. 'A queen.'

The priest cleared his throat. Her father was already standing next to Sybille. The wedding ceremony began.

Chapter Nine

A ragged cheer went up as Bernadette and Hugo arrived in the Great Hall for their wedding feast. It was already crowded. The hall had been transformed. Tables were spread with snowy white linen; candles glowed in glass lanterns; swags of greenery meandered along the hall walls and hung at table ends. In the roof corners, the ever-present banners of the household knights swayed brightly in the draughts.

'So this is where everyone is,' Bernadette said softly, smiling at a local lady who was trying to catch her eye.

Hugo led her to the place of honour at the centre of the high table on the dais and her heart thumped to see so many people looking her way. Her new husband saw her seated and lifted her hand to his lips in a courtly gesture that a month ago, Bernadette would have dismissed as play-acting. She had the sense that it still was.

'You do look beautiful.'

'It's the gown,' Bernadette said. 'It's silk.' She wanted to return the compliment by telling Hugo how handsome he looked but her tongue tied itself into knots. She, Bernadette, beautiful? Allis, tall, lovely Allis, with her blue eyes and blonde hair, was the beauty of the family. She, on the other hand... Hugo was simply being gallant because it was their wedding feast. He did not mean it.

Hugo took his place at her side. As the wine and ale began to flow, she realised he was shaking his head at her. 'It is not the gown, it is the woman inside it. You, Angel, are beautiful.'

A servant appeared, jug in hand. 'Wine, my lady?'

When their crystal goblets had been filled, Hugo slid it her way. 'I was relieved to see your father heeded my request to limit the congregation in the chapel.'

She sent him a startled look. 'That was your doing?'

'Aye, I asked Lord Michel to keep the service intimate. I was not sure he heard me.'

'Thank you, Hugo. That was thoughtful.' And incredibly heartening, she recognised. Not only was Hugo demonstrating that he understood her, but he was prepared to act to ensure she felt comfortable. She watched him glance apologetically around the hall.

'The feast you will have to endure.' His mouth tipped into a smile. 'There was no swaying your father on that score.'

'I understand.' Bernadette had attended Allis's wedding and the feast afterwards. She knew what to expect and it helped to have seen the ritual before. The fuss. Nonetheless, it was somewhat daunting when it was you rather than your sister who was the centre of attention. She sat quietly and, with Hugo a warm and watchful presence at her side, was able to endure it. Course after course was brought to the tables. Trout baked in tarragon sauce; roasted capons fragrant with sage; great haunches of beef with glistening onions.

'Do you care for some beef?' Hugo asked.

Sipping her wine, she shook her head.

'What about this pie?'

'I am not very hungry,' she murmured. 'I might try some fish.'

Hugo gestured for a servant and saw her served. Idly, Bernadette took some bread and picked at it. The air was redolent with the smell of wine and cinnamon and garlic. Despite Hugo's attentiveness, she was too unsettled to eat. More pies appeared. With their pastry tops cut to form crenellations, they looked like miniature castles. There were platters of cheese and grapes. Pastry wafers glazed with honey. Bowls of nuts. Pears. Noise ebbed and flowed, soon reaching thunderous levels, just as it had done at Allis's wedding.

At length the table on the dais was cleared of most of the food.

'You will not have to endure much longer,' Hugo murmured, resting his hand gently on her thigh.

She shivered. Dread of disappointing him was a

coil of fear inside, but she simply was not ready for the intimacy of the marriage bed. 'I know.'

'There will be music later, we should be able to escape then.'

His eyes were searching and warm enough to bring heat to her cheeks. His gaze dropped, fell to her mouth and briefly, to the pearl-encrusted neckline of the blue silk gown. When he looked back up, his gaze was dark. He looked hungry, and she knew it was not for food. He turned his gaze away and picked up the crystal wine glass.

Bernadette held back a sigh. Hugo desired her, and she had made him promise not to touch her. She felt like a charlatan. He was the best of men, and he was now her husband. Panic fluttered in her belly. She had never felt so confused. She wanted Hugo, she always had. *Hugo and I desire each other.*

Except desire wasn't enough. She needed space to accept her sudden change in status. Just over a sennight ago she had been preparing to leave the world and all its trappings behind her. And this—the feast, with all that went with it—was simply too much. It was overwhelming. Everywhere she looked there were expectations, the most alarming being that she was expected to give Hugo children. God willing, she would. If only those images of Mama's death would leave her. If only...

The blare of a trumpet dragged her from her thoughts. Guests were lining up to present Hugo and

Bernadette with gifts, beginning with those of the highest status.

Lord Robert Vaucluse of Carpentras came first. Bernadette had always liked Lord Robert. It had been a worry when Allis had refused to marry his son and relations between the two families had soured. His presence at Bernadette's wedding feast was heart-warming.

'Lord Robert.' Bernadette smiled. 'I am most happy to see you.'

'You are gracious, my lady.' Lord Robert was holding a box-shaped object that was wrapped in red silk and for an instant, she was reminded of one of the Wise Men in the Bible. Bowing, Lord Robert placed the box on the table in front of her. 'I am thinking that now you are a married, you may find a use for a trinket box.' His eyes danced. 'It came from the Holy Land, but it wouldn't have done for the convent.'

'Thank you, my lord.' Bernadette pushed back the silk covering. Made from olive wood, the box was inlaid with ivory and mother of pearl, set in the shape of flowers. 'It is charming, my lord. I shall treasure it always.'

It was fortunate that Lord Robert had come first, his familiar face had relaxed her. As their table filled with gifts—a set of pearl-handled eating knives; a brace of gilt goblets; several brooches and cloak clasps; a gold chain; various lengths of silk and damask; furs; even a cask of wine—Bernadette's nervousness eased. Everyone was so kind.

When the lords and ladies had paid their respects, the hall doors opened and, as was their family's custom, the villagers poured in to offer their congratulations. These gifts were humbler—a set of wooden spoons; a skein of embroidery silk; a pair of new shears; some ribbons; a set of pins...

They received them all with the same gentle courtesy.

As the last of the villagers headed toward the wine barrel, Bernadette saw Hugo staring at a wooden cradle, left by one of the villagers. He turned to her, lips twisting into a smile. 'One day, perhaps?'

Bernadette's heart jumped into her mouth. Impulsively catching his hand, she brought it to her lips and kissed it. His disappointment was palpable. She imagined Hugo would be a wonderful father, and the idea stirred an emotion deep within her chest that she couldn't yet place.

With the noise of merriment fading behind them, Hugo followed Bernadette up the curling stairs and into her bedchamber. He secured the door to fend off any mischief-makers and leaned against it. He had never been inside Bernadette's bedchamber. It smelt of beeswax and lilies. Candles flickered in wall sconces. The bed was wide, with a large canopy and blue velvet bed hangings looped back with golden braid. Happily, it was roomy enough for two, though judging by the frozen expression on Bernadette's face, Hugo wasn't confident she would be comfortable with him sharing her bed. Lord, he hoped she did not expect him to sleep on the floor.

He continued his appraisal of what she had agreed was now their bedchamber. A crucifix hung on the wall next to a shuttered window. There was a small fireplace. A vase of white lilies and star-like blue daisies filled the empty hearth. Hugo was vaguely conscious of other furniture—a coffer and a tall oak cupboard, polished to a deep shine.

Bernadette—his wife—was staring bemusedly at a painted screen angled across a corner of the chamber. The ribbons in her glossy hair were trembling. She looked alarmingly pale. Disconcerted, Hugo rubbed his brow. He had assumed that once they had removed themselves from the Great Hall, she would recover her composure. She had agreed to share her bedchamber with him on the understanding that he would make no demands on her person. He had sworn to keep his distance. It was a promise which was not going to be easy to keep, but he would not break his word.

'That screen is new,' she muttered. She swept towards it, and his gaze was caught by her long train hushing across the floor.

'Is your gown heavy?' Hugo asked, wishing to distract her. She didn't look happy.

'A little.' She sent him a tight smile. 'It's odd how quickly you get used to it though.'

A white garment hung over the top of the screen. Frowning, she picked it up and shook it out. A night-gown. Flushing crimson, she draped it over her arm and bent to examine the painted surface of the screen. Lilies were depicted on one panel, pink roses on the other. She peered behind it. 'Sybille has been busy.'

Hugo held in a sigh, not fooled for a moment. Bernadette was using the screen as a delaying tactic. For her peace of mind, he must make his intentions, or rather his lack of them, plain. It was harder than he imagined. He would never forget how sight of that wooden cradle sitting among their wedding gifts had transfixed him. The resolve to fill it with their children, with sons and daughters who had Angel's stunning brown eyes. But not yet. 'Angel, we are in our bedchamber, please know you can relax. You can trust me. I promised not to touch you and I will hold to that promise.'

She swung to face him, eyes wide with what he would swear was surprise. Truly, the low cut of her gown was a scandal. It took all of Hugo's willpower not to stare. To prevent himself from imagining the curvy body beneath, he looked deep into her eyes. Long-lashed brown eyes made brighter with tiny golden flecks, the most beautiful eyes in the world.

'I know,' she murmured. She was looking shyly up

at him, her cheeks tinted a delicious pink. 'Hugo, I've been thinking.'

He lifted an eyebrow. 'That bad, huh? I shall take it as a warning.'

A faint smile lifted the edges of her mouth. Heartened, he stepped closer. Taking the nightgown from her, he tossed it on to the bed and took her fingers in his. Her mouth drew his gaze, weakening his resolve to keep his distance. She was staring at the top of his jacket as if her life depended on it.

'Hugo, this evening I see that perhaps I put you in a difficult position by asking you not to consummate our marriage.'

His breath seized and for one blissful moment his heart leaped. He leaned closer and caught a subtle hint of fragrance. She must have made a scent out of lilies. Blended with a scent he recognised as being unique to Bernadette, it was unexpectedly heady for a woman who had intended to take the veil. He cleared his throat. 'You did?'

'Yes.' She placed her hand on his chest.

'Angel, you said you were not ready.'

She hung her head. 'I'm not, not really. Events moved so swiftly I haven't grown used to the idea of marriage.'

He nodded understandingly, even as that subtle fragrance wound round his senses. With every breath he could feel his resolve weakening. *Mon Dieu*, but this was going to be a challenging night. 'It is understandable, you can't help but be conscious of your mother's untimely death. You fear childbirth. Angel, please relax. I will not break my word by importuning you. I can wait.'

A shaky sigh left her. 'Thank you, Hugo.'

He lifted her hand, kissed it, repeated the gesture with her other hand and watched her eyes darken. More than anything he wanted her to trust him, and much as he wanted her, he would wait. 'There is passion between us, but we have no need to rush,' he murmured, leading her gently to the bed. He urged her to sit and when she complied, he found himself breathing more easily. She did trust him, she must.

Sitting himself, he pulled her gently on to his lap. 'Angel, I know little of what it is to be a husband. I am bound to make mistakes. But when eventually you decide to honour me with the gift of your body, I will do my utmost to please you.'

She leaned against him. A twist of dark hair tickled his neck and his pulse thudded. 'Thank God, the nuns did not cut your hair,' he murmured, reaching up to stroke it. Stroking her hair was astonishingly soothing and Hugo allowed himself to be distracted by it. When his fingers caught in the circlet of flowers he frowned. He would love to see her with it completely loose. Would she object? There was only one way to find out. 'Angel, how does this thing come off? Are there hairpins?'

'One or two.' She brushed his hand away, removed several gilt pins and set the headdress aside.

With a sigh of pleasure, Hugo wound his fingers into the glossy tresses, unravelling ribbons as he went. Free of the ribbons, her hair waved this way and that. 'I love the way it has a mind of its own,' he murmured. Arranging a shiny dark skein over her shoulder, he ran his hand down its length. 'You have always had beautiful hair.'

She gave him a look of disbelief, which he ignored. More than anything that look warned him that she truly was not ready to become his wife. Unfortunately, at that moment, Hugo's hand, having followed the flow of her hair, was scant inches away from her breast. That low neckline was such a temptation. All he had to do was slip his fingers down the neckline and…

No. He had sworn not to touch her.

'Hugo, I know our agreement has upset you and I am truly sorry.' Her cheeks darkened with what he recognised was embarrassment and she cleared her throat. 'I need to tell you about something that happened at the convent.'

He managed not to groan. 'Go on.'

'Occasionally, ladies are admitted, unmarried ladies who have no intention of becoming nuns. They stay for a while and then leave. You will know what I mean, Hugo, when I say that they come to the convent to hide their shame.'

'They are unmarried and with child?' Hugo asked. 'As Eglantine was?'

'Aye, just like Eglantine. Hugo, not all such women are as fortunate as Eglantine. Many are just like Mama, they do not survive their lying in. It is very distressing; I lost a friend that way.'

Hugo started. 'A friend?' He kissed the side of her head, inhaled her scent, and ignored the ache in his groin. He could wait, truly he could.

'Aye.' Blinking rapidly, she swallowed. 'At the convent she was known as Novice Marie, although I doubt that Marie was her true name. Of course, when she took her novice's vows, no one knew she was with child.'

'Mother Margerie would not have been pleased when she found out.'

Bernadette's head dipped in agreement. 'She was not. Marie's novice's robes were removed, but provided she agreed to help in the infirmary, Mother Margerie said she could stay until her child was born.'

'But Marie did not survive.'

'No.'

'And her child?'

'He—' Bernadette's voice cracked '—died too, bless him.'

There was a bright, glassy sheen in her eyes before she averted her head. Without being told Hugo understood that Angel had been present at Marie's death and witnessing it had been as traumatising as the ghastly tales Hortense had told her about her mama. He was at a loss as to what to say that might comfort her. He had no doubt that the gruesome stories about Lady Genevieve's lying in, and the ensuing guilt Bernadette had felt had driven her to Saint Claire's. It was bitterly cruel that similar horrors had awaited her there. 'I am sorry, Angel.' He sucked in a breath. 'Come, we should prepare for sleep. Would you like me to summon Violette to assist you?'

She looked up, face white and woebegone and shook her head. 'Thank you, Hugo, but that is not necessary. I trust you. I am sorry to disappoint you on our wedding night.'

He frowned. 'You could never disappoint me and as your husband I forbid you to think that you could.' He nuzzled her cheek. The heady fragrance of lilies weaved around him, a sensual smell unique to Angel which was utterly devastating. She was too innocent to know it, but he was completely in her thrall. 'Come, you cannot sleep in that gown.' He picked up the nightgown that Lady Sybille had made for her. 'If you cannot manage the buttons, I can help you.'

'Thank you, Hugo, but I believe I can manage,' she said, voice small. She rose, bent to kiss his cheek, and disappeared with the nightgown behind the painted screen.

Hugo scrubbed his face with his hands and tried not to look her way. Small rustlings fed his mind. How many layers was she wearing beneath the blue silk?

Truth be told, the gown was cut so low, how it had stayed in place was a mystery. She would scarcely need to unbutton it; the smallest tug would surely have it off her. It was a few moments before he realised he had been standing by the bed for far too long tormenting himself with imagining how much soft, creamy flesh would by now be revealed. If he planned to occupy that bed with her, he had best undress quickly.

He unbuckled his belt and sat down to remove his boots. He was unbuttoning his jacket when it occurred to him that his innocent wife's sensibilities might be offended by his usual practice of sleeping naked. Determined not to be banished to the hearth for the night, Hugo tore off the rest of his clothes, save for his linen shirt. That, thankfully, was long enough to hide most of him. Rose petals scattered as he flung back the bedcover and clambered into bed. He would sleep with his wife on their wedding night. In her bed.

Cautiously, he eyed the screen. The blue silk gown was hanging over it and her nightgown had vanished. Bernadette emerged, plaiting her hair. Her head was bent. Hugo's frown deepened. She was avoiding his gaze. Little did she know that the nightgown Lady Sybille had made for her was as fine as gossamer, it revealed more than it concealed and clung to every delicious curve. She finally looked his way and her pretty mouth pursed, but she did not ask him to remove himself from the bed. She simply went round all the wall sconces, putting out the candles and, sadly, with each extinguished candle a little more of her was hidden from his view. The shutters were closed and the gloom deep. Then she climbed on to the bed and the mattress dipped.

'Goodnight, Hugo.'

He smothered a sigh. 'Goodnight, Wife.' He had never felt less like sleeping. He lay there for some while with her scent beguiling his senses, listening to her breathing. It was soft and even, but although she was perfectly still, he knew that she was no more asleep than he was. He rolled over on to his side and her breathing hitched, just slightly. He rolled on to his back, rested his head on his hands and stared into the darkness, forcing himself to think about the wedding feast, about anything rather than face the idea that bedding his wife was likely to be more of a challenge than he had feared.

Goodness, Bernadette thought, Hugo was so warm. Lying against her, he simply radiated heat. She heard a slight groan, which was quickly smothered and allowed herself to relax. Hugo. Her husband. He shifted slightly against her, his breathing even. Steady. He was asleep. They had been married for several hours now and she was regretting that he had not kissed her properly. Oh, he had kissed her hand and the side of her head. But he had not kissed her mouth. She missed it. She fingered her lips, knowing she only had herself to blame. Hugo had wanted to kiss her, she had seen it in his eyes, but she had been too much of a coward to encourage him. Things might have got out of hand. And now...

He shifted closer, pressed against her and she heard another groan. Something was pressing against her, something hard that proved without doubt that desire was strong in him, even in his sleep.

'Hugo?' she hissed. 'Are you awake?'

Muttering incoherently, he rolled away, taking his warmth and most of the bedcovers with him. He was asleep. Bernadette tugged experimentally at them, and by way of much wriggling, managed to ease herself back under them. He did not wake, and he was, she discovered, lying on his back. Resting her hand on his arm, she shifted into his warmth and closed her eyes.

One evening, a month later

Bernadette was in the chapel, kneeling next to her mother's grave marker. She had been staring pensively at the gilded lettering cut deep into the white marble for some time:

> *Here lies Genevieve, Countess of Arles.*
> *Beloved wife and mother.*

The habit of coming to pray at her mother's resting place was ingrained into her. Some of her earliest memories were of kneeling here. Originally, Hortense had bullied her into coming. Ever since her wedding day and the upsetting night that followed, Bernadette came by choice, to find peace.

It was not the first time Bernadette had found herself wondering how different her life might have been had her mother lived. She and Hugo had only been married a few weeks and already she felt herself changing. Marriage had given her focus. Hugo was now at the centre of her life. He had made no attempt to cajole her into surrendering her innocence, which ought to be a relief. Far from it—she was beginning to regret his forbearance, for the result of it was that they both slept badly. Every blessed night.

If Hugo was irritable, she was more so. Last night she had snapped at him for clunking into her bedchamber long after she had retired. She had not even been asleep! He had known, of course. The look he had given her. Their marriage was in danger of foundering.

Heavy-hearted, she stared at her mother's ledger stone. She had become quite pragmatic—she would never know her mother. And Lady Sybille was a dear. She had not taken her mother's place, no one could do that, but she had filled a void in Bernadette's heart.

Bernadette had never told Hortense, but because she felt her mother's presence most keenly here in the chapel, she often imagined that she and Mama were conversing. Rather than praying, she told her everything. Naturally this included her recent marriage to Sir Hugo Albret of Nérac. She confessed her joys—how

pleased she was to have married him. And her fears—
that thanks to her fear of childbed, their marriage was
already in trouble. She asked questions. *Maman, will
he ever forget Allis?* Her mother remained silent, and
the question remained unanswered. With a resigned
smile, she kissed her fingertips and pressed them gently to the deeply carved lettering on the cold marble
tomb. *Goodnight, Maman.*

Chapter Ten

Bernadette was hurrying through the Great Hall when her father came hurtling towards her. 'Where the devil have you been?' he demanded. The lines on his brow told her that something was very amiss. 'I have been searching for you everywhere.'

'I was in the chapel. Papa, what is it?'

'I have news for you,' he said, mouth grim.

She felt the blood drain from her face. 'Hugo's been hurt?'

'Hugo is not hurt,' he said gruffly, and lowered his voice. 'Though this does concern him. Come, we cannot speak freely here.'

When they reached the estate office, her father closed the door, waved her to a seat and picked up a scroll. 'This arrived from my steward in Gascony this afternoon. You will recall that our family originally came from there. We have kept a small manor at Larressingle, Sir Gilebert stewards it for us.'

'Yes, Papa.' Bernadette gazed at the scroll, mind

whirling. A letter from Gascony? Hugo's family estate was also in Gascony but given the rancour that had developed between Hugo and his brother Lord Aleran, Bernadette couldn't think why Papa's steward would be writing to him concerning Hugo.

'When you agreed to marry, I decided to make enquiries into Hugo's kin in Nérac.'

Bernadette stiffened. 'Have you mentioned this to Hugo?'

'Of course not,' her father said, impatiently. 'After he told me about the rift between him and his brother, I realised he would have argued against it. I am not about to take orders from my captain. Frankly, the more I thought about their falling out, the more it troubled me. I could not let it rest.'

Bernadette found herself staring at the letter. 'What does it say?'

'In summary, I asked Sir Gilebert to ride to Nérac and speak to Lord Aleran.' Her father stabbed at the letter. 'It says here that his reception was cool to say the least. He was turned away at the gate.'

'Sir Gilebert was refused entry? How strange.'

Her father studied her through hooded eyes. 'You know something of Gascon politics?'

'I probably ought to know more,' she said. 'I do know that warring factions have been fighting for the upper hand in Gascony for years. You would think that Lord Aleran might welcome your steward as a potential ally.'

'Quite. Bernadette, I have some thoughts as to how best to proceed, but I should warn you. You may need to decide where your loyalties lie.'

Her skin chilled. That sounded ominous. 'Papa?'

Her father stroked his beard, eyes softening. 'You are a joy to me, Bernadette, and you always have been. It would give me great pleasure if you chose to make your home here.' He scowled at the letter. 'However, this communication from Sir Gilebert leads me to believe that Hugo needs to return to Gascony. If that were so, Bernadette, how would you choose? Would you remain here with your family, or would you accompany him?'

Bernadette searched her father's face, thoughts whirling like leaves in a storm. On the one hand, she adored her family. She would like nothing better than to live out her days at Galard. Her stomach twisted. Since marrying Hugo that future had seemed assured. She was fond of her husband, her father trusted him, and he was on good terms with everyone.

On the other hand, learning of the troubles Hugo had had with his brother Lord Aleran had opened her eyes to the unhappiness and sense of dislocation her husband had been hiding. How alone he must have felt! It was a realisation that made her wishes for a life of quiet contentment at Galard seem selfish indeed.

She sat very straight. 'Papa, please don't take this amiss. I love it here, but my place is with Hugo. If he decides to travel to Gascony, I will accompany him.'

Her father cleared his throat. 'Quite right, quite right.' His eyes were looking a little misty, but his smile was warm. 'It is plain you care about him.'

'I do, Papa, very much.'

'Excellent. Mind, I have a word of warning. In his letter, Sir Gilebert tells me that he is himself recently married. I have no idea how competent a housekeeper his wife will turn out to be. Given that our manor at Larressingle has for years been run entirely by my steward, I fear you may find it lacks what Sybille would call a woman's touch.'

Bernadette grinned. 'You mean it will be more of a barracks than a manor?'

'Exactly.'

'That doesn't worry me. Life at Saint Claire's was far from luxurious and if Larressingle turns out to be a bit rough at the edges, I shall enjoy setting it to rights.'

Her father gave an approving grunt. 'I hoped that would be your response.' He glanced at the door. 'Before we take this further, I believe Hugo should join our conference. Send for him, will you?'

'Yes, Papa.'

Hugo strode to the estate office. It was late in the day and the request to meet Bernadette and her father was concerning. Lord Michel was in the habit of issuing his orders well before noon so it must be urgent. When he entered the office and saw Bernadette's frown was mirrored by one on her father's face, his sense of foreboding deepened. Bernadette had been subdued when he had last seen her. Ever since their marriage there had been distance between them. His gut twisted. It did not seem likely she would discuss their marital difficulties with Lord Michel, but she and her father were close.

'There you are, sir,' Lord Michel said. He was fiddling with a scroll, which he slowly unrolled. 'Come in.'

Hugo seated himself next to Bernadette and touched his hand to hers. 'Angel, is all well?'

'Papa has news from Nérac.'

Hugo stopped breathing. How could this be? 'News from Nérac, my lord? You are in the habit of receiving word from my brother's holding?'

Something wary in Lord Michel's gaze set alarm bells ringing in Hugo's brain. 'No need to look daggers at me, Hugo, I have not presumed to write to your brother. However, since you have joined the family by marrying Bernadette, I have made a few enquiries on your behalf.'

A bitter taste filled Hugo's mouth and for a moment he quite forgot he was speaking to his liege lord. 'You did what?'

'I wrote to my steward at Larressingle,' Lord Michel continued smoothly. 'You may remember our family hold a manor there. It is only a few hours' ride from Nérac.'

'I remember,' Hugo said tightly. Suddenly, his every nerve was stretched to screaming point. Dread filled him. He did not need to be a seer to know that whatever Lord Michel had discovered was likely to raise challenges. Carefully he lifted his hand from Bernadette's. 'Pray continue, my lord.'

'In brief, I informed our steward at Larressingle, Sir Gilebert, where you are from and that you were fostered here. He tells me he believes something untoward is happening at Nérac. I should warn you that the last time Sir Gilebert managed to gain entry—and this was several years ago—he was told your brother the Count had had some kind of seizure. His wife—Countess Ragonde—was apparently in charge. You know of this already?'

'No.' Hugo was almost too choked to speak. His brother had been ill? It was hard to imagine. As a boy, Aleran had been intensely physical—strong and impatient with weakness of any kind. It was impossible to imagine him laid low with a seizure. His insides tightened. 'When did my brother fall ill? Has he recovered?' Despite the bad blood between them, Hugo did not wish Aleran ill.

'As I said, it is some years since Sir Gilebert was allowed inside the castle. After he received my recent letter of enquiry, he was again turned away.' Lord Michel's mouth tightened. 'My steward has not seen your brother and thus he has no idea of his present state of health.'

Aleran might be dead. Hugo found himself on his feet, betraying deep inner turmoil in a confused welter of words. 'My lord, I must leave for Gascony. I need to see for myself whether Aleran is dead or alive. I pray he is living. If so, I need to speak to Countess Ragonde. I have never met her, and I ought to ensure that she is capable of running Nérac. The estate could fall to rack and ruin.'

'And if Lord Aleran is dead?' Bernadette murmured. Her face was pale, Hugo could see that this news had shocked her too.

He looked blankly at her. 'That is unthinkable. Without a lord, the estate is liable to be ripped apart. If Aleran is no longer with us, Nérac will need a lord capable of protecting both the people and the land.'

'Just so,' Count Michel said, looking intently at Hugo. 'Nérac will need a new lord. From what Sir Gilebert tells me, it's possible it already has one.'

'He has an heir?'

Nodding assent, Count Michel smoothed out the letter. 'Jésu, Hugo, sit down. You are giving me a crick in the neck. I recognise that this is hard to hear but let me tell you the rest. If I can, I will do my utmost to help.'

Feeling Bernadette's eyes on him, Hugo glanced at her. Her brown eyes were filled with fellow feeling and something else, something he was unable to read. Jaw tight, he sat.

'Sir Gilebert,' Lord Michel continued, 'informs me

that a few years ago, your brother's wife gave birth to a boy named Dennis.'

'Dennis,' Hugo murmured. 'He will be far too young to run an estate like Nérac.'

'Aye, he will be a small child. Hugo, the rest of my steward's report is even more troubling. He says that on the day of his last visit years ago, the day he did gain entry, Nérac appeared rundown.

'Sir Gilebert was so concerned at what he saw that he issued a series of invitations to Countess Ragonde on the pretext of returning her hospitality. His invitations went unanswered. My recent enquiry prompted him to follow up with a further visit, but again the gate was barred to him. He was refused entry.'

Hugo rubbed his brow. His head felt as though it was stuffed with thistles. Aleran had been ill, and he had a small son. Regardless of the rift between him and his brother, Hugo found himself praying that Aleran was alive. One thought rose out of the confusion. Aleran needed his help. 'My lord, thank you for this intelligence. Does Sir Gilebert have anything further to add regarding my brother?'

'Unfortunately not. Your brother may be fully recovered, my steward has no idea. Strange rumours abound, but that is all they are, rumours.'

'So,' Hugo said slowly. 'Gascony beckons.'

The Count grunted. 'I thought that would be your response.'

Hugo sent Bernadette a bleak smile. Certain she

would not wish to leave Galard, he raised her hand to his lips. 'If I may, my lord, I will leave in the morning.'

'Of course,' Lord Michel said.

Bernadette also smiled assent. 'Very well.'

Hugo felt his mouth tighten. The idea of leaving Angel behind was deeply unsettling. Truth to tell, it was excruciating. He felt sick at heart, and her calm acceptance of their separation was pure torture. Releasing her hand, he shoved to his feet. 'If you will excuse me, I need to speak to Olivier.'

'Hugo, you will need a troop to go with you,' Lord Michel put in. 'Take your pick of my men.'

'You are very kind, my lord.'

Bernadette followed him to the door. 'I'll alert the kitchens, we will need food for the journey.'

Hugo came to an abrupt halt on the threshold. *We, she had said we.* 'Angel? You are surely not thinking of coming with me?'

With a scowl, she punched him lightly on the arm. 'I am your wife, Hugo. I belong at your side.'

He stared. 'You don't mind?'

'Of course not, you dolt. I'd much prefer coming with you to staying here worrying.'

The relief was so intense, Hugo stumbled. *Mon Dieu*, what was wrong with him?

After an early supper where Bernadette caught Hugo's concerned gaze on her more than once, and where, since they were at the high table within earshot of half the castle, private conversation was clearly inadvisable, Bernadette and Hugo repaired to their candlelit bedchamber. They had barely begun to cram clothing into saddlebags when a knock on the door interrupted them.

'Enter!'

Lord Michel stuck his head round the door and the candle flames swayed. 'I thought Violette would be helping you,' he said.

'She is busy packing her own things,' Bernadette told him. Her father was holding a document that was yellow with age and bore the imprint of several large seals. She had never seen it before. 'Papa, what is that?'

'This is for you. It is the deeds to Larressingle. The manor and village are yours. Please accept them as my wedding gift.'

Bernadette's jaw dropped. She and Hugo were being given a manor? Or rather, Hugo was, for as she could hardly forget that, once married, a woman's property belonged to her husband. Smiling, her father held out the calfskin. Hugo was staring at it as though bemused. His dark eyes were glassy, he looked astounded. Sensing that her husband was beyond speech, understanding that he was stunned to finally be given land, Bernadette flung her arms about her father. 'Thank you, Papa, thank you!'

'Come on, lad, take it.'

Hugo took the parchment, swallowing hard. 'Thank you, my lord. This means the world to us.'

Bernadette knew what he meant. Being gifted with the deeds of a manor would ensure that Hugo was no longer dependent on others. He would not have to draw down on her dowry unless necessary. Her father's next words confirmed it.

'Larressingle is close enough for you to visit your brother whenever you wish. You may like to know that regular markets take place in the town square. They are generally well attended and revenues from the markets will give you something of an income.' He sent Hugo a meaningful look. 'It will give you independence, lad. You need call no one master save your conscience. Be sure to keep these deeds under lock and key. There is a strongbox in the cellar at Larressingle, Sir Gilebert will show you where it is.'

'Papa, you are the best of fathers,' Bernadette said, hugging him to her.

Her father gave a jerky nod. Walking to the tall cupboard, he opened a door and closed it again. He frowned at the bed. 'I do hope you are not leaving the furniture behind.'

'I was not sure it was mine.'

'Well, it is.' He cleared his throat. 'It forms part of your dowry.'

'Thank you.' Bernadette looked thoughtfully at the bed. It would have to be dismantled before carting it to Gascony. Given that Hugo was anxious to reach Nérac with all speed, it was not feasible to take the heavier furniture quite yet. 'Papa, it will take far too long to dismantle the bed. In the interest of speed, the heavier pieces will have to be left behind.'

Her father nodded. 'Very well. I shall arrange for the rest of your chattels to be carted to Larressingle when you have sent word you are settled.'

Bernadette got barely a wink of sleep that night and nor, she could tell by the restless stirring, did Hugo. Lying in the dark, her mind was racing with thoughts of all they had to do the next day. 'Provisions,' she murmured.

Alongside her, Hugo shifted. 'I have organised provisions. And we shall not be riding through a desert, we can buy more on the way.'

'What about packhorses? We will need quite a few.'

A gentle hand touched her arm. 'Angel, try to get some sleep. That is all arranged.'

She finally fell asleep, her mind still doing cartwheels when Hugo, with a heavy sigh, pulled her into his arms and kissed her brow. 'Sleep, Angel, sleep.'

She pried herself out of bed before dawn and was in the bailey early enough to see pink clouds streaking the sky in the east. She and Violette were overseeing the loading of several packhorses when Hortense appeared, pack in hand. Plainly, she expected to be among their party. She looked down her nose at Violette.

'Why is Violette here?' Hortense demanded.

Bernadette braced herself for what was bound to be a trying conversation. 'Hortense, Violette is my maidservant these days.'

'Surely she is not going with you?'

'Of course she is.'

'Violette cannot ride.'

'No matter. She will ride pillion behind one of the men.'

Hortense harrumphed. 'My lady, you would do better to take me.'

Bernadette stiffened her spine. 'How so?'

'Your father must have warned you that Sir Gilebert has been running Larressingle almost single-handedly. It will not be fit for a lady.'

'Apparently, Sir Gilebert has recently married.'

'I'll wager that will make no odds,' Hortense said, lip curling. 'Especially if it was a recent marriage. Think, my lady. What will be the state of the manor after all these years with only a man to see to the housekeeping? You are bound to need me.' She looked towards the stable. 'Which of the animals shall I take?'

'I am sorry, Hortense, you are not accompanying us,' Bernadette said. Out of the corner of her eye, she could see that Hugo was listening. When he lifted an enquiring eyebrow, plainly prepared to step in, she gave a slight headshake. She could deal with this.

'My lady, your mother would want me to stay with you.'

'Would she?' Bernadette resisted setting her hands to her hips. 'And why is that?'

'Lady Genevieve needs your prayers.' Hortense sent a look of loathing in Hugo's direction. 'Now more than ever. And you, my lady, need counsel.'

'Thank you, Hortense, but I am a grown woman, a married woman. Henceforth, I shall rely on my husband for counsel. Be assured that I shall pray for my mother's soul as and when my conscience dictates. Mark this. Violette is coming with me. You are not.' She softened her tone. 'Hortense, this is not a journey for a woman of your years. We will travel fast.'

And travel fast they did, although with their cavalcade being so large, it took well over a sennight to reach Larressingle. To a man the troop was mounted and in addition Lord Michel had insisted they took several spare horses on leading reins. Bernadette's dowry was strapped to the back of a packhorse and surrounded by soldiers. After them came an astonishing number of baggage mules. Some were laden with food and drink, others with tents, sleeping pallets and blankets. Yet more mules bore saddlebags containing clothing, a few household items, a small travelling chest of Bernadette's and another of Hugo's.

The spare horses were extremely useful, because although Bernadette rode her pony Tansy for some of the way, Tansy was smaller than most of the horses and tired easily. At such times, Bernadette rode one of the larger mares.

When at last they reached the bridge overlooking the Larressingle moat, Bernadette was weary and saddle-sore. None the less, her spirits lifted.

'Larressingle,' Hugo murmured. 'We are here.'

They paused by the bridge. A fortified town, or *ville bastide*, Larressingle was designed to withstand the bands of marauders that terrorised Gascony from time to time. It did not appear to be a large place. Bernadette knew that the villagers who had originally served the manor would have built their houses around their manor, tucked safely within the encircling wall. Bernadette studied the wall. Thankfully, it looked solid. Sturdy. From her vantage point it curved gently away from the road.

'Larressingle is smaller than I expected,' she said.

'Aye. Your father told me as much.' Hugo grinned. 'Still, it's all yours.'

'Hugo, since we are married, by rights it is yours.' She smiled. 'I still find it hard to believe Papa gave you a manor.'

Earnest brown eyes held hers. 'Angel, please know I consider the manor yours as much as mine. Larressingle is *ours*.'

'Yes, yes,' Bernadette said, not really believing he meant it.

Hugo shook his head at her. 'Angel, I am determined that one day you will trust me enough to believe that when I say something I mean it.'

Aghast, Bernadette stared. 'Hugo, I do trust you.'

His jaw tightened and he said nothing more. He gestured for their party to cross the bridge and they rode into Larressingle.

Chapter Eleven

Sir Gilebert must have had word of their arrival, for when they reached the courtyard in front of the manor, he was there to greet them. Tall and wiry, with a thin brown moustache, Bernadette set his age somewhere between Hugo's and her father's. As Sir Gilebert introduced himself, she hoped she said the right things, but Hugo's comment about trust had caught her off guard. It was, she felt, completely unfounded. During their journey, she had naturally kept all personal comments to a minimum. Sleeping under canvas a few feet away from their men-at-arms was scarcely conducive to private conversation.

'Lady Bernadette, you are most welcome.' A wave of Sir Gilebert's hand sent servants scurrying. After Hugo and Bernadette had dismounted and Hugo had taken charge of Bernadette's dowry and assured himself that the horses were in capable hands, Sir Gilebert guided them into the manor. They passed through a shadowy passageway and into the hall.

The manor hall was modest in size. There was no dais, but it was far from the barracks Bernadette had suggested. The walls were wood panelled, and the hooded fireplace looked large enough to ward off the winter chills. A table was positioned in front of the fireplace and a second table was placed at right angles to the first. Hugo set the dowry box down.

A couple of maidservants entered bearing flagons and goblets. As they arranged them on the table, Bernadette was conscious of curious glances straying their way.

A comfortable-looking woman in her middle years glided towards her. 'You must be Lady Bernadette.' The woman dropped into a neat curtsy. A welcoming smile flickered into being and she turned to Hugo with another curtsy. 'And you have to be Sir Hugo.' A bunch of heavy keys hung at her waist, telling Bernadette that this woman ran the household.

'This is my wife, Celeste,' Sir Gilebert murmured.

'I am very pleased to meet you, Lady Celeste,' Bernadette said. 'I wish you both every joy and happiness.'

'Thank you, my lady. We wish the same to you.'

Sir Gilebert cleared his throat. 'If it pleases you, my wife will take the two of you to your bedchamber.' He nodded towards the table. 'When you are rested, refreshments await.'

Hugo nodded. 'Thank you, sir.' He laid a hand on Bernadette's dowry chest. He was responsible for her fortune, and he would not lower his guard until he had it safe. 'But before we do anything else, I need to secure this in the strongroom.' He also had the deeds to the manor tucked into the lining of his jacket. 'Lord Michel mentioned a strongbox. I need to see it.'

Sir Gilebert nodded. 'Come this way, sir. Celeste holds the keys to most of the manor, but you will understand that I alone hold the key to the strongroom and the strongbox.'

'*Bien sûr*. Of course.'

'We need a torch.'

A maidservant brought Sir Gilebert a torch and Hugo picked up the dowry chest and followed him into the passage and down a winding stairway. Like the rest of the manor, the cellar was built entirely in stone. The roof was vaulted. Light angled down from vents high in the walls and the air was cool. Several storage barrels lined the walls. Nets of onions hung from the roof alongside several bunches of what Hugo assumed were herbs. There was a distinct smell of rosemary. At the far end, lost in shadow, was a door, strongly banded with iron.

Sir Gilebert gestured between the rows of barrels at the shadowed door. 'The strongroom.'

Setting the torch in a bracket on the wall, Sir Gilebert produced a key and put his shoulder to the door. It groaned open. A substantial iron box faced them, the sole object in what was a much smaller chamber. The light was dimmer here, with only a slim vent to admit air and light. More iron banding secured the strongbox to the flagstones.

Sir Gilebert went back for the torch and set it in another bracket. Light shimmered across the vaulted ceiling and the dark retreated. He produced another key and bent over the strongbox. 'As you see, Sir Hugo, there are three locks. Once we are finished, I shall hand all three into your keeping. You alone will have access to this section of the cellar.' The strongbox lid was heaved back. 'This is where the bulk of the estate's revenues are kept,' Sir Gilebert said. 'The account books are in my office, and you are welcome to examine them at any time. You will find no fault with the accounting.'

Three leather purses lay side by side at one end of the strongbox. The other end was empty, leaving plenty of space for Bernadette's dowry. Having put the dowry into the strongbox, Hugo reached for one of the leather purses and weighed it in his palm. It was reassuringly heavy. His heart thumped. Lord, there was surely more coin in this purse than he could have earned in his lifetime. And thanks to his marriage it was his. Well, it was his and Bernadette's.

Catching Sir Gilebert's gaze on him, he smiled ruefully and replaced the purse. 'You can show me the account books later.' He reached into his jacket and withdrew the deeds. 'In the meantime, these are the manor deeds. Lord Michel has signed them over to my wife and I.'

Sir Gilebert took the deeds. 'I take it a scribe has made a copy?'

'Aye. Lord Michel is keeping that at Galard.'

'Very well.' The deeds were tucked into the side of the strongbox, and Sir Gilebert closed the lid and locked it. 'We can look over the deeds after breaking our fast tomorrow.'

'Of course.'

Without further ado, Hugo was handed the keys to the strongbox, Sir Gilebert reclaimed the torch, and they went back upstairs to the hall. Bernadette was still there, sitting at the table with Lady Celeste. Wine goblets in hand, they were discussing food stores.

'You need not worry that we shall run out of grain, my lady,' Lady Celeste was saying. 'We have a small store here for emergencies, but the bulk of the town grain is housed in a raised barn by the church. I shall point it out to you when we walk round Larressingle tomorrow. People will want to meet you. I can introduce you to some of the merchants and townsfolk.'

'Thank you,' Bernadette replied. Her eyes were brighter than they had been in some days. 'I would love that.'

A weight lifted from Hugo's shoulders. Bernadette had been quiet for the last sennight, so quiet that Hugo had assumed she was miserable at leaving Galard. It was good to see her giving every appearance of being content to be made lady of this manor. He needed to

know she would be happy while he dealt with the dis-
quieting events at Nérac.

Hugo accepted the goblet Sir Gilebert offered him
and drew him aside. Once he had ensured that suitable quarters had been found for Violette and their
escort, he got straight down to business. Hugo and
Bernadette held the title to Larressingle, though Hugo
was mindful that Sir Gilebert had acted as steward
on his own for years. Hugo had limited experience of
managing an estate, and the need for tact was clear.
He had no wish to put the man's back up. It was possible Sir Gilebert had come to think of Larressingle
as his own fiefdom.

'Sir Gilebert, I need to ride to Nérac as soon as
possible.'

Sir Gilebert nodded easily. 'I assumed as much. Do
you go tomorrow?'

'The day after will be soon enough. It will give the
men a day to settle in and check the horses over. Do
we have reserve horses in our stable?'

'We do indeed. Also, you might like to know there's
a livery stable next to the tavern. It has proved useful in the past.'

'A livery stable, eh? That sounds promising.' Reminded of the many times Angel had had to change
horses on the ride from Galard, Hugo glanced at her,
now engrossed in a conversation about household linens. Hugo understood that Bernadette was fond of her
pony, but it had been irksome for her having to switch

horses so many times. Tansy suited a younger woman and Bernadette could certainly handle a larger mare. He made a note to ask Sir Gilebert if the livery might sell him a suitable mount.

Sir Gilebert set down his goblet. He was listening to the conversation about linens. He addressed Bernadette. 'My lady, my wife and I are at your disposal. If you and your husband would care to explore the town tomorrow, we shall be delighted to escort you. You may prefer to remain in the manor, in which case I shall leave you with Celeste.'

'Thank you, I should like to see the town,' Bernadette said. She smiled at Celeste. 'And I would enjoy your company too. Is there a cloth merchant?'

'Yes, my lady, there is.'

'What about seamstresses?' Bernadette asked. 'Do we have any here in in the manor?'

Lady Celeste looked speculatively at her. 'A couple. I am a competent seamstress myself, but I am afraid designing a pattern is beyond me. Do you care to sew?'

'She loves it,' Hugo put in. 'Makes the patterns too.'

Lady Celeste's eyes lit up and she and Bernadette embarked upon a discussion of the various merits of English weaves and Flemish silks and Oriental embroideries...

Understanding that he had no further role in his wife's conversation, Hugo took a draught of wine and turned back to Sir Gilebert.

* * *

Shortly afterwards, Hugo and Bernadette were shown into their bedchamber so they might tidy themselves in readiness for supper.

The bedchamber was larger than Bernadette had expected, although the bed looked shorter than her bed at Galard. Noting Hugo's disparaging glance, she had to smile. 'I hope Papa sends our furniture soon. You are far too tall for that bed.'

Apart from the length of the bed, Bernadette had no complaints. A brightly coloured carpet covered a section of the wide-planked floor, an unusual luxury. A bowl of warm water sat ready on a side table. Unpinning her veil, so she could tidy her hair after she had washed, she went to the window to check out the lie of the land beyond the manor courtyard.

The villagers' houses ran one into the next, and the stonework was covered with grey and yellow lichen. The roofs formed a complicated patchwork. Roof tiles seemed to be made from a mix of grey timber and red clay. Some buildings were thatched with reed.

'Stop scowling at that bed, Hugo. Come and see.' She draped her veil on a chair back. 'Our bedchamber is positioned over the manor's main entrance.'

Hugo came to stand behind her. Setting his hands on her shoulders, he kissed the side of her neck. Briefly, she leaned against him. However, when he slid his hands about her waist, she tried to ease away and went to stand before a polished bronze mirror, hanging over a side table. Hugo came with her, hands warm on her hips. In the blurry reflection, she shook her head at him. 'Hugo, really. We look like a couple of vagabonds.'

'You look delightful, you always do,' he murmured.

Firmly, she shook her head. 'That is not true. I need to change my gown, this one is crumpled and dusty. I have smudges on my face and as for you—your hair looks as though it has not seen a comb in weeks. We must make ourselves respectable for supper. This is our manor, and we have responsibilities towards our retainers. Sir Gilebert and Lady Celeste expect us to act with dignity.'

'Dignity,' Hugo muttered. It was hard to think about dignity when all he wanted was to win her trust. Every night the yearning to make her his wife in more than name grew more and more painful. Even in their tent, lying on hard, stony ground he had ached to kiss and caress her, but he had not been about to seduce her with half their escort within earshot. She deserved better.

Tonight, he was determined that would change. Larressingle was their home. Angel had known him for years. She had agreed to marry him, she had not had to meet the horde of suitors. Tonight, he was determined to show her that her worst fears would not materialise, that he knew ways of keeping her safe. Heaving a sigh of frustration, he set about making himself respectable for supper.

* * *

That night, using the pretext of fatigue after so many days on the road, Hugo escaped with Bernadette as soon as he decently could.

'My thanks, Lady Celeste, for your warm welcome,' he said. 'Supper was delicious, I am particularly fond of chicken braised in wine.'

Angel murmured agreement and before she could blink, he had snatched up a candle and whisked her upstairs and into their bedchamber. A wooden wedge was attached to their door latch by a leather thong. Slipping the wedge into place, Hugo locked the door. When next he looked at her, she was standing with her back to the shutters. She had used the candle to light the wall sconces. Her eyes were wide—dark and wary. 'Angel, you are not afraid of me.'

Slowly she shook her head. 'No, of course not.' Her voice was firm. Too firm? Was she trying to convince herself? Conscious that she might find his greater height intimidating, Hugo sat on the bed, leaned back on an elbow, and held out his hand. 'Come here, Angel. I need to talk to you about our marriage.'

A pleat appeared in her brow, but she did as he asked and allowed him to take her hand. Nor did she resist when he pulled her on to the mattress next to him. 'Angel, do you trust me?'

Her fingers gripped his. 'Of course I trust you. Hugo, we have known each other nearly all my life.

You are my greatest friend.' Hesitantly, she touched his cheek. 'I married you, didn't I?'

He pushed himself to sitting. 'No, do not shift away. I will not hurt you.' Holding her in place, he smiled. 'I am hoping for a kiss. You have hardly touched me since our wedding day.'

'That is not true. We have slept together every night.'

'Aye.' He fought to keep his voice even. 'You have not welcomed much kissing though, and I know you like it.'

'I do, very much.' Lifting his hand, she kissed his knuckles and smiled sadly. 'It is just that I fear—'

'You fear we will get carried away.' She hung her head, nodding assent. 'Angel, I have given this some thought over the past few weeks. I accept you have a fear of childbed, but we cannot continue like this. Neither of us is sleeping well. We are making each other miserable.'

She bit her bottom lip in the way that invariably drew his gaze to her mouth, that kissable, tempting mouth. 'I am sorry, Hugo.'

'He stroked her cheek. 'If we are careful, there are ways we may enjoy each other without running the risk of you getting with child.'

She stared at his neck. 'I have been wondering about that.'

His eyebrows rose. 'You have?'

'Aye. I remembered something Mother Margerie said.'

'Mother Margerie?' He bit back a bark of laughter. 'What does that woman know of such things?'

'More than you may imagine. Listen, Hugo. While I was in the convent helping in the infirmary, I learned that there are more deaths in childbed in the convent than there are in, say, our village. It is my opinion that the mother's shame and fear about what will happen to the child makes the birth even more challenging than usual.'

'That sounds plausible.' Hugo had no notion where this was leading, but he knew better than to attempt to divert Bernadette when she was in full flow. He contented himself with stroking her hair.

'It is heartbreaking, because when the mother does survive, as often as not a wet-nurse is found, and the young lady returns home without her child.'

Hugo nodded. 'Many noble families deal with un-wanted children in this way.'

'It is very harsh.'

'It is horrible that a mother should have to endure that.' He ran his hand round the back of his neck. 'I had no idea Saint Claire's took in women in this way. Angel, must we talk about the convent on our first night here? I do not wish for you to be upset by this.'

'I am fine, Hugo, I assure you.'

He sighed. 'Very well.'

'The last time this happened, I was attending a

young lady whose baby was forcibly removed from her arms. She was beyond distraught and there was some noise, you understand. Mother Margerie came in. She told the girl, quite brutally, that her ignorance had brought her to this pass, and that if she didn't want it to happen again, she must either learn to be chaste or, if she insisted on fornicating, she must take pains to be careful. Mother Margerie hinted, very strongly, that there were measures that could be taken to prevent pregnancy.

'Hugo, is that what you are talking about? You know these measures?'

Hugo stared, his horror and shock momentarily doused by a rush of heat that went through him. 'I do.' He laid a hand on the side of her head and tried not to appear too eager. He did not want her to feel rushed. Bernadette had the most wonderful complexion, creamy and smooth. He pressed a swift kiss to her cheek. Provided he avoided leaving his seed inside her, she would not quicken. 'The main thing is to ensure you remain a virgin.'

She turned her face and their lips met. She tasted delicious, sweet and ripe. Hugo gathered her to him and when his lips drifted down her neck, he was rewarded with the faintest of moans. Unfortunately, she drew back and started toying with a button on his jacket. 'Hugo, I am afraid to confess that you have married an ignorant wife.' She rushed on, clearly embarrassed. 'I meant to ask Allis about such things, but I left it too late. I do not wish to disappoint you.'

'You could never disappoint me. You are forbidden to think that you could.' He nuzzled her cheek. The heady fragrance of Angel and lilies wove around him, a sensual spell that was unique and utterly devastating. She might not know it, but he was completely in her thrall.

'Hugo?' Small fingers gripped his jacket. 'You will have to teach me everything.'

Hugo smoothed away a twist of hair and in so doing, found his hand close to a tempting breast. Beneath the rush of desire, he was startled to discover a faint sense of disappointment. She had made it plain she was not ready for children. Despite his desire to become a father, he was determined to wait and pray that she would change her mind eventually.

Tonight, she was proving she did trust him. It was, he told himself firmly, a beginning. Besides, she wasn't alone in her ignorance. Hugo might indeed know how to avoid getting a woman a with child, but when it came to marriage itself, he was woefully unprepared.

He had learned nothing from his parents. His mother had died when he was scarcely more than an infant and he could barely remember his father. All Hugo knew about marriage he had learned from Lord Michel and Sybille. He was way out of his depth. And as for handling a wife who was consumed by fear of dying in childbirth—he had no idea where to start.

Shoving his hurt out of the way, he inhaled the intoxicating scent of lilies and smiled. Angel desired him, he would hang on to that. She was a sensual woman. Even better, she was not wearing much beneath the sumptuous gown she had worn to supper. From his perspective, more of her creamy skin was exposed than she probably realised.

She shifted slightly, angling herself so her breast sat squarely within his palm. A deliberate movement which invited further intimacies? It certainly felt like one. Her breast felt delicious, small and perfect. A dark pulse throbbed, and his mind filled with possibilities. This was their first night in their new home. If they gave each other pleasure, the bond between them would strengthen.

She pressed against him, wriggling with a shy and delicate wantonness such as he had never encountered. He was enchanted. Enslaved. Her lightest touch had fire running through his every vein. Angel was his wife. This passionate woman was his. Reaching for her bodice, he edged it lower, smiling as more creamy flesh came into view.

'Hugo, we will be careful?'

'Trust me.' He planted a row of kisses around her neck, just above the embroidery that ran along the neck of her bodice. With the fragrance of lilies filling his senses, he smiled against her skin. 'If we are careful, my love, we can avoid getting you with child.'

Hugo was eyeing the row of buttons at the front of Bernadette's bodice.

'I want to see you,' he murmured. 'Are those buttons decorative?'

'No.' Immediately, his hand left her breast and went to the top button. Faintly alarmed, Bernadette's eyes widened. She covered his hand with hers. 'We are to be naked?'

'I hope so.' The smile in his voice told Bernadette that, embarrassing though that question was, she was right to ask it. 'Angel, skin to skin is usually best.'

He shifted her to reach the buttons and Bernadette's mouth dried. Skin to skin. 'That sounds decadent.'

'It is, deliciously so.'

'Then why did Sybille make me that nightgown?'

Unnerved by the sensations Hugo's voice and touch were evoking inside her, Bernadette's mind worked. She knew vaguely what to expect. Vaguely. The ladies who had come to Saint Claire's had not been allowed much converse with the nuns and novices. With Mother Margerie impressing upon them the grave nature of their sin, they would not have dared flout her wishes.

Before going to the convent, Bernadette had overheard the castle servants gossiping about husbands and lovers. She had been desperately naive back then and none of what she had heard had meant much. Naturally, she had seen animals mating. She had found it almost comical.

How did things work when a man and woman joined? It must be roughly the same and yet... What a strange business it must be. It did not matter. None of it mattered. What did matter was that Hugo was smiling. Their conversation had banished the bleakness from his expression.

He had succeeded in working one of her shoulders completely free of her gown. He gave it a gentle, biting kiss before setting to work on the next button. His smile was warm. Expectant. 'Lady Sybille made that nightgown. The fabric is as thin as gossamer.' He shrugged. 'Wear it tonight if you wish. It will hide nothing. Come, kiss me.'

Bernadette laid her hand on his chest, felt a slight pull on her gown and it slipped a little further. He had undone another button.

Hugo grinned, and it occurred to her that he was having all the fun. She plucked at his jacket. 'Every button you undo has to be matched with me undoing one of yours.'

His eyebrows rose and he gave a wide smile. 'As you wish. I am two ahead of you. Have at me.' Leaning back to accommodate her, he gestured for her to proceed.

Her fingers were all thumbs and the first button revealed little more than an expanse of white linen shirt.

The second, her confidence increasing, she tugged judiciously at the linen beneath, revealing a small expanse of sun-browned skin.

Bernadette knew what a man's chest looked like; her father's knights sometimes trained bare-chested. Eager now, she hurried on, her fingers flying over the buttons. Another. Another. Another. When she reached the last button, she did not have to unclasp Hugo's belt, he had already done it. She had no idea where it went.

Stifling a moan, she tore his jacket from him. Somehow his shirt was gone. She had no recollection of removing it, but she found herself staring at his chest. *Mon Dieu*, Hugo was all lean muscle. Broad shoulders, wide chest, and lean stomach.

Dry mouthed, she swallowed. He was most beautifully made. 'You have collected a couple of scars,' she said, tracing them with her fingertips.

He shivered. 'Got those breaking up a tavern brawl in Arles.' A lock of fair hair fell over his eyes as he leaned towards her. 'You, madam wife, are a cheat.'

She looked blankly at him. 'I am?'

His eyes danced. 'We were meant to be taking turns with the buttons.'

'Oh.' He moved so quickly Bernadette had no idea how he managed it, but suddenly she was lying on the bed, while Hugo made rapid work of the remaining buttons on her bodice. He peeled her gown away.

'Lift up, *chérie*.' The gown vanished with a rustle.

The rest of Hugo's clothes went the same way, and they ended up lying on their sides facing each other. Half-excited, half-afraid, Bernadette was careful to train her gaze on his face. If she thought about what they were actually doing, if she thought about Hugo's more manly parts, well, her mind simply refused to go down that road. However, this was Hugo. It would be all right.

Eyes soft, Hugo reached for her and pulled her close. His musky scent—Hugo—surrounded her. It was oddly comforting. 'Come here, my love.'

Bernadette's thoughts began to scatter. Being in Hugo's arms in their new bed was utterly delicious. He was stroking her hair from her face, sending tiny shivers of sensation deep inside her. His expression, if she did not know better, was as tender as she could wish. His skin was so warm. Without thought, she pressed closer. Her body seemed to insist. She knew nothing, yet her body clearly had its own wisdom. She was not going to fight it.

'That's it,' Hugo murmured, raining kisses on her cheeks, her lips. Her breast. The sensations strengthened, shooting stars that reached into her core.

She heard a moan. Hers. How extraordinary. Without consciously deciding, she pressed closer. Instinct was warring with rationality. This would only work with Hugo. It was her last coherent thought. That most intimate part of him was pressing urgently against her. Inherent shyness had prevented her from looking at him there. He felt large, both hard and soft. She was not ready to touch him there and it didn't matter. Hugo knew what to do. He would keep her safe, all she had to do was surrender.

Hugo stroked his hand down her flank. He kissed her belly, and she allowed it. Revelled in it. More groans escaped. He nudged her thighs open and when his fingers touched her core, her last coherent thought was surprise. She, who had never thought to surrender to any man, would find complete surrender to Hugo terrifyingly easy. A month ago, such a thought would have been unthinkable.

Chapter Twelve

Bernadette and Hugo had spent their first day in Larressingle, exploring the manor and the town.

On their second morning, Bernadette woke late thanks to another chaste and extraordinary seduction, courtesy of her husband. Given how tired they had been after their journey, it had been exhausting greeting all the townsfolk. In bed Hugo had taken pains to satisfy her, yet when she opened her eyes, she felt bewilderingly frustrated. Still half-asleep, she allowed her thoughts to drift lazily through her mind. Her feelings were evolving at a startling rate. Being married to Hugo was at the root of the change. She could not fault him for his careful sensuality. *I am still a virgin. There is no chance I could be with child.*

Puzzled, she stared drowsily up at the bed hangings. A few days ago, she would have been thankful for that. She was afraid of childbirth and did not want children. Or did she? Once again she thought of the wistful way Hugo had studied the wooden cradle at their wedding feast. *Hugo wants children. He wants a family.* And so, she realised with a pang, did she. Provided they were his.

Her anxieties concerning childbirth were weakening, the desire to give Hugo the family he had yearned for was strengthening. Being apart from Hortense, and from any who had constantly reminded her of her mother's end, had slowly begun to release her from the fears that consumed her.

Above her, the unfamiliar bed hangings came slowly into focus. She was at Larressingle, where she was lady of the manor. It was another unexpected turn of the road of her life. Frowning, for she could hear voices outside, she pushed out of bed and hurried to the washbowl. Wrestling herself into her riding habit, she sped down to the hall.

Today they were meant to be going to Nérac. Hugo could not be thinking of going without her? Snatching a chunk of bread from a basket, she went into the courtyard.

Hugo was standing by a horse trough, deep in conversation with Sir Gilebert. He had mentioned taking a small escort, some of the men they had brought with them from Galard. Bernadette had not had his explicit agreement that she was going too, she had simply assumed that she would not be left behind. Hopefully an argument could be avoided.

Seeing her, Hugo held out his hand. He tugged her to him and gave her a swift kiss on the cheek. 'There you are, my love,' he said. 'I thought I would have to set out without bidding you farewell.'

'Farewell?' Bernadette's chin lifted. 'I am coming with you.'

Hugo stilled. 'I am not sure that is wise.'

Bernadette felt a flare of anger and fought to keep it from her voice. 'Hugo, I should like to meet your family.'

'So you shall, when I know it is safe for you to do so.' He slipped his arm about her waist and took her lips with a warm kiss and a gleam in his eyes that told her he was remembering what had passed between them the previous night. His expression sobered. 'However, given the lack of hospitality accorded to Sir Gilebert when he tried to visit and the reports he sent your father, I am not confident we will be well received.'

She gripped his hands. 'Hugo, you are *not* going without me. Think. The last news we had was that your brother was seriously unwell. Are you a healer?'

He grimaced. 'There are sure to be healers in Nérac.'

'You cannot know that for sure, you have not seen either the castle or town in years. Hugo, listen. I am no expert, but Allis taught me much and I learned more at the convent. Your brother is ill. If you find Lady Ragonde is not coping, are you confident you will be able to assist them?'

When Hugo exchanged rueful glances with Sir

Gilebert, Bernadette knew she had won this bout. She would be accompanying him to Nérac.

Sir Gilbert's lips twitched. 'I will ask Olivier to saddle Tansy,' he said. 'She should be rested enough for the ride to Nérac.' Receiving a resigned nod from Hugo, their steward headed towards the stable.

The Petite Baise river ran through Nérac. As they crossed the bridge and rode towards the castle, Hugo was blind to the streets he remembered from his childhood. Briefly, the acrid tang of the tanneries caught his nostrils. Holding his breath, he rode on. All he could think was that soon, he would be seeing Aleran. *Pray God he is alive.*

Once the stench of the tanneries fell behind, Hugo noticed that the town was unnaturally quiet. The narrow alleys that cut between the stone houses were almost deserted and many houses had their shutters up. The only sign of life was a cluster of housewives in one of the market squares. When he was young, the town had hummed with activity. Yet today...

He turned to Bernadette. 'This place is like the grave. I have never seen it so quiet.'

'Perhaps it is a local saint's day, and everyone is in church,' Bernadette said, smiling. 'There are so many saints' days, it is sometimes hard to keep count.'

Hugo nodded. That must be it. They continued in silence. Conversation was beyond him. As they approached the chateau, a cold hand closed over Hugo's heart. Aleran, he thought. Please God, let him be well.

Suddenly they were there. The walls of Nérac Castle stood firmly before them. A few hens were scratching about in the square in front of them. A cat prowled past the gate, which was closed. Hugo rode up to the gate, searching for the bell rope. It had been cut off and the shutter behind the iron grille of the peephole was firmly closed. Cold dread coiling inside him, he drew his sword and used the pommel to thump on the gate.

Bernadette felt for Hugo. It took a while for the peephole to open, but eventually an elderly serving woman peered out. She let out a gasp on sighting Hugo, and her wrinkled cheeks lost what little colour they had. 'It cannot be,' she said, lifting her hand to cover her mouth. 'You look so like the Count. Who are you?'

Hugo studied the woman, a pleat in his brow. He did not seem to recognise her. 'My name is Hugo Albret.'

The woman opened her mouth and shut it again, finally saying, 'Albret? B…but—'

'I am Lord Aleran's brother. Be so good as to admit us.'

The woman stared at Hugo a moment longer. The peephole scraped shut, the bolts rasped back, and the gate swung wide. The set expression on Hugo's face warned Bernadette to say nothing. She would get no sense out of him until he had found out how his brother fared. Was he still alive?

Nerves stretched tight with anxiety, deeply worried for Hugo, Bernadette forced herself to take stock of her surroundings. The castle was impressive. A wide façade spread out before them. Several stories high, it dominated a paved courtyard. Unlike at her father's castle, there were no workshops or buildings hunkered behind the curtain wall. Instead, several untidy piles of leaves had collected in the corners and there was a faint whiff of rotting vegetation.

She frowned. The leaves should have been swept away, but they had been there so long they were turning to mulch. A flight of steps led up to the sentry posts on the wall walkway. Where was the guardhouse? The stables? They must be behind the castle.

Gesturing for their men to remain in the yard, Hugo marched into the chateau so swiftly, Bernadette had to run to keep pace with him. They went up a flight of stairs and entered a large chamber on an upper floor. 'The hall?' she murmured.

'Family solar,' Hugo replied curtly. A muscle jumped in his cheek.

A row of glazed windows ran along a wall, and for a moment Bernadette was reminded of the alterations her father had made at Galard. Other than that, the interior of Nérac Castle was nothing like Galard. Her nose wrinkled. The smells in here were worse than those outside. The solar reeked of sour wine and despair. The air was stale. Heading for a window—they were all closed—Bernadette grimaced at the dust and spiders' webs wrapped round the handle and wrenched it open.

Poor Hugo. His brother's castle could not have been cleaned in years. The fireplace was clogged with ash; tables were greasy with candlewax and crumbs; the planked floor was sticky underfoot. It would be a miracle if the place was not infested with mice. Not to mention rats.

Hugo prowled to a table and stared at a collection of empty wine bottles that was piled up like driftwood. A mountain of discarded wine corks lay on the floor. Snatching up a bottle, Hugo sniffed it and set it down with a grimace. 'Lord, what on earth are they drinking?'

A shadow flickered briefly across an open door at the far end of the solar. Someone was watching them. A servant? It was impossible to say. Hugo stalked across and drew a woman into the light. She was wearing a crumpled scarlet gown that was far from clean and was trembling from head to foot.

Bernadette went cold. Servants rarely wore scarlet, that colour was usually reserved for the highest in the land. Who was she? If she was a noblewoman, where was her headdress? The woman's hair—it was impossible to tell whether it was blonde or light brown—hung lankly about her face, as dull and listless as the rest of her.

'Who are you?' Hugo demanded.

The woman stared vacantly up at him. Her mouth moved, but no sound emerged. Bernadette had a dreadful feeling that this was Lady Ragonde, Countess of Nérac. Suspecting her to be on the verge of panic, Bernadette walked carefully towards her. The Countess, if this was she, looked ill. Her gaze—her eyes were blue—skittered vaguely about the hall. It was almost as though she thought that if she did not look directly at Hugo and Bernadette, she could pretend they were not there. Her eyes were disturbing, her pupils were enormous. She had dark hollows in her cheeks and her skin was sallow. But it was the sinister blankness in her eyes that sent a chill down Bernadette's spine.

'Who are you, I say?' Hugo repeated, his voice almost a growl.

Bernadette stepped between them. 'Gently, Hugo,' she murmured. Hoping that the woman might, out of habit, respond to formality, she dipped into a curtsy. 'My name is Lady Bernadette of Larressingle, and I am delighted to meet you.'

She was relieved when the woman's eyes focused on her. Hugo, thank the saints, had the wit to step back.

'Lady Bernadette of Larressingle.' A faint frown appeared. 'I do not believe we have met.'

'No, indeed.' Bernadette smiled encouragingly. 'I understand you are the Countess of Nérac.'

The frown deepened. 'Aye, that is true. I am Lady

Ragonde.' Her focus briefly landed on Hugo before sliding away. 'And your companion?'

'This is my husband. Lady Ragonde, it is my pleasure to introduce Sir Hugo Albret of—'

Lady Ragonde went white and her hand shot to her throat. 'Albret, you say? Hugo Albret?' Staring at Hugo as though he were the devil incarnate, she scuttled back. 'Oh, no. No, no. This cannot be.'

'My lady.' Hugo gave his brother's wife his most charming bow. 'I am delighted to meet you.'

'Why…why are you here?' Lady Ragonde's fingers moved convulsively on her throat. Her fingernails were, Bernadette saw with a twinge of horrified compassion, none too clean.

'Lady Ragonde, you must not fear me,' Hugo said quietly. 'I am Aleran's younger brother. I have come because I heard you needed aid. Where is Aleran?'

'Aleran? He is…why, he is in his bedchamber. He has been ill for some while.' Swallowing hard, Lady Ragonde went to the table that was littered with discarded bottles, found a handbell and rang it.

Hugo sagged a little and glanced at Bernadette, the relief he was feeling writ large on his face. Aleran was alive. That brief exchange of glances told Bernadette that despite the bitterness and his long years of exile, the bond Hugo felt with his brother was unbreakable. He loved him still. Selfishly, her spirits lifted. If Hugo was capable of that after years of estrangement, there had to be hope he could eventually come to love his wife.

Outside, a cockerel crowed. As they waited for a servant to respond to the bell, Bernadette smiled at Lady Ragonde. Nérac Castle was uncannily quiet. Why, it was quieter than the convent in Greater Silence. There were no hurrying footsteps, no doors slamming, no whispers of laughter. Nothing. Just the cockerel outside and an oppressive silence. Where was the Countess's son, Dennis? In Bernadette's admittedly limited experience, young boys were not usually quiet or retiring.

'Is Dennis about, my lady? I would love to meet him.'

'Dennis? You will have to wait a while. He is playing in the garden with his nurse.'

'How old is Dennis?' Bernadette asked.

'He is three years old.' With an irritated glance at the door, Lady Ragonde rang the bell again. 'Where is everyone?'

'Perhaps the servants are out of earshot.' Bernadette said.

'Never mind.' Lady Ragonde set the bell back on the table with a clack. 'I shall take you to Aleran myself.'

'Thank you, my lady, that would be much appreciated.' Hugo bowed and gestured for his brother's wife to precede him out of the hall.

They passed along a dusty corridor. Bernadette

couldn't help but think that wherever the servants were, no cleaning had been done anywhere. A tapestry caught her eye. It was so dirty and moth-eaten, it was hard to see the design. Making out a tree and what might represent a deer, Bernadette guessed she was looking at a hunting scene.

Lady Ragonde paused briefly at the foot of some stairs. 'After Aleran fell ill, it was decided that we should occupy separate bedchambers. Aleran's bedchamber is up here.' Lifting her skirts, she started up the stairs.

Struck by the Countess's odd turn of phrase—*it was decided*—Bernadette frowned thoughtfully. The Countess seemed to be implying that she hadn't been the one to do the deciding. But if it had not been her decision, then who had done the deciding? Sensing a mystery, Bernadette skirted round several dust balls clustered at the foot of the stairs and followed. They went up one flight. Two. As they reached a small landing at the top, more questions bubbled up in Bernadette's mind.

If the servants were as lethargic as appearances suggested, why on earth would Aleran—Count of Nérac, after all, even if he was infirm—be relegated to such an out-of-the-way bedchamber? It was practically in the attic. It was the attic. The Countess didn't seem capable of making decisions. Someone else, Bernadette was sure, had put Lord Aleran up here.

Why? Wondering whether the Count was capable

of calling for assistance and whether anyone would hear him if he did, Bernadette watched his Countess lift the latch and they went inside.

The chamber was cramped and very basic. It had a sloping ceiling with heavy beams running across it, and a small, glazed window. A table sat on either side of the bed and a wooden chest at the foot.

The Count of Nérac was abed, lying slightly askew on a bank of pillows. His skin had a grey tinge, his cheeks were sunken and his lips faintly blue. Appalled, Bernadette fought to keep her expression neutral. Little more than skin and bones, the poor man looked to be at death's door. None the less, his resemblance to Hugo was marked. It was there in the shape of that distinctive nose and in the line of his jaw. Or what she could see of it through an untidy beard. The Count's eyes were brown, just like Hugo's. The Count stared at Hugo, mouth working. Hugo simply stared. Shock had turned him to stone.

Bernadette went to the bed, saying briskly, 'My lord, you do not look very comfortable. Permit us to straighten you.'

Moving to the other side of the bed, Hugo bent to assist. Between them they lifted his brother, plumped up his pillows, and set him straight. Lord Aleran was alarmingly easy to move. As they tended to him, his gaze alternated between Hugo and Bernadette. Reading no emotion on the Count's face, none whatsoever, Bernadette's sense of foreboding deepened. Whatever

ailed the man, it had to be more than an apoplexy. To
be so thin, he must also have a wasting disease.

'Aleran—' Hugo's voice was strained '—allow me
to present Lady Bernadette of Galard. My wife.'

Bernadette gave a quick curtsy. 'Actually, my lord,
my title now is Lady Bernadette of Larressingle.' Noticing a jug covered with a cloth and a clay cup on a
bedside table, Bernadette pulled the cloth from the
jug, and sniffed. 'Ale,' she murmured. And if she were
not mistaken it had been sitting too long. She looked
directly at Count Aleran. 'My lord, you are thirsty, I
am sure. I will send for fresh ale and ask the kitchen
to provide some soup. I shall also arrange for a chair
to be brought, so that Hugo may sit with you.'

The Count looked at her and heaved a sigh. Clearly,
he was too weak and weary to think of eating.

'Thank you, Angel.' Hugo glanced warily at Lady
Ragonde who was standing silently at the foot of the
bed, twisting a strand of her hair round her finger.

'I would like to stay,' Lady Ragonde said. Her voice,
though faint, was filled with longing. It was almost,
Bernadette thought, as though Lady Ragonde had
been barred from entering her husband's bedchamber and was using Hugo's appearance as an excuse to
see him. Dismissing the idea as preposterous, Bernadette linked arms with the Countess and guided her
gently to the door.

'My husband wishes to see his brother on his own,

my lady. It has been years since they have seen each other, I am sure you understand.'

As Bernadette closed the door behind her, a bleak-eyed Hugo blew her a kiss.

Once on the landing outside the Count's bedchamber, Bernadette was startled to see Lady Ragonde curl her fingers into fists.

'You mentioned finding my husband ale,' the lady said. 'This way, if you please.'

With a swish of her skirts and a sense of purpose Bernadette was pleasantly surprised to note, Lady Ragonde retraced her steps. Down the stairs, past the first landing and the moth-ravaged tapestries, before finally coming to a halt before a solid-looking door on the ground floor.

'This leads to the cellar,' Lady Ragonde said, producing a key and unlocking the door with a distressingly shaky hand. 'The ale is usually kept here, with the wine.'

The cellar was dark as ink. Muttering under her breath, Lady Ragonde had difficulty striking a light, but eventually Bernadette found herself gaping at what she could only call criminal disorder. Barrels were stacked from ground to ceiling and not one of them looked sound. Wood was split or rotten, the contents had clearly been seeping out of most of them. The smell, of rancid oil and a mouldy, fruity smell, had her covering her nose and trying not to breathe. A small shadow shot across the floor and vanished into a crevice. A rat. There were probably dozens. This was not the result of recent neglect.

Bernadette swallowed down her horror. The Nérac cellar was a lesson in how not to store provisions. It was impossible not to compare it with the one at Galard. The Galard cellar, while full, was orderly. Her stepmother Sybille, she thought, shaking her head, would be outraged.

Lady Ragonde slipped behind a listing barrel and Bernadette heard a clink. When she re-emerged, she had a wine bottle in either hand. They were identical to the discarded bottles Bernadette had noticed earlier in the solar. The Countess glanced at Bernadette and froze. 'What are you staring at?' she asked.

'I thought we were finding ale for Count Aleran. Until I am confident the water in your well is clean, your husband should be drinking ale.'

'Oh, yes. Ale. Of course.' Lady Ragonde looked about vaguely. 'I would swear it used to be kept here. Lord knows where it has gone. Never mind.' She brightened. 'They will have some in the tavern.'

The Countess's behaviour was as extraordinary as her appearance. Curious to see what she might do next, Bernadette held her tongue and followed her back to the solar. Lady Ragonde put the bottles on the table and set about opening one with an ease born of long practice. 'Will you join me in a drink, my lady?' she asked.

'Thank you, but I shall have one later. I need to go to the kitchens to see about that broth for your husband. And if there is no ale to be had, I shall make him a tisane. It will tide him over until the broth is ready.'

Nodding, Lady Ragonde poured a generous measure of wine into a cup and drained it. When she filled her cup a second time, Bernadette felt a frown form. The Countess seemed to crave the stuff, yet Hugo had said it smelt odd. Could the wine be the source of Lady Ragonde's ills?

Walking over, she plucked the cup out of Lady Ragonde's hand. 'The kitchens, my lady? Your husband needs to eat.'

Lady Ragonde blinked. 'We have to go straight away?'

'The sooner the better.' Bernadette would be sure to investigate the wine, but that could wait. 'Your husband needs that broth.'

It was a struggle persuading Lady Ragonde to take her to the kitchens. The longer Bernadette spent with her, the more she felt certain that something ailed the Countess that was almost as bad as the infirmity that had laid the Count low. The Countess's hands, when they were not twisting her lank hair or smoothing down her shabby red skirts, shook continually. It was hard to hold her gaze for more than a moment, leading Bernadette to the conclusion that the poor woman had lost her concentration. She did not appear to be being deliberately difficult.

'The kitchen, my lady?' Bernadette asked for the third time.

'Ah, yes, this way.'

The kitchen was empty save for an elderly woman kneading dough. The main fire was not lit and the spit empty.

'Good evening, Mistress,' Bernadette said, brightly. 'Is that bread for this evening?' She had hoped for more than bread and cheese for supper, but it would be better than nothing. 'Where's the bread oven?'

'And who might you be?' the woman asked.

Seeing that Lady Ragonde had fallen into one of her dazes and looked unlikely to respond, Bernadette smiled. 'I am Lady Bernadette of Larressingle. I am married to Lord Aleran's brother.' She made a show of looking about the kitchen. 'Please don't tell me you are the only person here. We hoped for supper this evening.'

'We? How many others have come with you?'

'My husband and I brought a sizeable escort. There are several horsemen.'

'Several?' The woman bit her lip. 'There is only me in the kitchen, mistress—I mean, my lady. We do not eat much at supper time. The castle guard dine at the tavern.'

Bernadette softened her voice. 'You need help. What is your name?'

'Barbe, my lady.' Barbe glanced awkwardly at the Countess, who watched in silence from the side of the kitchen with her dull eyes and restless, trembling hands. 'Help would be more than welcome.'

Very little persuasion was needed to encourage their men to help in the kitchen. The simple threat of them going without supper was enough. Bernadette wasn't surprised. The first lesson her father taught new recruits was invariably self-reliance. It was the same the world over. Every soldier worth his salt knew how to cook a basic meal. Which was all to the good, because in no time at all the kitchen fire was crackling, a tisane had been sent up to the Count, and orders had been given for the making of chicken broth. Unfortunately, it would be impossible to bake any loaves until morning, Barbe's dough would not prove in time. Instead, Bernadette set a couple of men to making flatbread while the dough Barbe had been making proved under a cloth. Another man was charged with finding two chairs and taking them to the Count's bedchamber.

Bernadette turned to her sister-in-law. 'Lady Ragonde, I believe supper will take about an hour. Do you think Dennis will be back from the garden by now?'

'He should be.'

'Good. We can wait for him in the solar. If you wish, I could sample that wine.'

Lady Ragonde led the way back to the solar so fast her feet might have been winged. She wasted no time drawing a cork. 'Here you are, my lady,' she said, shoving a cup into Bernadette's hand and filling another for herself.

Watching the Countess down her wine like a trooper, Bernadette sniffed hers cautiously. It did smell odd. And it was impossible not to see that the instant the Countess had finished hers her whole demeanour relaxed. It was as though…

Bernadette smelled her wine again and surreptitiously dipped a finger in to taste it. Ugh! Hugo's assessment was correct, it tasted all wrong. Bernadette put her cup down. She was about to recommend that Lady Ragonde chose a different wine from the cellar when light footsteps sounded outside the solar.

A small child burst in. '*Maman! Maman!* A cat got in the garden. Jeanette found kittens!'

This had to be Dennis. A bundle of energy, he ran eagerly towards his mother, before pouting. 'Wanted to bring them in. Jeanette said no.'

A fresh-faced young woman entered, carrying a hoop and ball. Mercifully, Jeanette was clean and neatly dressed. She looked every inch the ideal nursemaid. After discovering the Count in such dire straits and the Countess seeming to be ill herself, it was a relief to see someone so normal-looking. For all that Dennis was scowling at his nursemaid, it was obvious that he harboured no ill will towards her. There was a good bond between this child and Jeanette.

'The kittens are very young, little lord,' Jeanette

said, her sweet voice and manner confirming Bernadette's assessment of her. 'They need their mother.'

'Maman, you come see. Tomorrow? Please?'

Lady Ragonde smiled. Setting her cup on the table, she sank on to a bench and lifted Dennis on to her lap. 'Of course I will, sweet boy. I shall look forward to it.' She smoothed the child's hair out of his eyes and kissed his brow. 'I am glad you enjoyed yourself. Remember to thank Jeanette for taking you to the garden.'

'Thank you, Jeanette.'

Jeanette bobbed into a curtsy. 'You are welcome, little lord.'

Lady Ragonde bounced Dennis on her knee. With a squeal of delight, the boy snatched at his mother's hair to balance himself. Lady Ragonde gasped with pain, but Dennis received no chastisement. His mother deftly freed her hair from his grasp and the bouncing continued. After witnessing the general air of dilapidation and the apparent low morale of both Lady Ragonde and poor Barbe, it was a delight to see this side of things. Appearances, Bernadette reminded herself, could be deceptive. All was not right at Castle Nérac, but Countess Ragonde loved her son.

The mood shifted after Jeanette held out her hand. 'Come, little lord, it's time for your supper.'

Obediently, Dennis slid from his mother's lap. As he left the solar, he looked back. His mother was already on her feet, reaching for the wine bottle. *'Maman?'*

'My love?'

'Do not forget.'

'Forget what?' the Countess asked.

'Tomorrow. Garden. Kittens!'

'I will not forget.'

Hairs prickled on the back of Bernadette's neck. This household was most peculiar. One moment all appeared normal and the next...

'Lady Ragonde?'

Wine sloshed over the lip of the Countess's cup as she turned towards her. 'Lady Bernadette?'

'We are sisters now. I would be honoured if you would call me Bernadette. All this formality is rather wearing.'

The Countess smiled. 'It is, isn't it? You may call me Ragonde, if you wish.'

'Thank you.'

Ragonde sipped her wine more temperately. 'It will be nice to have a sister. I've always wanted one.'

Ragonde's eyes were hugely dilated. Bernadette stepped closer to make sure. Yes, here was proof. Whatever ailed Ragonde was more than a liking for wine. Bernadette glanced at the heap of discarded bottles. That wine was drugged. In one sense it was a relief to know that Dennis's mother was not simply drinking to forget her woes.

Unfortunately, if Ragonde was dependent on it, the path ahead of her was going to be rocky. Bracing herself, Bernadette reached out and took Ragonde's wine cup from her.

Ragonde gave her a shocked frown. 'What are you doing? Give that back, I'm enjoying it.'

'My lady—Ragonde—I am certain this wine is tainted. You should not be drinking it.'

'Tainted? What are you talking about?' Ragonde spluttered. 'It tastes better than any other.'

'There must be some drug in it, I am sorry.'

'That is not possible, Raoul brings it for me.'

'Raoul?'

Ragonde clenched her fists. 'Raoul is Aleran's cousin. Baron Raoul Sérillac of Fourcès. He is the best of men. He is extremely concerned about Aleran's illness, and he adores Dennis. He is a frequent visitor. He is always bringing toys for Dennis. That hoop you saw. A hobby horse. Some years ago, Raoul realised how much I enjoy this blend of wine and he started bottling it, especially for me. He never fails to ensure it's carted over whenever our stocks are low. Please, hand me that wine. I need it.'

'You need it?' Bernadette stilled; she was certain she was on the right track about the stuff being drugged. 'How so?'

'It stops me fretting. It calms me and I worry less.'

Bernadette nodded. 'It helps you cope with Lord Aleran's illness?'

'Aye. Please, Bernadette, give me my wine cup.'

'I cannot do that,' Bernadette said cheerfully. She

gripped the cup and took a firm hold of the remaining bottle. 'Come, let's go to the cellar and see if we can find something else to your taste.' Ignoring the rage putting sparks in her sister-in-law's dull eyes, she left the solar.

Chapter Thirteen

It was well past midnight when Hugo fell into bed. He and Bernadette had installed themselves in a disused bedchamber that might have been pleasant if it had not been so neglected. A single candle burned on a stand. Angel, who had been a perfect treasure, had asked Olivier to sweep it clean. She had even persuaded a resentful and irritable Ragonde to dig out some bed sheets.

The linen was reasonably clean, it smelt only faintly of must, but that Hugo could cope with. What had him in knots was seeing Aleran at such a low ebb. Hearing his sister-in-law's rage when Angel had tipped that disgusting wine into the garden had been the final straw. He was more than happy to let Bernadette deal with her.

'Did you have to get rid of that wine today?' Hugo asked, smothering a yawn as he looked across the pillows at her. 'Ragonde has the screech of a fishwife.

So much so, I was convinced that a brawl had erupted in town.'

'Waiting would not have been wise,' Bernadette said. 'I suspect that wine has been tampered with. I did not care to tip it into the gutter lest an animal drank it. It could well kill a cat or even a small child. I took it into the garden and poured it into the earth. I cleared the whole cellar.'

Hugo rolled his shoulders to ease out the kinks. 'Was that when Ragonde began shrieking?'

Sombre brown eyes held his. 'I am afraid so. She demanded I send to the tavern for a different wine.'

'There is nothing wrong with her lungs, the commotion carried all the way to the attic. Had I known you were still with the woman, I would have come down to assist you.'

'It was not necessary. I can cope with Ragonde.'

'I hope so. Lord, what is wrong with her?'

Bernadette shifted on the bed, gave him a concerned frown, and took firm hold of his shoulder. 'You are exhausted. Lie on your front, if you please.' As soon as he complied, she kneeled over him and began to tease out the knots.

In a trice, he was groaning with relief. 'Angel, thank you, that is heaven.'

'You are welcome. You must not worry about Ragonde,' Bernadette murmured, as she probed the worst of his tension with unerring accuracy. 'I believe I have worked out what her problem is. She is in for a bumpy ride, but if we can wean her off that wine, I trust she will recover.'

By the time Angel had expounded her theory that the wine was laced, possibly with poppy juice, and that she believed Ragonde had become dependent on it, the tightness in Hugo's shoulders had vanished. He was having a hard time keeping his eyelids open. 'Where the devil did the stuff come from?' he mumbled.

'Ragonde told me your cousin Raoul supplies it.'

'Cousin Raoul?' Hugo yawned. 'What reason could he possibly have for doctoring the wine?'

The mattress shifted and the bedchamber went dark as Bernadette put out the candle. Then her warm, welcome weight eased down beside him. 'That I have yet to discover.'

'Come here, woman. We will talk about this tomorrow.' Hugo curled an arm about her, kissed her on the brow, and an instant later was asleep.

Five challenging days later, Bernadette woke before daybreak to the sound of weeping. Gut-wrenching moans echoed mournfully along the empty corridors like a keening ghost. With a groan she pushed upright. There had been similar disturbances each night since they had arrived. Ragonde was fighting her demons and Bernadette could not leave her to fight them alone. Quietly, she swung out of bed and groped for her leather slippers.

Hugo's voice came softly out of the dark. 'Ragonde having bad dreams again?'

'It would seem so.' Shivering, Bernadette fumbled for her shawl, draped it around her shoulders and struck a light. 'I had better go. This may be more than a craving for your cousin's wine. Perhaps this time she will be able to tell me what it is all about.'

Hugo sat up. 'Shall I come with you?'

She shook her head. 'Best not. She is calmer when I am alone.'

'Thank God for small mercies.' Hugo sent her a shameless grin and disappeared under the covers.

Light in hand, Bernadette hurried down the corridor. Faint light glowed beneath Ragonde's door. She could hear voices. A woman's and then...

She pushed open the door. Her sister-in-law was sitting up in bed with Dennis in her arms. Tear tracks glistened on Ragonde's cheeks, and her son was sucking his thumb so hard his cheeks were hollow. His nursemaid Jeanette was standing uncertainly by the wall and the relief on her face when Bernadette entered spoke volumes.

Dennis took his thumb from his mouth. '*Maman* sad.'

'I can see that,' Bernadette said. 'I hope to help. Jeanette, Dennis needs his rest and so, I am sure, do you. I shall attend to Lady Ragonde.'

'Thank you, my lady.'

Dennis held out his arms. Jeanette approached the

bed and whisked him out of the chamber. When the door closed behind them, Bernadette allowed Jeanette's footsteps to fade before continuing. 'Would you like me to fetch you a tisane, Ragonde? I have one that will help you sleep.'

'Chamomile doesn't work.' Clumsily, Ragonde shoved a strand of hair out of her face. At Bernadette's instigation, she had bathed, and her hair had turned out to be a pretty honey brown. 'I know what will make me sleep,' she said sullenly. 'And it is not any tisane.'

'If you are referring to Baron Raoul's wine, you know you cannot have it. Besides, it is all gone.'

'I never had this difficulty sleeping when I drank Raoul's wine. I wish you hadn't poured it away. Bernadette, I beg you, send to Raoul tomorrow. I need that wine. It keeps the nightmares at bay.'

Bernadette went to sit on the edge of the bed. 'Ragonde, you are doing so well, don't spoil it now. Believe me, already you look healthier.' And that was the truth. Ragonde's skin was clearer, and her eyes were no longer dull. Purple smudges lingered beneath her eyes, but Bernadette had faith they would fade eventually.

'I feel like death,' Ragonde admitted, shakily. 'The slightest sound makes me jump. And the dreams I am having! The nightmares.' Covering her face with her hands, she ended on a wail. 'I can't bear it. I simply can't.'

'I believe you are through the worst of it. Ragonde, it might help to talk about the nightmares. Can you remember the detail?'

Ragonde lifted her gaze and her lips worked. 'Y-you will think me mad.'

'I doubt it.' Bernadette laughed. 'We all have strange dreams.'

Ragonde stared blankly at the door, such misery in her expression that Bernadette's heart went out to her. She knew without being told that Ragonde was thinking about her son. Was she worrying about the effect her behaviour was having on him? She must be.

'Ragonde, you need not concern yourself about Dennis. He knows you love him, and he loves you. That is all that matters. Love will carry you through.'

'Will it?' Ragonde gave a harsh laugh. 'It's no good, Bernadette. I know you mean well, but you cannot mend my dreams.'

'Try me,' Bernadette said.

A tear trickled down Ragonde's face and she brushed it away. 'Very well. I have the same dream every night. The birth pangs are upon me, and I am deep in travail. Finally, my baby is born. Bernadette, in my dreams the child is not a boy, it is a girl. The most beautiful girl.' Her voice broke. 'The worst of it is, I recognise this dream. It feels so real.'

'It is possible you have had the dream so often it has become familiar.'

Ragonde hesitated, then touched Bernadette's hand.

'It is not that, but I am at a loss to explain it.' She paused, brow wrinkling. 'If only I could remember more. I have a dim memory of the birthing being hard.'

Bernadette thought about her mother and sighed. 'Aye. Not all mothers survive their travail. Please, go on.'

'I would like to remember more. I saw Dennis and then I was given a drink to help me sleep.' She smiled reminiscently. 'Dennis was such a sweetheart I could not fail to love him.'

'Who was the midwife?' Bernadette asked. 'Was it someone here in the castle?'

'No, she came from the town.'

'Do you remember her name?'

'Fayette, I believe.'

Bernadette marked the name. She would make enquiries later. Ragonde's dream, particularly its repetitive nature, was oddly disturbing. 'You have given me much food for thought.'

'Have I?' Snatching her hand away, Ragonde swallowed. 'You think my mind has gone. I can see it in your eyes.'

Knocked back by the bitterness in Ragonde's tone, Bernadette stared. 'Ragonde, that is not true.' As she spoke, the word 'changeling' jumped into her mind. Might Ragonde's dream reflect what had actually happened? Could she have given birth to a girl and the girl had somehow been exchanged for a boy? Was that possible?

Surely not. Stories about changelings, where one baby was stolen at birth and another put in its place, were common. But this was reality. Mind spinning, she stared at Ragonde. From the first, her sister-in-law had not struck her as being the most reliable of witnesses. Yet something was obviously very amiss, and Bernadette was coming to see that it might be more, far more, than concern over Lord Aleran's incapacity.

There was no way Dennis could be a changeling. Everything in Ragonde's demeanour suggested that she accepted Dennis as her son. She clearly adored him. Her dreams of giving birth to a girl had to be a meaningless fantasy—the result of being deprived of the poppy juice she had become used to. That must be so. Or perhaps the baby girl was the child she could now never have.

Frowning, Bernadette thought of all the wine bottles she had emptied into the earth. There had been so many! It was one thing to give a woman wine laced with poppy juice when she was in pain, but to go on doing so? How did Aleran's cousin Raoul benefit by continuing to supply Ragonde with doctored wine three years later? Did he want Ragonde to lose her wits?

'Ragonde, is Baron Raoul married?'

'No.' Ragonde's mouth twisted cynically. 'Raoul told me, shortly after I married Aleran, that he loved me and would never marry. Raoul always had a strong sense of the dramatic. I never believed him. I have heard he keeps more than one mistress.' She covered her face with her hands and sobbed.

Bernadette's breath stopped. 'Are you saying you and Baron Raoul—?'

'No!' Ragonde shuddered. 'Never.'

Well, that was a mercy. Bernadette rubbed her brow. She needed to think. Above all, she must discover if something sinister lay behind Ragonde's dreams about having a daughter. Such dreams, the product of a dis-ordered mind, could not be taken as gospel. By all accounts, Ragonde had been given drugged wine for years. Why? To addle her mind? To what end? Again, the word 'changeling' sounded, clear as a bell. She must ask Hugo what he knew about his cousin. Was he ambitious? Ruthless? Baron Raoul might not have stolen Aleran and Ragonde's daughter and put his son in her place, but a county was at stake. Murder hap-pened every day for less than that.

If Dennis was the baron's son and if he had been ex-changed for Ragonde's daughter, he could not be per-mitted to inherit the county. He was not the true heir. Girls could not inherit, which meant that if Ragonde and Aleran's only child was a daughter, the county would not go to her, it would go to the next male heir.

Hugo might be Aleran's heir! Hugo.

Bernadette let out a shaky breath. The implications of all this were devastating. If Dennis was not Aleran and Ragonde's son, what had happened to their daughter? It did not bear thinking about. True or not, this must be investigated.

'Ragonde, I need to tell Hugo about your dreams.'

'Must you?' Ragonde's shoulders dropped. 'He will think me a complete madwoman.'

'I am sorry, Ragonde. Hugo has to be told.' Unwilling to discuss the extent of her suspicions against the baron before speaking to Hugo, Bernadette shifted, put her arm about Ragonde and hugged her. 'Listen, you stopped taking that wine mere days ago, I suspect the after-effects are still twisting your thoughts.'

Ragonde sniffled. 'At present, Bernadette, all I can think about is the baby girl in my dreams. Please don't tell Hugo. Not yet.'

Bernadette hesitated. Ragonde was already in distress, she didn't want to add to her woes. Yet she could not in all conscience keep this to herself. If Dennis wasn't Ragonde and Aleran's son, the entire county was in danger. This was an age when succession quarrels, particularly those involving a county so rich and ancient as Nérac, often led to war. If a rapacious neighbour got wind of the fact that Dennis was not the true heir and that Nérac was in disarray, warring lordlings would waste no time in banding together. In the battle for supremacy, the entire county could be laid waste.

'Ragonde, do not despair. Your mind may just take longer to fully recover.'

'At present, Bernadette, my thoughts are a shambles. I am pulled in so many directions, I feel as though I am on the rack.' She wiped a tear from her cheek. 'I am sorry to be troublesome.'

'You are not troublesome, merely troubled,' Bernadette said. 'We shall continue this discussion tomorrow. For now, we need sleep.' She lifted an eyebrow. 'If I make a tisane, will you drink it?'

'Thank you, I will.'

The second time Hugo was dragged from sleep, the grey light of dawn was creeping into the bedchamber. Angel was sitting on the edge of the bed, shaking his shoulder.

'Hugo, please waken. *Hugo!*'

Scrubbing his face, Hugo sat up and eyed her blearily. 'I am awake.'

'Here.' A platter of bread and cheese was dropped unceremoniously into his lap and a cup thrust into his hand.

He sniffed the cup. Ale. 'What is this?'

'Breakfast.'

Taking a gulp of ale, Hugo yawned. 'I thought we had agreed to breakfast in the solar.'

'Not today,' Bernadette said. 'We need privacy this morning.'

'That sounds ominous. I assume Ragonde upset you. What did she say?'

Bernadette sent Hugo a look that could only be described as sour. He stared; he'd never seen her look at him in such a way. She must be exhausted. 'My apologies, Angel. That was ham-fisted of me. Have you had no rest?'

'Not much. Hugo, we are breakfasting here because there are urgent matters that you need to know about, and it is vitally important we are not overheard.'

Having thus ensured she had his full attention, Bernadette climbed on to the bed, stretched out beside him, and launched into an unnerving account of what she believed ailed his sister-in-law. His wife was clearly so tired that her account was garbled. And so far-fetched as to be incredible.

'Let me get this straight,' he said when she came to a halt. 'You have not changed your mind about Raoul tampering with Ragonde's wine?'

'I have not. Hugo, I am beginning to suspect that drugged wine was given to her to stop her realising what had happened after she birthed her child.'

'So this drugging of her wine has been going on for years? Since Dennis's birth, in fact?'

'I believe so.'

'Angel, correct me if I have this wrong, but you also appear to believe that Ragonde might have given birth to a girl, not a boy.'

'I do. She has been having dreams which suggest this, though at present she does not appear to believe they reflect reality.'

'And you do?' Hugo gaped at her. 'Angel, this is madness.'

'Ragonde said you would think her mad.' Her mouth tightened. 'I never thought you would think it of me. Hugo, please bear with me. At first, I thought Ragonde was having difficulty differentiating between the world of her dreams and reality. That, so I understand, is common with those who take poppy juice.'

Startled, Hugo drew his head back. 'You have experience of dealing with such things?'

Placidly, Bernadette nodded. 'A girl was brought to the convent in a terrible state. A charity case. She had been found begging near one of the churches. She was painfully thin and close to death. The woman who brought her in had tried to give her food, but the girl invariably waved it away. I never learned exactly what happened to her before she came to Saint Claire's.'

She gave a rueful smile. 'I remember her arrival because it was one of those rare instances when Mother Margerie showed herself capable of compassion. It was she who found out that the girl had been given poppy juice. She would never reveal her full story, but I can imagine it.'

Hugo grimaced, he too could imagine. All too well. The world was full of brutes ready to take advantage of a frail and delicate girl. 'What happened to her?'

'She was put in the infirmary and under Mother Margerie's orders, brought back to reality. She was bathed and fed and gradually her senses returned.

It took time, Hugo, but in the end, we had a healthy young woman on our hands, instead of a wraith.'

'Where is she now?'

'She is still in the convent. She is not ready to leave. Mother Margerie has assured her that she may stay there for as long as she wishes.'

Hugo fell silent for a space, deep in thought, before saying, 'You see a marked similarity between Ragonde and this girl.'

'Aye. Thankfully, Ragonde is not so sick. She is thin, but not starving. And she is certainly capable of conversation, which the girl in the convent was not, initially at least.'

'So, you are confident Ragonde will make a full recovery?'

'I believe so.'

It was obvious that Bernadette was taking Ragonde's dream of birthing a girl as pure truth. Hugo wasn't so sure. His head throbbed with all the problems stacking up around him, the most pertinent being his concern for Aleran. And there was something else, something niggling at the back of his mind, only he was too damned tired to grasp it. He kneaded his forehead and then he had it. The question they should be considering wasn't whether Ragonde and Aleran had had a daughter or a son three years ago...

'Perhaps we should start by looking further back,' he muttered.

'Further back?' A line formed on Bernadette's brow. 'What do you mean?'

'You recall my telling you about the letter I received from Aleran, telling me never to return home?'

'Of course.'

'I got that letter years ago, and naturally I assumed that Aleran was in good health when it was written—in other words that he was in full control of himself, body and mind. What if that were not the case? Supposing Aleran's apoplexy took place shortly before I received the letter?'

Bernadette's gaze was puzzled. 'Hugo, I am not sure what you're saying.'

Hugo laughed and even to his own ears it sounded harsh. 'Angel, if we do nothing else today, we must find out from my sister-in-law when, precisely, my brother had the attack that laid him low.'

Bernadette winced. 'You suspect she had carnal relations with someone other than Aleran? Hugo, I thought of that. I asked her whether she had been intimate with your cousin and she was appalled. I do not believe she could betray Aleran in such a way.' She searched his face and sighed. 'You really do mistrust her.'

He reached for her hand. 'I'm sorry, Angel. It is obvious she is hiding some dark secret.'

'She was drugged, Hugo! Drugged. Over a long period of time. She was drugged so long it stole her wits.'

He looked at her, unmoved. 'That is all rather convenient, is it not?' He softened his voice. 'Angel, try to understand. I must speak to Ragonde. If Aleran was struck down before I received that letter, then he has been incapacitated for many, many years.'

'I don't suppose you recognised his handwriting?'

'He did not write that wretched letter. A scribe wrote it, but it was signed and sealed with his seal.'

'Anyone might use a seal. Could the signature have been forged?'

'It is possible. Angel, you've seen Aleran. Even with us ensuring that he has been fed night and day since we got here, he is little more than skin and bone. He can scarcely move, and he cannot speak. How on earth could a man in that condition father a child?'

'Perhaps your brother was not so ill at the beginning. Perhaps he had more than one apoplexy. Perhaps—'

Hugo withdrew his hand. 'Angel, enough. I have little faith in anything Ragonde says. Need I remind you that Aleran is young to be struck down with an apoplexy. *Mon Dieu*, this is no minor thing. The succession of Nérac is in question.'

Tossing the platter with the remnants of his breakfast on to the side table, he got out of bed. 'As soon as we are dressed, we must find Ragonde. I need to know when Aleran first became ill.' He splashed water on his face and reached for his shirt.

'Hugo, I am certain Ragonde believes Aleran fathered her child.'

'You, Angel, are an innocent.'

Her eyes glittered and she sprang out of bed. 'And you are far too suspicious.'

'I have a right to be suspicious. And the more I hear about my sister-in-law, the more my suspicions are aroused.'

Chapter Fourteen

As Hugo and Bernadette approached Ragonde's bed-chamber, Bernadette sent Hugo a tight smile. Hugo recognised that look. 'Angel? You have something to say?'

'Hugo, I will do my best to stand back while you speak to Ragonde. However, please bear in mind that she is not fully recovered. The slightest setback over-whelms her, and it will feel less of an inquisition with only one of us asking questions. There is no sense re-ducing her to speechlessness.'

'Good point,' Hugo murmured. 'I am fully con-scious that this will be an awkward discussion.' The succession question overrode all else. Until that was resolved, the fate of the Albret lordship hung in the balance. He felt appallingly conflicted. Personally, he needed to know exactly when Aleran had first suf-fered his apoplexy. Given the severe after-effects and how weak his brother had become, it was a crucial question.

Gripped with a painful mixture of dread and hope, Hugo found himself wishing for the impossible. He wanted Aleran to have had his stroke before Hugo had received that damning letter. Not that Hugo wished Aleran to have suffered ill health for so many years, naturally, but because it might imply that Aleran had no hand in repudiating him in so final a way.

The letter had been penned by a scribe and though he had had his doubts, it bore the family seal, and so Hugo believed its validity. He let out a short breath. He was being ridiculous. His main task this morning must be to discover whether Dennis was his brother's son.

Unfortunately, Hugo was all too conscious of the mortification Ragonde would feel should he instigate a detailed discussion of intimate matters. It simply was not done for a lady to talk about such things with a knight she barely knew even if he was her husband's brother.

The obvious answer was that Aleran was not Dennis's father. In which case, Dennis was not the Albret heir. It would perhaps be politic to open with a less contentious subject. There were certainly plenty to choose from. He tapped on Ragonde's bedchamber door.

'Come in.'

His sister-in-law was sitting on a stool, combing her hair. As they entered, she flicked her hair over her shoulders and rose. Comb in hand, she turned enquiringly towards them. She certainly looked more presentable than she had done when he and Bernadette had arrived. She had washed her hair. Her gown was clean. It was a heartening transformation. Bernadette had worked wonders.

'Excuse the interruption, my lady,' Hugo said. 'I wish to clarify the sequence of events following Aleran's apoplexy, and I thought you would welcome Bernadette's presence.'

'Thank you, Sir Hugo, that is indeed thoughtful,' Ragonde said. 'I will help if I can.'

'When did Aleran first become ill? Was it before or after Dennis was conceived?'

'Before, sir. Many years before.'

Many years? Hugo's mouth dried. The urge to demand precise dates was strong. He tamped it down. *Keep it simple.* This was no time to satisfy personal concerns over whether Aleran had been incapacitated when Hugo had received that ghastly letter. It was crucial he discovered whether Dennis was Aleran's son. God willing, they could untangle the rest later.

'My lady, this may cause distress, but I need to understand what measures you took when Aleran was first struck down.'

Ragonde was staring pensively at a blue cloak on a peg. Anything, Hugo suspected, was easier for her than meeting his eyes. 'I sent for your cousin Raoul. He came straight over, and I sought his advice. He was most helpful.' His sister-in-law swallowed. 'I was terrified Aleran might die.'

'I am glad you did not face it alone,' Hugo murmured, even as he was wondering exactly how helpful Raoul had been. As a boy, his cousin had been hotheaded and belligerent, prone to act first and ask questions later. He had always been ambitious. In those days, winning had mattered above all else.

Had he changed? As a man, had Raoul learned the significance of justice? Of honour? Hugo had not seen Raoul in years, but his cousin's reputation today was questionable. Still, it wouldn't do to judge him on hearsay. Hugo would have to meet him and come to his own conclusions.

'So, Raoul advised you,' he said. 'In what way?'

'He was all consideration. He arranged for Avryll to come and nurse Aleran.'

Hugo, who had not seen much evidence of Avryll caring for Aleran, felt a frown form. 'Avryll is one of the townsfolk?'

'No, Avryll is from Fourcès.'

Hugo stiffened. 'She is a retainer of Raoul's?'

'Aye.' Ragonde bit her lip. 'Was it wrong to accept Raoul's help, sir? I thought, with him being Aleran's cousin…' Her voice trailed away.

Hugo looked thoughtfully at Ragonde. It was certainly strange that Raoul should have established one of his maidservants in Nérac Castle when he might simply have encouraged Ragonde to use one of her own retainers or, failing that, a suitable woman from the town.

At present, though, his sister-in-law didn't strike him as strong-minded enough to withstand the blandishments of a man with Raoul's reputation. She must have been shocked beyond bearing at Aleran's illness. Had Raoul taken advantage of her weakness?

'Pray continue.' Hugo was conscious that his smile was becoming strained. 'What else did Raoul do?'

'He sent Barbe recipes for gruel for Aleran,' Ragonde told him. 'And when some of our retainers drifted away—'

Hugo's stomach tightened. 'Your retainers drifted away? Were they coerced?'

'I… I do not believe so, but I couldn't swear to it.' Ragonde gazed earnestly at him. 'Hugo, we have been protected. Raoul sent his men-at-arms to stand in for the men who left us.'

'He did, did he?' A rush of rage brought bile to the back of Hugo's throat. 'Jésu.'

The comb jumped in Ragonde's fingers, and she ducked her head. 'You are angry. I am sorry.'

'Raoul had no right to station his men at Nérac, none whatsoever.' Hugo's nostrils flared. He fought to remain calm. 'Are his men still here?'

'I think so.'

Heaven help them, this was worse than Hugo could have imagined. 'My lady, how many of the soldiers stationed here answer to Raoul?'

'At present? I am not certain.'

Hugo swore under his breath and Ragonde took a

couple of hasty steps back. Hugo had been so appalled by Aleran's appearance that ever since their arrival a couple of days ago, he had been glued to his brother's bedside, trying to get him to eat and seeing that he was washed and shaved when clearly, he should have given more attention to the state of the castle garrison.

He had, as a matter of course, cast his eye over security procedures. He had interviewed the castle guards; he had asked their captain to conduct a review of the armoury. Not once had it occurred to him that the some of the soldiers with whom he had spoken might not be Nérac men.

Ragonde was eyeing him so uncertainly Hugo attempted to moderate his tone. It was not easy. 'My lady, this is frankly outrageous. When did Raoul's men turn up? Immediately after Aleran fell ill?'

'Oh, no. Apart from sending Avryll, Raoul kept his distance until Dennis was born.' Ragonde took another backward step. 'I'm telling the truth, Sir Hugo. I swear it.' Her voice trembled. His sister-in-law was as flustered as a woman could be. Guilt? Or her craving for poppy juice? Either way, it added up to Hugo not trusting a word she said.

'Tell me, my lady, did the King transfer Aleran's authority to Raoul?'

'I do not believe so. Is that possible?'

'Of course it is possible,' Hugo grated out. He reminded himself that Ragonde must have been very young when she married Aleran. Notwithstanding, as a lady married to a count, she ought to know these things. 'If a lord is incapable of fulfilling his duties, which include supplying levies for his overlord, his lands may be gifted to someone else. In exceptional circumstances—usually when there is a male heir—the lord's wife may act as his deputy until the heir is old enough to succeed.'

Ragonde blinked. 'In much the same way that a lady might take over the ruling of her castle if her lord is away fighting for his overlord?

'Just so.'

Bernadette cleared her throat. 'Hugo, as I understand it, the district surrounding the Albret patrimony has been mired in conflict for years. Clashes between the Crowns of England and France have made matters worse, giving the more powerful and ruthless noblemen the opportunity to behave like robber barons.'

'Thank you, Bernadette,' Hugo said drily. 'I may not have lived here for years, but I am aware of local politics.' He was also aware that his wife had deliberately drawn Hugo's fire on herself to deflect it from Ragonde. Well, he wasn't about to be deflected. He looked searchingly at his sister-in-law. 'My lady, do you remember if either of the Kings intervened?'

'I would remember that, I am sure. They did not intervene.'

'That is a mercy.' He let out a breath. 'Which means that you, Lady Ragonde, remain in command. Unless, of course, you ceded that privilege to my cousin? Have you done so?'

Ragonde stiffened. 'Certainly not. I would never do such a thing.'

Hugo grunted. For the first time in this discussion, he felt a flicker of hope. It appeared the woman had some backbone.

'I would never sign Aleran's birthright to someone else,' she said, fiercely. 'I do not have that right.' She paused thoughtfully. 'After Dennis was born, Raoul did visit more regularly.'

'To help with military matters, such as manning the garrison?' Hugo asked.

'Aye. He also found extra retainers.'

'I dare say that was when Raoul began sending his wine over,' Hugo muttered, eyeing her sharply.

'Aye, it was around that time.'

Hugo opened his mouth to press his sister-in-law for more information but Bernadette was shaking her head at him. His wife had mentioned the necessity of treading warily with Ragonde and her argument had merit. For the time being he would hold himself in check.

'Clearly, I should have spent less time with Aleran over the past few days,' he said. Even to his own ears his voice was bitter. The revelation that half the men stationed at Nérac answered to his cousin demanded immediate action on his part. 'I need to interrogate the garrison commander. We must know whether the allegiance of the men stationed here is questionable. I am praying that at least some of the guard remain loyal to my brother.' With a curt bow, he left the chamber.

Ragonde turned to Bernadette and her shoulders sagged. 'I hope he is not very angry.'

Bernadette's stomach was churning. Hugo was wild with fury. His brother was a count and Baron Raoul's men should not be stationed at Nérac Castle. Thank God, Hugo had had the sense to leave before he lost his temper. He must truly be enraged not to have questioned Ragonde about her fidelity. It would happen, she was sure. Meanwhile, she would do her best to pour oil on troubled waters. She drew in a calming breath. 'Hugo is concerned for Aleran,' she said, quietly.

Ragonde was staring pensively at the door, running a fingernail back and forth along the tines of her comb. The poor woman was worried to distraction. She needed something absorbing to take her mind off her woes. What might she enjoy?

At Larressingle, Lady Celeste had been delighted to start on clothing for the household—perhaps Ragonde might react in the same way. Bernadette could certainly assist her. Furthermore, if Ragonde relaxed a little, she might reveal more about the events following Aleran's apoplexy and Baron Raoul's involvement.

Hugo's approach had been quite blunt. Subtlety might prove more fruitful.

She made a show of peering through the window. 'The year is turning, Ragonde. The cold will be upon us before we know it. I believe the servants would welcome warm clothing.'

Interest flickered in Ragonde's eyes. 'I used to enjoy sewing.'

'Do you have any fabric in storage? I am a reasonable seamstress, and I would love to help.'

'We did have some.' Ragonde's face fell. 'I think the mice got to it.'

'Never mind. Do you have keys to the castle strongbox?'

Ragonde put her comb down and her hand went to the keys hanging from the chatelaine at her girdle. 'Aye.'

'Then all is not lost. Let us see if we can find enough coin to buy a few bolts of cloth.'

The strongbox was in a small side room to one side of the cellar. The lock was a little stiff, but it opened without too much trouble and Bernadette was pleasantly surprised to see several bulging leather purses. Ragonde hesitated before picking one up and loosening the leather ties. It was filled with silver. She poked uneasily at the coins nestled inside. 'We should ask Aleran before spending this.'

'Ragonde, your husband is in no position to accept or deny your request.'

Her sister-in-law's face set in obstinate lines. She returned the purse to the strongbox and locked it back inside. 'Be that as it may, I shall still ask him. I have never taken anything from the strongbox without his permission.'

Bernadette blinked. That explained much. The ragged linen, the worn clothes. 'So not once since your husband fell ill have you taken coin from the strongbox?'

'Not once.'

Bernadette and Ragonde went up to the Count's bedchamber. He was awake and Avryll was at his bedside, attempting to spoon broth into his mouth. Or was she? Bernadette had the distinct impression the woman had only snatched up the bowl because she had heard their footsteps approaching.

'Thank you, Avryll.' Firmly, Ragonde took charge of the bowl. 'That is all for now.'

Avryll went out and Ragonde took her place at the bedside, spooning broth carefully into her husband's mouth. Her demeanour was so loving that Bernadette knew that Hugo's suspicions regarding Ragonde's fidelity were baseless. Ragonde adored her husband.

'Lord Aleran is looking much better,' Bernadette said, taking a seat on the opposite side of the bed.

'That is Hugo's doing, he has been most attentive.' Ragonde shot a dark look at the door. 'He is far more attentive than Avryll. I believe I shall send her back to Raoul. Jeanette has a sister, Elaine. I shall solicit her help.'

Bernadette felt a burst of optimism. Ragonde was beginning to use her initiative. It was heartening to see. Better yet, Aleran's eyes were bright. He appeared to be following their conversation, and when Ragonde mentioned their plans to buy linen and fabric to clothe the servants in the coming winter, his mouth definitely relaxed. Not only did he understand them, but he approved.

They sent for Elaine. When she arrived, Ragonde was happy to leave Aleran in her hands. She and Bernadette returned to the strongbox. Ragonde was smiling as she removed a purse. 'I have not been to market for an age,' she said. 'I shall enjoy buying cloth again. The first thing I shall do is hem a set of sheets for Aleran's bed.'

'And after that?'

'A tunic for Dennis.' Ragonde gave a little skip. 'We shall buy fabric for the whole household. I wonder if Elaine sews, I must remember to ask her. Everyone needs a new set of clothes. And most of the linen needs replacing.'

'We shall be busy.' Bernadette smiled. Progress. Hugo would be delighted.

Hugo stumbled into his bedchamber in the foulest of moods. A cold supper hours ago had been followed by several weary hours interrogating the men-at-arms.

Bernadette was already abed. She sat up, rearranged the pillows behind her and smiled sunnily at him. Her smile faded. 'Hugo, what's amiss?'

'Everything.'

'Meaning?'

'I can confirm what Ragonde told us. Many of the men in the so-called Albret garrison answer to Cousin Raoul.'

A glossy dark curl had escaped Bernadette's braid. She twirled it round her finger. 'Oh, dear. I was hoping you'd find otherwise.'

'I am afraid not. The entire castle is in disarray.'

Bernadette sent him a small smile. 'Not entirely.'

'Oh?'

'Your brother is much improved. Thanks, I am sure, to your care these past days. Furthermore, Ragonde has dismissed Avryll.'

'The maidservant planted by Raoul? Jésu, I was so taken up with the state of the garrison she completely slipped my mind.'

'Ragonde has dealt with her. She has been dismissed. A local woman has taken her place, Jeanette's sister Elaine. Hugo, I wish you had seen Ragonde this afternoon. It was as though she had awoken after a long sleep. She got rid of Avryll without a qualm. She is planning to buy new linens for Aleran, and we are to make winter clothing for the household.'

A wave of weariness washed over Hugo. Was his trusting wife in danger of being taken in by Ragonde?

Until Dennis was proved without doubt to be Aleran's son and heir, he wouldn't trust the woman an inch. 'Angel, do be careful.'

Bernadette nodded, then frowned. 'Careful?'

He rolled his shoulders and came to stand at the end of the bed. 'I question Ragonde's motives. This sudden burst of activity could be an attempt to throw you off the scent. She could be distracting you.'

'Hugo, I am sure you are wrong.'

'I doubt it. Angel, think about it. Aleran has been ill for years. Believe me, he can hardly move a muscle.'

'Hugo, he truly is improving. You should see him with Ragonde. It is lovely to see.'

'I thank God he is eating and that you have found someone reliable to care for him. Can he move?'

Her eyebrows lifted. 'You know he cannot. In time, perhaps, but—'

Hugo cut her off with a chopping motion. 'Angel, stop. Think. Aleran cannot lift a finger. He cannot speak. He has been like this for years. The idea of a man in his condition having carnal relations with his wife beggars belief.'

'You think Ragonde committed adultery?'

'She must have done. Dennis cannot be my brother's son.'

Bernadette folded her arms across her breasts. 'Hugo, I trust Ragonde. I believe her.' She dragged in a breath. 'Furthermore, the longer I spend with her, the more I like her.'

'You like her. *Mon Dieu.*' Relieving some of his frustration by throwing off his clothes, Hugo stomped to the washbowl. His wife's way of finding good in everyone was enough to drive a man to drink.

Reaching for the drying cloth, he wiped his face and tried again. 'Angel, it is vital we find out whether Ragonde remained faithful to Aleran. Vital. How did she conceive? The question must be asked, and I accept that it will be better received coming from you.'

Bernadette's mouth fell open. 'You want me to ask how they made love?'

'Precisely.'

'I cannot ask that! It is far too intimate.'

'That is the nun in you speaking.' He shoved his hair out of his face. 'Bernadette, you must leave your maidenly scruples behind you. You are a married woman and the succession of the Albret patrimony is at stake. Dennis must have been conceived through an adulterous relationship. Given dear Cousin Raoul's involvement, my money is on him.'

Bernadette's lips thinned. 'Hugo, you didn't see Ragonde with Aleran today. You could not hope to see a more loving wife.'

'Love?' Hugo snorted. 'This is not about love; you cannot trust love. This is about power. Power always transcends love.'

She rocked back, white-faced.

'And in this case,' he pressed on ruthlessly, 'with the Albret tradition of the first male heir inheriting the entire estate, Ragonde had a strong motive to give birth to a boy. Think, Angel. Do you honestly think my brother could father a child?'

Bernadette's expression was priceless. He could see doubt fighting with her desire to believe Ragonde. In her heart, Bernadette must have been wondering how it was that Aleran, whose apoplexy had paralysed him so severely, could have fathered a child.

'Ragonde might have found a way to stimulate intimacy in Aleran,' she murmured.

Hugo replied equally quietly, 'It might also be argued that desperation could lead Ragonde to foist another man's child on him. She could pretend to the world that it was his and since Aleran is unable to speak, he is no position to refute her. I agree that such an act on Ragonde's part would be shockingly immoral, but she would have much to gain from taking such a route. She might consider the loss of her integrity a small price to pay.

'In the event of Aleran's early demise, her position as mother of the heir to the county would be secure. A girl would not be half as useful. If Aleran failed to father a boy, on his death the estate would pass to the next male heir. Angel, it comes to this—either you ask Ragonde how her baby was conceived, or I will.'

Angel glowered at him for the space of several heartbeats before relenting. 'This is a conversation

Ragonde would prefer to have with me. I shall ask her on the morrow.'

'Thank you.'

The next day Hugo muttered something about sending to Larressingle for reinforcements and strode off, leaving Bernadette to find Ragonde. It was the moment of truth. Bernadette had mentioned to Ragonde that she needed to speak to her on a matter of some importance and Ragonde had searched her face. 'You wish to be discreet?'

'That would be best.'

'Very well, we shall talk in my bedchamber.'

So, here they were, sitting on the edge of Ragonde's bed, with Ragonde looking expectantly at her. Acting on instinct, Bernadette took her sister-in-law's hand and cleared her throat. 'Ragonde, I have been wanting to ask you a question. I fear you will find it insulting, and I beg you to forgive me, but ask it I must.' She bit her lip. 'I understand that Aleran had his apoplexy several years ago.'

'That is true, he did.'

'And he has been paralysed ever since?'

'Aye.'

'How then, did you go about getting with child?'

Ragonde's cheeks went scarlet. Briefly, she closed her eyes. 'Do you know, I have been dreading that question ever since I became great with child. Yet before now, no one has asked it.' She let out a sound that was half-laugh, half-moan. 'I don't quite understand why not. Bernadette, Aleran is not totally paralysed. After he fell ill, I discovered there were ways to…to please him.'

'Really?' Bernadette recognised that they were both likely to find this conversation awkward. Even so, she was intrigued. She leaned forward. 'Would you care to explain?'

Swallowing, Ragonde gave her a candid look. 'You have not been married long, are you sure about this?'

'Certainly.'

'Men,' Ragonde said, her cheeks bright with embarrassment, 'are incredibly responsive to what they see. The naked body of a woman can arouse them, especially if the couple are married and care for each other. Women's carnal responses, as I am sure you will have discovered, are usually a little different. At least they are in my case. Most women respond more on an emotional level. I suspect you are the same.'

'You are speaking of love, I believe,' Bernadette said. Which Hugo did not believe in.

Ragonde smiled. 'I see you understand exactly.' At which point, she launched into an explanation that left Bernadette hot, flustered, and filled with ideas so shockingly bold, they felt as though they belonged to someone else. Ragonde described how Aleran was able to be intimate with Ragonde, and how their love making could still be pleasurable despite his ailments.

Also, how the act of love making was both emotionally and physically fulfilling. It left her wondering.

If she tried similar tactics on Hugo, would their intimacies become more emotional?

After an enlightening and thought-provoking conversation, Bernadette and Ragonde went upstairs to see Aleran.

'Thank you, Elaine,' Ragonde said, dismissing Jeanette's sister when they arrived. 'We shall remain with the Count for the moment. We will call you if we need you.'

Bernadette and Ragonde ended up spending the afternoon there. Between them, they changed the Count's bedlinens and helped him to eat and drink. That done, Ragonde settled at his side, took his hand, and began to talk. She talked about Dennis and Jeanette, and her plans to set the castle to rights. Bernadette sat with them, ostensibly hemming a sheet in the light of the window, while quietly observing how well they related to each other. The longer Bernadette sat there the more convinced she became that Hugo was wrong about Ragonde. Ragonde had not betrayed Aleran.

Once, when Ragonde briefly released her husband's hand, Bernadette thought she saw movement in Aleran's fingers. It was almost as though he wanted to reach for his wife. Catching her breath, she stared. No, his fingers were quite still, she must have imagined it.

Chapter Fifteen

Shielding her candle, Bernadette reached their bedchamber. She had not seen Hugo for hours and the more time passed, the more nervous she became. He must be made to see that Ragonde was an honourable woman who loved her husband, and she had thought of a way of persuading him. Would it work? She pushed open their bedchamber door.

'Hugo?' Silence greeted her. Bernadette had been praying that whatever wrongs he found in the garrison could soon be set to rights but given how long he was spending there it looked as though her hopes were ill founded. She sighed. He was too caught up with military matters to spare much time for his wife. Their marriage was young and already they were beginning to argue. The way Hugo had stormed off...

Was this how their marriage was going to unfold? At first, Bernadette had hoped he would involve her in everything. This was Hugo, her friend. Of course, he hadn't promised love, but at the least she had expected a partnership. Unfortunately, since coming to Nérac, on the rare occasions they had been alone, they had often been at odds with each other.

She sighed. She could do with some familiar company. It was a pity she had left Violette at Larressingle. If Violette was here, she would have someone to talk to. No, no, she was becoming maudlin, and it would not do. Squaring her shoulders, she set about lighting more candles.

Thanks to her sister-in-law she had a plan. She was going to stick to it.

When the chamber was aglow and the candles arranged to her satisfaction, she sat down in front of the mirror and straightened her veil. Late though it was, Bernadette was not going to prepare for bed quite yet. Not until her husband came in.

She had been extremely uncomfortable delving into the carnal aspects of Ragonde's past. It had been intrusive, to say the least, although now she was extremely thankful she had done it. She had learned much. And rather than tell Hugo what Ragonde had said, she was going to demonstrate.

She was reasonably confident he would fall for it. He had already shown himself to be a passionate man, and if Ragonde was correct, she should easily prove her point. *I might not have Allis's stunning beauty, but Hugo is attracted to me. And even if he is tired and angry, I have a strong suspicion passion would overcome that.*

She called Ragonde's words to mind. 'Men,' Ragonde had said, 'are incredibly responsive to what they see. The naked body of a woman can arouse them, especially if the couple are married and care for each other.'

Bernadette sat before the mirror, staring blindly at its gleaming surface as she wondered whether it was wrong of her to set out to arouse her husband when she was aggrieved with him for being so judgemental about Ragonde. It felt oddly wicked. And arousing, definitely arousing.

As Hugo himself never tired of reminding her, convent life was behind her. Her life as Hugo's wife was what she made of it. She would never truly hurt him and he, despite his occasional high-handedness and his ridiculous insistence that love was not to be trusted, would never hurt her. She was smothering a yawn when quick footsteps came down the corridor. Spurs chinked and her fatigue vanished.

Hugo brought the chill of the night into their bedchamber. He drew up short to see her sitting before the mirror and flung his cloak over a peg. The mirror blurred his image. Staring at his hazy outline, Bernadette reached up, found the tie on her veil, and undid it. Her heart thumped. 'Is all well?' she asked, turning to face him.

Hugo did not answer straight away. His mouth was tight, he really looked distracted. He unbuckled his sword and set it down at his side of the bed, as was his habit. Then he sat and began dragging off his boots.

'Hugo, what happened?'

'Nothing I did not expect,' came the curt reply. He disrobed quickly and got into bed. Naked, despite the early autumn chill. 'I do not expect you learned anything of note from Ragonde?'

'I did actually. Allow me to demonstrate.' Bernadette's cheeks burned. Suddenly she felt appallingly shy. Self-conscious. She reminded herself that she and Hugo were married and from the outset there had been heat between them. Being distracted by his brother's problems had not led Hugo to forget his promise to her. At Larressingle, he had shown himself to be the kindest, most considerate of lovers. Not for a moment had he forgotten her fear of childbirth.

Sadly, since coming to Nérac, they had started to drift apart. Which put her in a strange position. She was still relatively innocent, and she wanted to demonstrate what must have happened between Ragonde and Aleran. To be sure, Hugo had given her pleasure, and she had done her best to return it. But tonight, despite the distance that had developed between them, or perhaps because of it, Bernadette was tempted to take things further. Her fears of childbirth were fading.

Her mouth dried. She was very much afraid she was falling in love with him. Hugo wanted children, and she wanted Hugo. Perhaps if she gave him the children he longed for, he would begin to forget Allis. The affection between them had not died, she told herself. It could be revived.

She and Hugo would never truly belong to each other until she gave herself to him. Besides, in the face of what they had discovered at Nérac, her reservations regarding childbirth seemed overwhelming, as if she sometimes couldn't escape everything that Hortense had subjected her to. She wanted a proper marriage. With Hugo. No other man would do.

Rising from her seat by the mirror, wishing he were in a better mood, Bernadette went to stand at the foot of the bed. Thanks to the way she had arranged the candles, the light fell directly on her. With careless deliberation at variance from her normal tidy self, she dropped her veil on to the floor.

Hugo's eyes widened. 'Angel?'

'All you have to do is lie there,' she murmured. 'Remember, this is a demonstration of what I learned from Ragonde.'

'Very well.' He pushed himself up on the pillows and put his hands under his head. His voice was slightly hoarse. She had definitely caught his interest. She sent him an arch look, eased out of her surcoat and let that fall too. When her belt, slung low at her hips, fell with a soft clunk on to her surcoat, Hugo swallowed. The tightness of his mouth eased, and a slow smile formed. 'Angel, come here.'

'No. Tonight, Hugo, you must consider yourself utterly helpless. Utterly in my thrall.'

He laughed. 'I am already in your thrall.'

'Good. Lie still. You are forbidden to move.' Coming to his side of the bed, she slapped his hand aside as it came to rest lightly on her hips. The longing for him to touch her burned brightly inside, heating every inch of her body. But that could not come, not yet. 'You cannot move, remember?' She laid her finger on his mouth, frowning slightly when he kissed it. 'You are also forbidden to speak.'

His eyes gleamed. He was looking at her hair. 'Not even,' he whispered in a sensual voice that sent warmth to her toes, 'to implore you to unbind your hair?'

'Not even then.'

Hugo tried. He lay like a stone as she perched on the edge of the bed and removed her shoes. He said nothing when she tossed them into a corner. Nor did he speak when she rose to lift up her skirts and roll her stockings down. His throat worked, and when she drew off her kirtle and shift, she heard a distinct groan. She raised her eyebrows at him and gently shook her head. His body gave a slight jolt as—totally naked—she climbed in beside him and eased over him, resting a hand on that wide, well-sculpted chest.

Again, his hands drifted to her hips. His eyes were dark with desire. 'Angel, I am warning you, you are playing with fire.'

As Ragonde had intimated, Bernadette could feel he was ready. Very much so. Proof, not that she needed it, that desire was strong on both their parts. And, of course, that a man could be aroused by the sight of a naked woman. She smiled into his eyes and her heart ached.

'Angel, you are driving me insane.'

'No speaking, sir.' Every pulse throbbing, still braced on her hand, she was leaning forward to kiss him when his grip tightened and before she knew it, she was lying on her back staring up at him. 'Oh.'

He grinned and slid his leg between hers. 'Oh, indeed. My lady, you have had your fun. If you wish to consummate our marriage, it is your turn to lie still while I ensure that you are ready. You wish to proceed?'

'I do.'

She could not lie still, of course, any more than he could. She wound her arms about his neck when he kissed her mouth. She parted her lips with a moan of pure relief. When his attention shifted to her breasts, she wriggled and squirmed and when, finally, he positioned himself over her, she was as ready as a woman could be.

He eased slowly into her, with each tender shift and sway bringing them closer until finally full intimacy was but a breath away. They stayed on the brink for a moment, staring into each other's eyes as though they had been bespelled. Hugo's expression was almost fierce. Undaunted, Bernadette gripped his shoulders, and he sank into her. They were one.

It was easier than she had expected. Her body welcomed him in and there was no pain. Far from it, her breath was quickening. Hugo's too. He smothered a moan and when he began to move, a subtle tensing in his body encouraged her to find a rhythm. Hugo's breathing matched hers—desperate, eager.

'Angel, you feel like heaven.' Hugo's eyes were glazed. It was obvious he had forgotten this had begun as a demonstration. Looking at him, with love warming every inch of her, Bernadette was having difficulty remembering herself. What had begun as a demonstration of how a woman could seduce a man had turned into something altogether different.

Dizzy with need, she rocked to and fro. *We are one, at last we are one.* She loved the feel of his chest against her breasts. She loved everything. Beneath him, she wriggled this way and that like the wanton she was whenever he touched her.

It did not take long, for either of them. The world was lost in a bright rush of stars, and Hugo shuddered and collapsed on top of her, panting. Then he shifted to his side and pulled her close. With a relieved sigh, she rested her head on his chest.

Silence. Then, 'Angel, what happened to your anxieties?'

'I am not sure.' She looped a strand of hair behind her ear and nuzzled his chest. She could hardly say that their marriage was, for her at least, no longer one of convenience. She had surprised herself with her eagerness to join with him and she had no doubt what that meant. She had fallen in love with him. It was the most inconvenient thing she could have done. Particularly since she did not know whether he still had feelings for Allis 'My fears are not entirely gone.'

'I see.'

He didn't really understand, his eyes were puzzled, and Bernadette did not want to admit that she hoped full physical closeness would strengthen their marriage. It had been magical, even though it was likely one-sided. She nudged his chest. 'Anyhow, you are forgetting, that was a demonstration.'

'Hmm. Once you began making a dance out of removing your clothes, I am afraid I forgot everything save how much I desired you.' His hands were in her hair as, idly, he began to remove the hairpins that had not fallen out, sending them tinkling to the floor.

'That was the point, Hugo.'

A broad shoulder lifted. 'There is no need to be irritated, I liked it very much.' Hugo paused and a teasing note entered his voice. 'Perhaps we need to try it again.'

They made love again and for Hugo their second time was as overwhelming as the first. Angel was incredibly responsive and a joy to bed. Later, as she lay tucked up against him, he found himself studying her face. Why, he had no idea, for he knew well what she looked like. Her eyes were closed, though he did not believe she was sleeping. Those luxuriant eyelashes were hiding her thoughts. He frowned at her mouth. It was turned down into a pout he felt impelled to kiss away. He wanted her smiling secretly to herself and instead she looked worried.

He had had no doubt that she desired him, and that passion had swept her away as much as him, but all was not right in her world. At present, her expression was that of a woman who regretted what they had done. She did not look content. What was she thinking? Was she worrying about possible consequences? A shiver ran through him. Her fear of childbirth remained. It was the last thing he wanted.

Turning away, he slipped out of bed to pinch out the candles. Returning to their bed, he gently drew her into his arms. He liked sleeping close to her, but it instilled a fear within him. He could not afford to fall in love. As sleep pulled him under, his last coherent thought was that it might be too late to prevent that happening.

Sewing in her brother-in-law's bedchamber with Ragonde was a helpful distraction when one suspected one's husband was doing his best to keep his distance.

Admittedly, much of the time it was Bernadette doing the sewing. Ragonde was more than content to sit by her husband, holding his hand. Talking. She had been deprived of his company for too long. By now Bernadette was hemming her second pair of sheets.

On Ragonde's insistence, this set was destined for the bedchamber Bernadette shared with Hugo.

As though making up for lost time, Ragonde kept up a constant flow of chatter. She told Lord Aleran that she had ordered the solar to be swept out and the floor scoured. The kitchen too. She mentioned that on sunny days, old tapestries were taken outside so the dust could be beaten from them. 'They will be repaired, Aleran,' Ragonde said. 'All the furnishings. I am determined Nérac Castle will be restored to its former glory.'

As Ragonde chattered away, Bernadette kept a watchful eye on the Count. His face had filled out, his skin looked healthier, and that horrible tension had gone from about his eyes. The more Lord Aleran recovered, the more marked the resemblance became between him and Hugo. It was there in the shape of the jaw. That distinctive nose. There was no question but that satisfying food and regular attention from his increasingly talkative wife were responsible.

'Dearest, I've asked Jeanette to bring Dennis up later, he—' Ragonde broke off abruptly and her eyes widened. She stared at the hand lightly clasped in hers. 'Bernadette, did you see that? Aleran moved! I swear his hand moved.' Leaping to her feet, she bent over her husband and stroked his head. 'Dearest, can you do that again?'

A lump in her throat, Bernadette set aside her needlework and leaned closer. 'My lord? If you can move your hand, please show us.'

And there it was, almost too small to be noticed, but Lord Aleran made a definite, deliberate movement. At the same time, he made a low, growling sound. That too was clearly deliberate. Bernadette felt herself smiling. He was truly recovering! Hugo would be so happy. She glanced at Ragonde and to her astonishment saw that her sister-in-law's face had drained of colour. The surprise, she supposed.

'Ragonde, try asking Lord Aleran a question.'

Ragonde gulped. Her eyes were glassy with tears, and it took her a moment to find her voice. 'Dearest, you understand us, don't you?'

Again, Lord Aleran made that growling noise. It was a small thing and it seemed to tire him for he was breathing harder than he had been a moment ago. Frowning, Bernadette wondered if he had been able to make that sound ever since the apoplexy had struck, only lack of proper nourishment had left him too weak to manage it.

Ragonde stared at his hand. 'He can definitely move his hand.' A tear spilled over. 'Thanks be to God, Aleran is recovering. Aleran, my love, can you speak? Please, try.'

The Count's mouth flickered in the faintest of smiles.

'I imagine it is too soon for speech, Ragonde,' Bernadette said. 'In a few weeks, perhaps, if we continue to look after him.'

Spotting that subtle movement in his hand again, an idea leaped into Bernadette's head. She captured the Count's gaze. 'My lord, if we provide quill and parchment, do you think you could make a mark?' Lord Aleran's hand made a weak stabbing motion. 'That, I believe, is a yes. Ragonde, I do believe your husband is trying to communicate.'

Excitement carried Bernadette to the door. 'Ragonde, wait here. We need pen, ink and paper. I shall fetch it.'

Ragonde blinked. 'You are thinking we can converse with Aleran using pen and paper?'

'Yes! Don't you see? We can start by asking simple questions, ones that can be answered with a plain yes or no. Later we can move on to more tricky topics.'

'Tricky topics,' Ragonde repeated in a strange, flat voice. Her cheeks had yet to regain their colour. 'Bernadette, you must tell Hugo.'

'Naturally.' Hand on the doorframe, Bernadette studied Ragonde's strange pallor. 'Ragonde, you look as though you have seen a ghost. What is wrong?'

Ragonde avoided her gaze. She stared at her husband's bedcovers as though her life depended on it, hands clasped so tightly Bernadette could see the white gleam of bone. 'Bernadette, can we keep this from Raoul? If he learns that Aleran is on the road to recovery, there is no knowing what he might do.'

'The baron will hear of this eventually.'

'But not for a while. Please, Bernadette.'

The anxiety in her sister-in-law's voice ensured that Bernadette could only give one answer. 'If that is your wish. At present, I will only tell Hugo.'

'And you will make certain he keeps this to himself?'

'Yes, yes,' Bernadette said, not quite understanding why Ragonde was making such a fuss about Raoul. Unless—could Hugo's suspicions be well founded? Was Baron Raoul Dennis's father? No. Absolutely not. Ragonde idolised her husband. Hugo could not be more wrong on that score. 'We can decide later when to tell the baron.'

'Bless you,' Ragonde said.

Bernadette hurried away to find Hugo and to fetch her writing things.

Hugo had closeted himself the estate office, where he was looking over the account books. One look at his face and Bernadette knew he was in dire need of good news. He looked up scowling and she grimaced. 'Oh, Lord, what have you found now?'

He directed a gesture of pure frustration at the books. 'The estate accounts have been woefully neglected. There have been no entries for years.'

'What?' Bernadette leaned over the desk and drew the ledger towards her. A glance at the final listing had a frown form. She ran her finger over the entry.

'This would have been made at about the time Dennis was born.'

'My thoughts exactly.' Hugo leaned his head on his hand and kneaded his brow. 'Before then, they are meticulously neat. It is my guess that the earlier entries are in Ragonde's hand. The fact that none have been made since Dennis was born is yet another mark to set against her. It really does not look good.'

Bernadette held his gaze and some of the delight she was feeling over Aleran's progress seeped away. 'You might try to see Ragonde in a better light.'

'Angel, with evidence like this, it is not easy.'

She laid her hand on his. 'Hugo, it is important for you to understand that the drugged wine would have clouded Ragonde's mind. I doubt very much she would have been capable of keeping the accounts any more than she could run the household.'

'That woman,' Hugo said, shaking his head, 'is nothing but a liability.'

'Hugo, the accounts can wait, we can discuss them later.' Bernadette closed the ledger with a thump and pasted a smile on her face. 'Something wonderful has happened. You, sir, are coming with me. Hurry, Hugo.'

Bernadette took Hugo's hand and fairly towed him out of the office. Her eyes were sparkling with happiness. 'Angel, what's happened?'

'It is Aleran. You will see.'

After a brief detour to their bedchamber where she

unearthed her portable writing desk and handed it to him to carry, she hurried upstairs, bursting with suppressed excitement. Hugo guessed his brother must have improved. 'For pity's sake, Angel, what has happened? You have me on tenterhooks.'

'Patience, Hugo.'

Mystified, Hugo entered his brother's bedchamber on Bernadette's heels. Aleran was awake, lying in his usual position. Everything looked as it usually did. Aleran looked calm. He actually looked contented. It was such a relief.

'Where on earth has Ragonde gone?' Bernadette murmured. She gave a small shrug. 'Never mind, she will be back presently, I am sure.' Establishing herself in a chair at the bedside, she held out her arms. 'My writing desk, if you please.'

Hugo passed her the writing desk and while she busied herself opening it, he took the chair on the opposite side of the bed and smiled warmly at his brother. 'I hope the ladies have not overtaxed you.'

Aleran grunted. Hugo froze. It was the first real response he had had from Aleran since coming home. 'Aleran?' He stared at Bernadette. 'Angel, did you hear that?'

Face lit with excitement, she nodded. 'I am praying there is better to come. Here, take this.' Reaching across the bed, she handed him a piece of parchment. 'Put that under your brother's hand.'

'His hand?' Utterly bemused, Hugo did as he was

bid. Rising, Bernadette came round to his side of the bed, a trimmed quill in one hand and an ink pot in the other.

'We will likely get ink all over the bed,' she said, 'but in this instance, I don't believe anyone will care.'

'Angel, what the devil is going on? You are surely not expecting Aleran to write?'

'Not exactly.' A dark glance was flung at the door. 'I do wish Ragonde had waited. I wanted her to be here for this, but it cannot be helped. Hugo, I am testing out a theory. By the by, irrespective of whatever happens here, Ragonde has asked me to make sure that no one in the castle knows Aleran is making such excellent progress.'

'Why is that?'

'I believe she is concerned that word doesn't reach your cousin.'

Tension balled in Hugo's gut. Whatever he thought of Ragonde, her fear of Raoul was probably well founded. 'Angel, I accept Ragonde does not trust Raoul.'

'You acknowledge he drugged her wine?'

'Let us say I agree it is possible.'

Angel nodded; she was studying Aleran. 'Hugo, we need to converse with your brother. Pay attention, you may need to help.'

With that, she put the quill in Aleran's fingers. Hugo wasn't surprised when his brother immediately dropped it. Nor was he surprised when Bernadette sent Aleran the sweetest of smiles. 'Never mind. Try again, my lord, if you please.'

Aleran did try. His fingers trembled as he strained with the effort. A couple of false starts later he succeeded. The quill remained put, wavering a little, but in his grasp.

Hugo held his breath as Bernadette put her hand over Aleran's and guided it gently to dip the quill in the inkpot. When she had it positioned so the tip hovered over the parchment on the bedcover, she took a deep breath.

'My lord, I propose to ask a few questions. It will be easier if you could answer with a yes or a no.'

Aleran grunted.

'For the present, a sharp slash can signify yes and a simple cross no. Do you think you can do it?'

Hugo's nails gouged crescents in his palms as she watched the quill form a wobbly slash. Suddenly everything changed. Bernadette had but to start proceedings when Aleran took over. Questions and answers came thick and fast.

'My lord, you are feeling much recovered?'

'Slash.'

'We are so happy. Hugo was devastated when he heard you had fallen ill.'

Aleran grunted. His gaze flickered towards Hugo and back to the parchment. Painstakingly determined, his hand crawled over the parchment. Slowly three words emerged. 'Why…so…long?'

Sick with remorse, Hugo let out a shuddering breath. 'I think you are asking me why I did not come home when I heard you were ill.'

A grunt.

'Aleran, you will have to forgive me.' Hugo's voice was rusty, distorted with emotion. 'The truth is, it took me years to discover that you were ailing.'

Under his brother's unblinking stare, Hugo made his full confession. He told him about the letter that had arrived at Galard all those years ago when he had been a boy. He explained that it had made no mention of Aleran's infirmity. 'Far from it, the letter led me to understand that you wished to break off all connection with me and that I was no longer welcome here at Nérac. I was told, very plainly, to make my own way in the world.'

Aleran made a choking sound. His eyes brimmed and his hand formed a clumsy row of crosses on the parchment. 'No. No. No.'

The last cross was a little faded, the ink was running dry. Bernadette noticed of course, dipping the quill in the ink pot again and returning Aleran's hand to the parchment.

Hugo sent Aleran a remorseful smile. 'I suspected that something was wrong, even though it appeared you had signed the letter. It was also sealed with your seal.'

Another cross splattered on to the parchment. 'No.'

'It was forged?' Aleran made the slash for yes and

Hugo felt his mouth twist as he continued. 'I wrote back several times over the years, but I never had a reply. Mercifully, after Bernadette and I married, Lord Michel received tidings from his steward at Larressingle, Sir Gilebert. You know of him, I believe.'

Aleran actually dipped his head at this point and Hugo continued, explaining to his brother all that he had heard and the concern that had in the end brought him back to Nérac.

Hugo and Aleran talked, and though Aleran never uttered a word in Hugo's mind it was definitely a conversation. In the next half hour, he learned enough to dispel any lingering doubts concerning his cousin's perfidy. Raoul might not have caused Aleran's apoplexy, but he had played a large part in the ill fortune that had befallen the Count and Countess of Nérac since then.

'It will not be easy, getting unscathed through the briars, Aleran,' Hugo warned him. 'But I give you my oath I will do my best to ensure that we win through.'

Bernadette gave a small cough. 'Ragonde should be back by now.' She pushed to her feet. 'She really ought to see this. I am going to fetch her.'

Chapter Sixteen

Bernadette went to the nursery. Jeanette and her sister Elaine were about to take Dennis into the garden, and they had not seen Ragonde. It was the same story in the kitchen. Ragonde had disappeared. A terrible suspicion had Bernadette chewing her lip.

Ragonde was back to her normal self; a self Bernadette was delighted to find was wholly unrecognisable from the demoralised wraith she and Hugo had first encountered. Ragonde was a loving, determined woman and she might have decided to investigate whether her recurring dream—the one where she had given birth to a girl rather than a boy—was based on reality.

Baron Raoul had been poisoning her with that terrible wine for years, and the dream might have made Ragonde question why it had been necessary for him to continue doing so. From there it was no great leap for her to wonder whether the baron had stolen her daughter and replaced her with Dennis.

As she hurried down the corridor to Ragonde's bed-chamber, Bernadette found herself wondering whether this new, determined Ragonde would find courage to go to the baron's holding in Fourcès. She might. Particularly if she knew that Hugo had lost patience with her. Hugo had questioned Ragonde's fidelity. Ragonde was bound to feel she could not rely on him to assist her. This new Ragonde would not sit idly by, twiddling her thumbs. She would want answers and she would act without Hugo's support.

In similar circumstances, Bernadette would do the same. If she suspected that she had a daughter, she would fight tooth and nail to find her. A shiver ran down her spine. She did not want to think of Ragonde going to Fourcès. Yet it was a distinct possibility.

Heart in her mouth, she burst into Ragonde's bed-chamber. A scattering of coins gleamed on the floor. It was obvious that someone had been counting them and had dropped a few. That someone—it could only be Ragonde—had either been too careless or in too much of a hurry to pick them up.

Ragonde was not a careless woman. The true Ragonde—the woman who smoothed back her husband's hair with a loving hand; the woman who had dismissed the idle creature sent to serve him; the punctilious woman who sought her husband's permission to take even a penny from his treasury—that woman would not be so careless.

Ragonde has gone to Fourcès. She is searching for answers.

Bernadette checked the row of pegs on the wall where Ragonde usually hung her cloak, and her fears were confirmed. The blue cloak was gone.

She hurtled towards Aleran's bedchamber and had reached the bottom of the stairs when she had the most terrifying thought of all. Hugo had not seen his cousin since he had been a boy, but with every day that Aleran recovered the family resemblance between the brothers became more marked. They had the same distinct profile. If Hugo set foot in Fourcès, he was bound to be recognised.

Bernadette sagged against the handrail. What could she do? She could not tell Hugo. He would immediately grab an escort and chase after Ragonde. The uproar when he was seen was bound to be appalling. Blood would be shed. *It would be safer for Hugo if I went without him.*

Straightening, Bernadette altered course and crept like a mouse to her bedchamber to collect her riding boots, her cloak, and her purse.

God was with her. Sir Gilebert had obviously just arrived from Larressingle. Both the castle courtyard and the stable yard were thronging with horsemen, all clamouring for space for their horses. In the confusion, Bernadette managed to secure the assistance of two of the burliest grooms, brothers named Gui and

Pierre. Shortly afterwards, the three of them rode unhindered and, she prayed, unnoticed, out of Nérac.

Fourcès.

Modest in size, Baron Raoul's castle sat on a mound at the heart of the town. It was encircled by merchants' houses and workshops. Shutters were open and stalls were out. Housewives were picking over apples and plums, and the tavern was doing a brisk trade. If Bernadette had not been so concerned to escape unobserved, it would be an idyllic scene.

As she glanced about her, she was assailed by misgivings. Had she done the right thing coming here? How would Hugo react when he realised? The cramp in her stomach warned her that Hugo was likely to be furious and she found herself praying that he would be so distracted by Sir Gilebert's arrival that it would be several hours before he noticed her departure. Hopefully, by that time, she and Ragonde would be on their way home.

She ran her gaze along the curved walkway in front of the shops. The walkway and workshops were roofed over to provide shade and to keep off rain. There was even a pavement, doubtless to protect people from mud on wet, wintry days.

She sent up a swift prayer. Please Lord, let us escape Baron Raoul's notice. So many prayers. She was a bundle of nerves.

Leaving the horses with Pierre in a livery just off

the main street, Bernadette and Gui walked back to the covered walkway in front of the castle. It did not take long to spot Ragonde's blue cloak. The tavern was tucked in between a butcher and a silversmith, and she was sitting on a trestle outside it, doing her best to appear inconspicuous. Her hood was up, and her face was barely visible. When she noticed Bernadette, she swiftly slid along the bench in a futile attempt to conceal herself behind a supporting post of the walkway roof.

Bernadette slipped on to the bench beside Ragonde and gestured for Gui to sit opposite them. 'Ragonde, it is no use trying to hide,' Bernadette murmured, keeping a wary eye on a brace of guards deep in conversation at the end of the walkway. 'I am glad I caught up with you. It is dangerous here, we ought to leave.'

Ragonde's eyes flashed, and she shrank deeper into her hood. 'You are wasting your time. I have concluded that my dream was a true one. I birthed a daughter. I am not going home until I know what happened to her.'

Lightly, Bernadette touched her sister-in-law's hand and ignored the voice inside her urging her to leave Fourcès with all speed. 'Rest easy, Ragonde. With your permission, I shall try to help.'

'Excuse me, *madame*,' an unfamiliar voice cut in. A serving girl stood by their table, a cup on her tray and a plate of pastries. Swiftly, she set the cup at Ragonde's elbow and addressed her. 'The child you were enquiring about?' She nodded towards the castle gate. 'Look, she is leaving the castle now. The girl with the black puppy. Dotes on that animal, she does.'

Ragonde turned to stare. Bernadette followed her sister-in-law's gaze and her breath stuck in her throat. The child was small. All high cheekbones and huge eyes, she looked half-starved. Her clothes were filthy and worn almost to rags. They had been patched several times and the hem was unravelling. Most telling of all, her nose—sharp as a blade—was a miniature copy of the Albret nose that lent such distinction to the profiles of both Aleran and Hugo.

Ragonde would have risen, but Bernadette laid a hand on her arm and shook her head. 'Wait,' she muttered.

'Who is the woman with her?' Ragonde asked brokenly.

'Her name is Emma,' the serving girl replied. 'She was a friend of the child's mother.' The serving girl's face went hard. 'Sad to say, the little girl does not fare well in the castle. Every now and then she goes to stay with Emma. I dare say it's the only time that poor mite eats properly. Emma brings her here occasionally. We feed them well.'

Ragonde made a strangled sound, and a large tear rolled down her cheek. 'Do you know the child's name?'

'Laura.'

'Laura,' Ragonde murmured. Holding the serving

girl's eye, she drew a coin from her purse and slid it towards her. 'Would you be so good as to fetch whatever Emma usually orders for Laura and herself.'

The girl beamed. 'Of course, *madame*. It will be my pleasure.'

Happily, the guards at the end of the walkway had ambled off. Realising Ragonde was about to invite Emma and Laura to join them, Bernadette stood. 'I believe I should be the one to approach her.'

Ragonde caught her breath. 'Be wary of what you say.'

'Rest assured, I know better than to shout our names from the roof tops.'

Shortly afterwards she returned to the table with Emma, Laura and the black puppy. 'Emma, I should like you to meet my sister-in-law,' Bernadette said softly. 'And this is Gui.'

Emma nodded warily at Ragonde and Gui. After the barest hesitation she took a place next to Gui with Laura clinging to her, all eyes. The serving girl reappeared with a plate of cakes and another of sausages. A small jug of wine and a cup of honeyed milk were set down next to them. The puppy gave a hopeful whine and its tail flickered. It had seen the plate of sausages.

Forcing a smile, for Bernadette was increasingly nervous about sitting by the inn in full view of Baron Raoul's castle, she slid the plate of cakes towards Laura and racked her brains to find a way of get-

ting Ragonde and Laura somewhere less conspicuous.
'We've milk and cakes for you. The sausages are for
your puppy. Will you allow me to take him?'

The little girl nodded. Bernadette took the puppy,
set him on the ground and gave him a sausage. Beside her, Ragonde was struggling to keep her composure. Not once had her sister-in-law's gaze left Laura's
face. She was desperate to drag the child on to her
own knee.

'Would you care for wine, Emma?' Bernadette
asked. Emma had a piercing gaze and a narrow face.
It was the face of a woman who had seen much in this
world that she did not like. She was quite definitely
on her guard. Which was, Bernadette told herself, no
bad thing. As no reply was forthcoming, Bernadette
filled the cup anyway.

Emma's mouth tightened. 'I have never seen any of
you before and I cannot think why you would invite
strangers to join you.'

Bernadette kept her gaze firmly on Emma. 'I shall
be blunt, if I may.'

'Please do.'

'I understand that you are not this child's mother
and that you care for her from time to time. Why is
that?'

Emma's face darkened. She gave a bitter laugh and
jerked her thumb towards the keep at the top of the
mound. 'Laura belongs to the baron.' With a derisive

sniff, Emma lowered her voice. 'He is her father, not that you would know that from the way he treats her.'

'Yet you are apparently able to care for her. Why is that?'

Emma's hand strayed towards her cup and she took a sip of wine. 'Her mother Nicole, our great lord's mistress, was a friend.'

'Was?'

Emma's shrug was far from casual, it held a world of grief. 'Nicole died the day Laura was born.'

'And you mourn her still.'

Nodding, Emma stroked Laura's tangled hair. 'The baron knows full well where she goes. He pays no mind. He is happy to have her out from under his feet.' Emma took a sausage from the plate and passed it to Laura. 'Sometimes it is weeks before he even notices.'

'Weeks? Goodness.'

'Aye. If he is feeling generous, he leaves me a little *pourboire*, a tip to help defray costs. It is better than the alternative.'

'The alternative?' The words slipped out before Bernadette thought to hold them back. Emma had been a good friend to the baron's mistress, Nicole, so it was possible they had chosen the same way to earn their daily bread. Flushing, she waved her question aside. Her days in the convent had taught her that hard choices were often forced on women if they were to survive. 'Forgive me, Emma. Forget I asked that.'

Bernadette was saved further embarrassment by a

nudge at her skirts—the puppy had wolfed his sausage. He let out a hopeful whine. 'Laura, may I give your puppy another sausage?' Mouth full herself, Laura nodded absently.

The two guards had sauntered back, and she was watching them. It was impossible to miss the way the little girl turned her head and shrank against Emma. Bernadette felt a distinct prickle of alarm. The poor child. 'Are those men looking for Laura?' she muttered. What might they do if they saw Laura and Emma speaking to strangers? They really had to get away from here.

Emma shrugged. 'It is hard to say, but I doubt it. Men from the castle garrison often drink here.'

'In that case, we should leave. Emma, when you've finished your wine, I would be honoured if you would direct us to your house.'

'House?' Emma shook her head and Bernadette was relieved to see that she seemed to have passed some kind of test. Despite her tactlessness, Emma understood she meant well. 'Lodgings more like. Mind, they are not fancy.'

That was an objection swept aside with a smile. 'Emma, I spent years in a convent where poverty was the nuns' watchword. Are your lodgings close?'

'They are a little way from the square, behind the livery.'

'Excellent.'

Laura looked up and pointed at the cakes. 'Take cakes, take cakes.'

Emma's harsh face eased into a smile. 'Never fear, my cherub, those cakes are definitely coming with us.'

Emma's lodgings proved to be a single chamber on the upper floor of a wooden house that had a distinct lean to it. Leaving Gui in the street, Emma led the way, carrying Laura. Ragonde followed with the precious cakes wrapped in a cloth and Bernadette came last, helping the puppy scrabble up the rickety stairs. Beneath their feet, the floorboards groaned.

The chamber was furnished as sparsely as a nun's cell. There was a bed, a small cot and a battered coffer. Clothing hung on pegs. A basket held a couple of hanks of green wool, a pair of knitting pins and a child's cloth doll. A rug was folded beneath the cot, presumably for the puppy. Mercifully, everything looked clean.

Bernadette smiled. 'You must have taken lessons from our Mother Superior,' she murmured. 'Where do you cook?'

Emma lifted a shoulder. 'I share a cooking fire below with other tenants. This must seem humble to someone like you, but in the main our great lord—' at mention of the baron her tone was laced with acid '—leaves Laura and me to our own devices. And that is how we like it, is it not, my cherub?'

Laura nodded.

Ragonde thrust the cakes at Bernadette and pushed forward, clearing her throat. 'Excuse me. Bernadette, we are no longer in the eye of the town, and I should like to hold Laura. Emma, with your permission?' She held out her arms.

Emma looked to Laura. Laura, who had clearly come to her own judgement about these strangers, gave a shy smile.

Eyes swimming, Ragonde took the child, holding her as though she was the most precious thing in the world. 'Well met, Laura,' she whispered. A single step took her to the bed. She sat down on the edge of the mattress, reached into the basket, and picked up the doll. 'This is pretty, is it yours?'

Ragonde and Laura embarked on a conversation involving the doll and whether it was a girl or a boy. Knowing how hard it must have been for Ragonde to have held herself in check at the tavern, Bernadette knew better than to intrude. She turned back to Emma, who was staring curiously at her.

'What is your name, *madame*?' Emma asked. 'Why have you not introduced yourselves?'

Bernadette cleared her throat and jerked her head towards the child playing with Ragonde. 'We cannot say, not yet. Emma, for your well-being and that of the child's, I beg you not to press us on this.'

'Laura's safety is in question, that is plain,' Emma said. 'Madame, I may not be of your rank, but I am not stupid.' Biting her lip, she subjected Ragonde to a thorough study before looking back at Laura. Her gaze was sharp as a needle. 'It is odd, the baron is clear that she is his get, so why do I see a resemblance between Laura and this lady?'

'Coincidence?' Bernadette said. Emma's probing was making her decidedly uncomfortable. She moved to a narrow window, half obscured by a leather curtain to keep out draughts, and peered out. With the houses being so close to each other, she could see little of the street. Gui was completely out of sight, all she could see was the heads of passers-by on the opposite side. She could hear a faint hammering; a smith was at work nearby.

Emma sniffed and her gaze returned to Ragonde. 'There is a resemblance. Something about this lady's expression and the shape of her face—' She broke off with a gasp and her skin went grey. 'Holy Mother, I know who you are and why you are here.'

'Please, Emma, name no names,' Bernadette said quickly. 'Even if you have stumbled on the truth, we will not corroborate your conclusion.'

Emma's eyes were wide with panic. 'Blessed Virgin, you would not want this aired in the town square. God help us, I knew the baron was a fiend when I overheard him saying that Laura, like the puppy, was a runt.'

Bernadette let out a horrified gasp. Fortunately, her sister-in-law was so engrossed with her daughter, she had not heard.

'The baron has said far worse than that, my lady. I overheard him tell Laura that she was not worth her keep any more than the puppy.'

'Emma, please.' Bernadette swallowed down a bitter rush of rage. Baron Raoul was a complete monster. How could he be so cruel? 'It is vital you do not address me as my lady.'

'Very well, I shall address you as mistress.'

'Thank you. The last thing we want is to put you or anyone in danger. We are hoping to restore Laura to her rightful place.'

Emma's mouth worked. 'That would be best.'

At that moment, heavy footsteps pounded up the stairs. The door rattled and Gui charged in. 'My lady, we are discovered.' Taking her by the elbow, a familiarity Bernadette knew was prompted by urgency, he turned her to the window.

There on the opposite side of the street, head turned up towards the window, stood an elderly woman with wrinkled cheeks. It was the same woman who had opened the Nérac gate for Hugo and Bernadette on the day they arrived. Like Avryll, whom Ragonde had dismissed, she must answer to Baron Raoul.

Hugo was closeted with his brother who was still holding the quill when he heard his squire bellowing below stairs. 'Sir Hugo! *Sir Hugo!*' Recognising the distinct edge of panic in Olivier's voice and wondering what on earth might have caused it, for Olivier was usually the most carefree of fellows, Hugo strode to the door and called down to him, 'Up here, Olivier.'

Olivier thundered up the stairs. 'Sir, you are needed in the stables,' he blurted breathlessly. 'At once.'

Hugo stared. Olivier really did look worried. 'Not a fire, surely?'

'No, sir. But it is urgent. I overheard the grooms talking. Apparently, Lady Ragonde set out earlier and when Lady Bernadette learned of it, she ordered a horse to be saddled and followed her.'

Ice filled Hugo's veins. 'She did what?'

'Lady Bernadette has gone to Fourcès.'

For a moment Hugo could not move. He stood like a stone, glaring at his squire, and even though he could read Olivier like a book and could see the truth in the lad's eyes, he heard himself saying, 'Why the devil did no one stop her?'

'Sir Gilebert's arrival has caused chaos down there, sir. It was pure chance I heard the grooms talking. Both Lady Ragonde and Lady Bernadette have gone.'

'This had better not be one of your tricks, Olivier,' Hugo said. He did not want to believe it. If only half of Bernadette's suspicions proved to be true, the two women were in grave danger.

'It is no trick, sir. The grooms are convinced both ladies have gone to Fourcès.' Olivier hesitated. 'Lady Ragonde set out alone, but Lady Bernadette did take Gui and Pierre with her.'

Aleran made a choking sound and the quill jerked

in his hand. Swiftly replenishing it with ink, Hugo straightened the parchment.

Aleran wrote two words. *'Notre fille.'* Our daughter.

Hugo stared. 'Aleran?'

More words appeared. 'Her dream.'

Mind roiling with fury and dread, Hugo gouged his nails into his palms. 'A dream is not proof, Aleran. Good God, it certainly is not enough to justify the pair of them haring off to that hornets' nest.'

Jésu, Angel had gone to Fourcès with but two grooms for protection. Grooms. To be sure, Gui and Pierre were burly men, but two grooms were no match for trained guards. Hugo looked at his brother and gave a curt bow.

'Aleran, I will bring them back, I assure you. In the meantime, I shall send Elaine up to you. Please note, I will be posting a handful of my men at intervals on the landings below. They will remain there for your protection until my return. And as you have heard, Sir Gilebert has brought reinforcements. He is efficient and conscientious. With him acting as your deputy, you may be confident the interests of Nérac are safe.' He gripped his brother's shoulder. 'I shall return as soon as I can, but given the distance between Nérac and Fourcès, that is not likely to be today. *Au revoir.*'

Chapter Seventeen

Heart in her mouth, Bernadette stole another look into the street. The hammering had stopped, and an eerie silence had fallen. Both the passers-by and the elderly woman had gone. Abruptly the silence was broken by the tramp of heavily booted feet. A chill shot through her. Ragonde was holding on to her daughter as though her life depended on it. Emma's face was like chalk. 'Whatever happens,' Bernadette said, softly, 'we must do our best not to alarm Laura.'

Emma nodded. 'Amen to that.'

Hugo had given the standard emblazoned with the Albret coat of arms to Olivier, and he and his troop galloped into Fourcès behind it. He was acting for his brother; he was entitled to use it. He was gambling that sight of the Albret standard—a dazzling gold sun on an azure field—would serve as a potent reminder that Aleran and Hugo belonged to the senior branch of the family. It should encourage any waverers among

Raoul's men to think twice about offering resistance as well as being a not-so-subtle reminder that Raoul should not be terrorising Bernadette and Ragonde.

At the gate his cousin's men gawped uneasily at the flaming sun on the standard and waved them on. Hugo signalled to the troop to draw rein by the castle mound and assessed the lie of the land. He had a dim recollection from his boyhood of the area beneath the castle being a hive of activity. Merchants had set up shop at the foot of the mound. There was a tavern. A butcher. A baker.

Today, he found himself scowling. The tavern door was shut at a time when trade would usually be brisk. And the stalls in front of the merchants' houses had been put up. All were firmly closed. His scowl deepened. No one was about. Not a soul. Except…

A door on one of the merchant's houses opened a crack. Someone was watching them, their face lost in shadow. 'Lord Aleran?' came the wary whisper. 'Are you well? We heard you were ailing.'

'I am not Lord Aleran. I am his brother, Sir Hugo Albret of Larressingle, and today I am acting in his stead.'

The door opened another inch and the voice warmed. 'Welcome, sir. You and your brother are as like as peas in a pod.'

Hugo managed a wry smile. 'So I am told. Do you know my cousin's whereabouts?'

The man pointed. 'The baron led a troop of foot soldiers that way, towards the livery. The look on his face was so disturbing, we closed the shops. He and his men have yet to return.'

'My thanks.'

The door closed softly and, cold sweat running down his neck, Hugo gave the signal for his men to ride in the direction of the livery. He was appalled to realise his hand was shaking and he knew beyond a shadow of a doubt that it had nothing to do with confronting Raoul. His heart was banging against his breastbone because of Bernadette. Had she been hurt? What might Raoul do to her? *Jésu.* He had never felt so desperate in his life. He forced himself to focus. Raoul must be confronted.

His mind took flight as, suddenly, he knew exactly what to do. He looked at his sergeant. 'Mathieu?'

'Sir?'

'The narrow streets will work to our advantage,' he said. That and his cousin's arrogance. Whoever had alerted Raoul to Bernadette and Ragonde's presence in Fourcès must have told him they were practically unguarded. His cousin, it seemed, was courageous when faced with a couple of unarmed women.

'Mathieu, the baron has no idea we are here. I shall ride round to the other end of this street with half of the men. You must stay here with the others until you hear a blast of the horn. When you hear it, block off this end of the street. Not one of my cousin's troopers are to be allowed to retreat. Understood?'

'Yes, sir.'

A shout outside brought Emma to the slit in the wall that served as her window. Heart thudding, Bernadette pressed close. The voice was harsh and clipped. 'Emma, I know you are there. I am told you have visitors from Nérac. Bring them out, I want to speak to them. And do not forget my daughter. As you see, my men have torches. If you defy me, they will fire the house.'

'That, I assume, is Baron Raoul,' Bernadette said. He was tall like his cousins, but there the resemblance ended. His hair was dark, and his nose fleshy. He had none of the features Bernadette had come to associate with the Albret family. She disliked him on sight, which was not surprising. This was the man who had drugged Ragonde and stolen her daughter.

Emma threw a desperate look her way. 'My lady, the soldiers will not hesitate to fire the house. If they do, half the town may burn with it.'

'Very well,' Bernadette said. Her hands were clammy. Surreptitiously she wiped them on her skirts before stiffening her spine. 'We have no choice but to go outside. I shall go first.'

'No, my lady,' Gui spoke firmly. 'I will go first.'

Bernadette shrugged. 'Thank you, Gui, but please take care. Do not take risks. Ragonde, can you manage with Laura?' Ragonde nodded. Emma scooped up the puppy, and with Gui in the lead, they started down the stairs.

The baron's men crowded round the doorway so closely Bernadette could smell the ale on their breath. Gui's arms were caught and wrenched behind him. 'That is *not* necessary,' she said, bristling. 'We are offering no resistance.' Simultaneously a horn sounded. She could also hear hoofbeats. Strangely, horses were thundering at them from two directions at once. And there, flying bravely at one end of the street, was the Albret standard.

Baron Raoul swore. '*Mon Dieu*, what is this?' Before the baron's foot soldiers had time to react the horses were upon them.

'Hugo!' Hugo was charging towards them on Clovis. Bernadette was never so relieved to see anyone in her life. Her breath left her, and her legs weakened. 'Thank God, Hugo is here.'

Hugo flung himself off Clovis and spent the next half an hour issuing orders. Having seen Bernadette was unharmed, he was determined not to look her way again. If he did, he was not sure he could behave like a civilised man. He wanted to shake her, he wanted to kiss her senseless, and he could do neither. A dark fury burned inside him. How could she have been so foolish as to run off after Ragonde without a word?

First things first. Cousin Raoul's hands were bound. Hugo ordered him to be marched back to the hall to await interrogation. A handful of Raoul's men put up a fight, and while he brought about their capture, Hugo managed not to look at his wife. He would deal with her when he calmed.

The offending men were put in chains and sent to the dungeon below the castle. As for the rest of the Fourcès guard, sight of the Albret standard seemed to have knocked the fight out of them. Within half an hour, Hugo had secured the town.

Anger still riding Hugo like a demon, he studied the ragged mite in his sister-in-law's arms and reached for calm. 'Who is this child?' he asked, though the tightness in his belly told him he that he already knew the answer.

His sister-in-law met his gaze squarely. 'This is Laura Albret,' she replied. 'My daughter.'

'My lady, you have my sincere apologies for doubting you.'

Relaxing, Ragonde flushed and sent him a gentle smile. 'It is understandable, considering everything you found when you reached Nérac.' She leaned her cheek against Laura's head. 'Hugo, will we go home this evening? Aleran would like to see his daughter as soon as possible.'

'See her he shall, but not today,' Hugo said firmly. 'It is a ride of several hours and we have already pushed the horses hard. I would not have them lamed.

Tonight, we sleep in Fourcès. We shall return to Nérac on the morrow, after I have assured myself that the town is secure.'

Bernadette could see the storm building in Hugo's eyes and wondered when it would break. They were ushered into the hall of his cousin's castle, a bleak chamber that was more like a barracks than a hall, particularly with the arms of the vanquished guards piled up on the trestles by Hugo's men. There was little comfort on view. From the corners, cowed-looking maidservants shot them wary glances. Clerks and servants stared wide-eyed when the Albret standard was brought in.

Calling for a scribe, Hugo had a couple of chairs set up behind one of the tables and before she knew it a court was in session. Her husband thumped on the table with the hilt of his sword and Baron Raoul's interrogation was underway.

'By what right do you hold me?' the baron growled.

Hugo indicated the Albret standard. 'By the order of the Count of Nérac. You, Raoul Sérillac of Fourcès, are charged with sedition. Do you deny placing your illegitimate son, Dennis, in the place of the daughter of the Count and Countess of Nérac?'

'Of course I deny it!' The baron's cheeks flamed as he strained against his bonds. 'I have never heard such utter hogwash. Release me at once.'

'Hold!' A shout from among the townsfolk gathered

in the entranceway drew all eyes. 'Allow me to pass, I beg you. I must speak to Sir Hugo.'

A subdued muttering arose as a man elbowed his way through and came to stand before Hugo. 'Sir Hugo Albret?' the man asked. Without waiting for a response, he fell to his knees and covered his face with his hands. 'I have come to beg forgiveness. I did not want to do it. I—'

The baron jerked convulsively. 'Hold your tongue, Perceval, if you want to keep it.'

'Gag my cousin, Mathieu,' Hugo said coldly. He ignored the ensuring struggle and caught the newcomer's gaze. 'And you are?'

'The town apothecary, sir. Forgive me, you must forgive me. I did not want to do it, but I had no choice.'

'You have committed a crime?'

'To my everlasting shame, I have, though you must believe me, I was forced into it.'

'And the nature of this crime?'

The apothecary moistened his lips. 'It concerns a tincture I supply to the baron. It is often given to women in childbed, sir. To ease the pain.'

Ragonde gave a sharp intake of breath and glanced at Bernadette. 'Proof,' she whispered.

'Perhaps.'

The apothecary gulped. 'I am always careful to stress that the tincture is to be given sparingly. Too much and the woman can slip into a sleep from which there is no awakening.'

It was Emma's turn to stare at the apothecary. 'You mean as happened to my friend Nicole?'

The apothecary sent a terrified glance to the baron, whose cheeks, now that he had been gagged, had gone purple. 'I never ask what the baron needs the tincture for, but I suspect so.'

Bernadette could keep silent no longer. 'What is this tincture made from?' she asked. 'Poppies? Was it poppy juice?'

Miserably, the apothecary nodded. 'I know I should not have supplied it so freely, but the baron threatened the life of my wife. I had no choice.'

After an almost imperceptible glance at Bernadette, Hugo drew his head back. 'Your wife was threatened, Perceval? Where is she?'

'In the town prison, sir. She has been there three years, since Nicole died.'

'She has been there so long?' Hugo grimaced. 'Thank you for your testimony, Perceval, I need to investigate further before I can release her. Do I have your surety that you will not abscond?'

The apothecary gave a sad smile and nodded. 'I will not abandon my wife.'

Hugo stared thoughtfully at the apothecary and a muscle twitched in his cheek. 'Of course not. One further question. If this tincture was mixed with, say, wine and taken in smaller doses over a long period, what would the effect be?'

'It would cloud the mind. I believe it would be

addictive. The long-term effects can be most demoralising.'

Determined to do everything he could to ensure a peaceful conclusion to the end of his cousin's rule, Hugo finally announced that he and the rest of their party would have to stay in Fourcès for a few days. Noticing Ragonde shudder at the thought of passing the next few nights in Baron Raoul's castle, Hugo recalled the lodge next to the church of Saint Laurent. Would that be preferable? Ragonde assured him it would indeed.

Which was how that evening, Bernadette found herself sitting on the edge of yet another bed that was scarcely large enough for her, let alone for her and Hugo. The guest chamber was cramped and cell-like, but the bedlinen smelt fresh. A jug of water and small washbasin had been placed on a shelf. The storm she had seen in Hugo's eyes would break soon; she was sure.

She finished plaiting her hair and stared pensively at Hugo's back. He had disarmed and was perched on the end of the bed, his head in his hands. He was exhausted. He had not said a word since they walked in. Setting his anger with her aside, she knew he had much on his mind. Knowing Hugo, he would be worrying about Aleran, who with the best will in the world was plainly unable to fulfil his obligations as Count of Nérac.

And then there was Dennis. What would happen to Dennis once the world knew that he was the illegitimate son of a man who was likely to be executed for treason? It was obvious that Ragonde and Aleran were going to acknowledge Laura as their daughter. However Aleran decided to proceed, Hugo was now his heir. Sooner or later Hugo would become Count of Nérac. It was a lot for him to digest.

She stared down at her hands, locked tightly together. She spoke quietly. 'Hugo, are you all right?'

'I am well enough.' With a sound of exasperation, he jerked round, eyes fierce. 'Or I would be, if I could rely on my wife to act in a reasonable manner.'

'Hugo, I am sorry I displeased you—'

'Displeased me? You left without leaving as much as a word about where you had gone. You are the most stubborn and wilful woman alive. Do you have no thought for anyone's feelings other than your own?'

'Of course I do!' Drawing back, Bernadette met him glare for glare. 'Hugo, I had to go quietly. I was thinking of you all the time.'

He gave a bitter laugh. 'That, my lady, is a lie. If Olivier had not chanced to hear a conversation in the stables, no one would have known you were chasing after Ragonde and that she was heading here. How hard would it have been to tell me? I am your husband. You owe me your loyalty, though plainly you only remember that when it suits you. Why sneak out alone? Why did you not confide in me?'

'I am not sure why you care, sir.'

'And what does that sullen look mean?'

She folded her arms beneath her breasts. 'Hugo, I know you will never forget Allis. You married me for my dowry, and because you hoped that I would one day give you children.'

'That is absurd.'

'Is it?'

'Angel, stop trying to distract me. For pity's sake, why leave Nérac without telling me?'

'Because, you pig-headed fool, what I had learned of your cousin's character did not lead me to think he would take kindly to you turning up on his doorstep.' She looked earnestly at him. 'I know he has not seen you for years, but you and Aleran are so very alike. He would have known you in an instant.'

Hugo stared at her for a long moment. 'You were concerned for me?'

'I was afraid you would be killed! Of course I was concerned.' She paused and lightened her tone. 'I was not to know that you would storm in behind the Albret standard and take over the entire town.'

Hugo sighed and scrubbed his face with his palm. 'We both need sleep.'

'Assuredly.'

No more was said until they had crawled under the covers. Hugo pinched out the light. 'Goodnight, Angel.'

'Goodnight.' Bernadette lay in the dark, listening

to the familiar sound of Hugo shifting about to find a comfortable sleeping position in a bed that was far too small for him. It was a good sign that he was calling her Angel again, although it hurt to know that he seemed determined to keep his distance. *I love you, Hugo.* In all the years she had known him, she had never seen him livid with rage, he who was invariably measured in all things. But today, with her...

Hugo let out a sigh and the altered rhythm of his breathing told her he was asleep. She rolled towards him. He had spoken with such intensity. Such passion. Her breath stopped. A man who did not care would never have reacted so fiercely. Such a man would chastise his wife and let the matter drop. Hugo must care for her more than he was prepared to admit. But did he love her? Gently, she laid her hand on his broad shoulder and prayed that he did.

The next day, Hugo began by questioning the apothecary's wife. After corroborating her statement with several townsfolk, Hugo had no doubt that her husband was innocent of malicious intent. The woman was freed on the condition that the apothecary recorded his own testimony concerning the tincture that Baron Raoul had coerced him into providing.

Meanwhile, Bernadette went in search of Ragonde and Laura. They had slept in one of the nearby cells in the lodge, but they had not broken their fast in the refectory, and when she went to their cell, she found it empty. She ran them to earth in Emma's lodgings. Ragonde and Laura were sitting next to Emma on her bed.

'Ragonde, what have you been doing? I have been searching for you everywhere.' Laura gave a little giggle and pranced forward, the puppy at her side. The child's rags had gone, and she was wearing a blue tunic over a cream undergown. Her hair was shining; it was a beautiful honey gold, just like her mother's.

'Someone has been to the bathhouse, I see.' Bernadette swung Laura into her arms and the child let out a delighted squeal. 'And you have been shopping. What a pretty tunic.' With the puppy jumping up and down at her knees, she settled Laura on her hip.

'We have indeed,' Ragonde said. She and Emma were smiling, and as Bernadette smiled back, she saw that Emma too was wearing new clothes. 'We even took the puppy to the bathhouse. Everyone must look their best when we arrive back at Nérac. By the way, Emma has agreed to come with us. She will be Laura's nursemaid.'

Bernadette nodded. It made perfect sense. Laura would settle more easily, and Emma had already proved how much she cared for Laura. 'I am glad.'

Ragonde touched her daughter's head and her smile dimmed. 'Bernadette, I cannot help but worry when I think of the future. I fear for Aleran. And although Dennis is not our son, I have come to love him. What will happen to him?'

'Ragonde, have faith in Hugo. If we pull together, all will be well,' Bernadette said. Ragonde nodded and smiled, but her eyes remained clouded.

Chapter Eighteen

⁓⁓⁓

They finally reached Nérac four days later, and during that time Bernadette had hardly seen her husband. Each night he met her in their chamber at the lodge and though he was scrupulously polite, he remained distant. As for her, she was hopeful. Being hopeful was, it seemed, a tiring business.

By the time they reached Nérac castle, she was exhausted. Sir Gilebert came out to the stable to greet them and as their party dismounted, Bernadette overheard Hugo offering him the stewardship of Nérac. Without as much as a look in her direction, Hugo clapped the man on the back and off they marched, doubtless to the estate office. She watched them go with a heavy heart.

In their youth, Hugo had not told her everything. He had never mentioned the rift with his brother or his lack of land, but he had liked and trusted her. This taciturn stranger worried her. Sighing, she left him to his conference with Sir Gilebert. She would not impose upon him until she knew she was welcome.

Ragonde had sped upstairs to see Aleran with Laura and Emma. Doubtless introductions were being made.

Disconsolately, Bernadette went to the solar. It was a pleasant surprise to find Lady Celeste there, examining one of the large tapestries on the table. 'Lady Celeste, how lovely to see you,' Bernadette said, warmly. 'I had no idea you were here.'

'Gilebert sent for more men from Larressingle. He said new recruits were needed for the garrison. When he also mentioned that the housekeeping needed attention, Violette and I wanted to lend a hand,' Lady Celeste said.

Bernadette felt her mood lift. 'Violette came with you?'

'I believe she is cleaning your bedchamber.' Lady Celeste patted the tapestry. 'I have been sorting through the wall hangings and I think this hunting scene is salvageable.'

'I like that one,' Bernadette said. 'It is too late to start work on it today. We can buy threads for it tomorrow.' She waited for the flare of excitement that usually accompanied a project such as this, but it did not come. There was just a dull ache in her chest and the nagging worry that with all Hugo had to face now he was heir to the county, he might find it hard to move past his anger.

* * *

'Hugo?' Ragonde appeared in the estate office doorway as Hugo was deciding how best to approach Aleran on that most thorny of topics, namely his brother's inability to fully discharge his duties as Count. The County of Nérac had long supported the King of England rather than the King of France. This meant that King Edward of England was their overlord.

Hugo had, of necessity, sent a full report of events at Fourcès to the King's lieutenant, Sir Francis of Ingham. Given the seriousness of Raoul's crimes, they expected a visit from him soon.

'Aleran wishes to speak to you in our chamber.' Ragonde grimaced apologetically. 'Perhaps I should make it clear that I know what Aleran wishes to say, and that he has asked me to speak on his behalf.'

Rising, Hugo nodded. With his wholehearted agreement, his sister-in-law had wasted no time in moving Aleran's bedchamber to an apartment on the ground floor. Her belongings had been taken into the new apartment. After too many years apart, Ragonde and Aleran were once again living as man and wife. Laura, Dennis, and their nursemaids had adjoining chambers. Overall, it was a much more convenient arrangement.

'Very well, I shall come at once.' Hugo followed Ragonde to Aleran's apartment. Bernadette was already there, sitting in one of three chairs ranged around the bed. She looked very serious. In fact, Hugo thought, noting the tension around Aleran's eyes, so did his brother. Smiling at Aleran, he took the chair next to Bernadette and looked expectantly at his sister-in-law. 'Ragonde?'

'As you are both aware, Aleran has asked me to speak for him. He has reached several conclusions, and we need to discuss them.' Ragonde took a deep breath. 'Aleran is recovering. It seems likely that he will become stronger, but he is fully conscious that he will not be able to fulfil his duties as Count. Hugo, you are his heir. You have proved yourself the most able of men and it is Aleran's ardent wish that you succeed him. The King's lieutenant, Sir Francis of Ingham, must be informed.'

Hugo gave his brother a crooked smile. 'I have already written to him, though I confess I feel uncomfortable depriving you, and any sons you may have in the future, of the county.'

Ragonde nodded. 'Aleran knew you would feel that way. He hopes you will take comfort from the fact that he has not been able to fulfil his duties for years and that this change is long overdue. Hugo, you know better than anyone that a count has many active duties. He must be a strong leader, capable of rallying his troops. He must be prepared to fight; he must sit in court and make judgements, as you did at Fourcès. The present state of affairs is unsustainable.'

Hugo rubbed his forehead and glanced at Bernadette. 'Angel, this will affect you as much as me. Do you agree with this conclusion?'

'I do.' Bernadette turned to Aleran. 'My lord, I wish with all my heart that you were well enough to remain Count and I know Hugo feels the same. He bitterly regrets the years of estrangement—'

Aleran made a convulsive moment and looked meaningfully at Ragonde, urging her to continue. 'Hugo, Aleran is anxious to know whether you accept that Raoul must have forged the letter you received all those years ago?'

'I do, of course.' Hugo looked earnestly at his brother. 'God knows I wrote back, dozens of times. You would think that one letter at least would have reached you.'

'We believe Raoul intercepted them,' Ragonde said.

'Knowing Raoul of Sérillac, I expect he burned them,' Bernadette murmured. 'Even all those years ago, he wanted to come between you. Thankfully, he failed.' Reaching across, she took Hugo's hand. Winding her fingers with his, she gave him a look that he had no difficulty interpreting. *Love can be trusted. Love can be true.*

And just like that, the band of tightness that had for years encased Hugo's heart, eased and fell away. Love could be trusted. It could be true. As he smiled into his wife's face, which was alight with love for him, he wanted nothing more than to drag her upstairs, declare himself and prove how much he adored her. Love, he realised, had been staring him in the face for years. The moment the meeting with Sir Francis was over and their status was confirmed, he would do just that.

'When do you expect Sir Francis to arrive?' she asked.

'My guess is that he will be here tomorrow.' Lifting her hand to his lips, he kissed it. His mind was spinning. So much was unresolved, and all he wanted to do was declare himself. Another night of chastity would not kill him. And then her fingers squeezed his and in response to the sudden clenching of his heart, he found himself on his feet. He could wait no longer.

'Hugo?'

'Ragonde, Aleran, you will excuse us. Angel, come with me.'

Hugo said nothing more until they reached their bedchamber, where he shoved the door open so forcefully that for a heart-stopping moment, Bernadette thought she had misread him. Violette, arranging a vase of lilies in the light of a wall sconce, gave a startled gasp. 'Good evening, Violette,' Hugo said. His voice was rusty. 'That is all for tonight.'

'Very good, sir.' Violette gave the lilies a final tweak, dropped into a curtsy, and made for the door.

'Thank you, Violette,' Bernadette murmured. 'You have worked wonders in here and the flowers are lovely.'

'You are most welcome, my lady.' Violette went out, and in the pause that followed Bernadette smiled uncertainly at Hugo.

'Angel, come here.' He set his hands at her waist

and drew her towards him until they were standing toe to toe as they had done when she had asked him to kiss her in the stable at Galard. The light gleamed on his blond hair. His smile was crooked, his dark eyes gleamed, and Bernadette would swear the green flecks in them were dancing. 'I have a confession to make.'

Her eyes widened. 'A confession?'

Cupping her cheek, he stroked her lip with his thumb. 'Aye. When we married, we agreed to care for each other. I thought we might eventually share a little passion and companionship. Our marriage was, to an extent, one of convenience.'

'You needed my dowry,' Bernadette murmured. 'I needed to escape marriage to a stranger.'

'Angel, I was like a blind man, stumbling about in the dark.'

Bernadette stiffened, then relaxed. 'And now?'

He leaned in and kissed her ear. 'You brought light into my life,' he whispered. 'You are my heart. My guiding star. I love you. I have always loved you.'

Breath seizing, Bernadette reached up and wound her arms about his neck. Their lips met in a warm and thorough kiss that was frustratingly delicate. Tender though it was, her blood was soon on fire for him, so much so that when he drew back, she was unable to prevent a murmur of protest.

'Behave, Angel. I have not finished my confession. I am sorry it took me so long to see it. In part it was because I first loved you as a friend.' Broad shoulders lifted. 'It took a while to see that the nature of my feelings had changed.'

'You told me, quite recently I might add, that you do not trust love,' Bernadette said, lightly. 'Perhaps that is why you never saw it, even though it was staring you in the face all along.'

'All along? Truly?'

Half laughing, she thumped his chest for emphasis. 'Yes, Hugo, all along. Even back when you yearned for Allis—'

Strong fingers clamped round her wrist. 'No. Bernadette, that is not true. I *never* desired Allis. I will admit to kissing her. Once.'

'Behind the stable,' Bernadette murmured. 'I happened to see you.'

'You did, did you?' His grip tightened. 'It felt all wrong. Angel, Allis is like a sister to me. I love her of course. As a sister. My love for you is of a different nature entirely. You are my world. Whatever the future brings, I know that with you at my side life will be rich beyond measure. I am bound to make mistakes, we both are, but together I am certain we can win through.'

Slightly overcome by this speech, Bernadette leaned her head against him and swallowed. Frowning, he tilted up her chin and peered down at her. 'I declare myself and you have nothing to say?'

'I love you, Hugo,' she murmured. 'I always have.'

His frown vanished and a grin appeared. 'That will

do for me.' He scooped her into his arms and tossed her on to the bed. 'Now, my love, I intend to devote the next few hours to convincing you how much I adore you. Agreed?'

Smiling as she had never smiled before, Bernadette opened her arms to him. 'Agreed. You may convince me to your heart's content.'

The next day, the King's lieutenant, Sir Francis of Ingham, surprised them. Bernadette was in the garden with Violette and the children when the rich blare of trumpets filled the air.

'Whatever's that?' Violette asked.

'That, I believe, is Sir Francis of Ingham. Heavens, it is well before noon, he is earlier than we expected.' Dismayed, Bernadette looked down at her gown. The puppy, which Laura had decided to name Tadpole, had jumped up at her and her skirts were covered with paw prints. 'I cannot greet the King's lieutenant looking like this, what will he think? Violette, please come with me. I need your assistance.'

Upstairs, Violette flung back the lid of Bernadette's travelling chest and moments later several beautiful garments were spread out on the bed. Bernadette's mouth fell open. 'Where on earth did you get these?'

'When you and Sir Hugo left Larressingle, Lady Celeste and I visited the cloth merchants.'

Amazed, Bernadette fingered an undergown in pale gold silk. Next to it lay a damask overgown in a wonderful leaf-green. The open sides were edged with soft white fur and the stitching was perfect. There was a cloak to match the overgown, leaf-green and lined with the pale gold silk of the undergown. More garments peeped out from beneath the leaf-green cloak.

Puzzled she looked at Violette. 'Who made them?'

Violette beamed. 'Lady Celeste and I.'

'Violette, they are incredibly lovely, but I definitely recall Lady Celeste telling me she was unable to make a pattern.'

'That is true.' Violette grinned. 'One of the merchants' wives helped us. As you can see, she is very talented.' She stepped closer and her tone became confidential. 'Lady Celeste and I decided that as Lady of Larressingle you needed clothes more fitting to your status. And now you are to be a countess you will need them even more. Do you like them?'

'I love them, thank you! Violette, we must hurry. I shall wear the leaf-green overgown with the gold silk undergown.'

'Very good, my lady.'

The plan was that they would receive Sir Francis in Aleran's apartment. In preparation, the tall curtains had been looped back so the sun streamed in, splashing over the floor in squares of light. A settle had been set up for Aleran, who was propped up with cushions, Ragonde at his side. Hugo was wearing the cloth of gold jacket he had worn at their wedding.

When Bernadette entered, his eyes widened. Striding across, he took her hand and bowed over it. 'Angel, you are beautiful.' The whisper was for her ears alone and when he lifted his eyes to hers, she saw them flare. Dark and hungry. Full of promise.

A trumpet blared and a man walked in. It had to be Sir Francis. He was tall and spare with short brown hair that was greying at the temples. He had a moustache, and his clothes were serviceable rather than showy. Everything about him spoke of economy. The same could not be said of his squire and the heralds who marched in his wake.

Bernadette caught the flash of red, gold and blue on the heralds' tunics. The golden lions of England were quartered with the *fleur de lis* of France. 'Goodness,' she murmured. 'Sir Francis has brought his heralds inside.'

'This is an official conference.' Hugo placed her hand on his arm as Sir Gilebert ushered the King's lieutenant in. 'Sir Francis is openly displaying his credentials, so that the world will know about the decisions made here today.'

'Sir Francis, welcome.' Sir Gilebert gestured Sir Francis to where Aleran and Ragonde were sitting. 'May I present the Count and Countess of Nérac, Lord Aleran and Lady Ragonde.' Turning to Hugo and Bernadette, Sir Gilebert continued. 'And this is Sir Hugo and Lady Bernadette of Larressingle.' Introductions complete, pleasantries were exchanged, and refreshments offered.

'Later, I think.' Coolly, Sir Francis waved away the refreshments. 'When our business is concluded.'

Sir Francis was a thorough man, he was not to be hurried. A scribe appeared and was established in a corner behind a table covered with inkpots, quills and parchment. 'Everything must be clearly noted,' Sir Francis said. 'The King has invested me with the authority to make a judgement today and he requires a clear exposition of my decision.'

As soon as Sir Francis understood the extent of Aleran's incapacity, he demanded to see for himself how Aleran managed to communicate. More quills and parchment were brought. Sir Francis was an intelligent man, and it did not take long for him to agree to hear Ragonde's testimony. Taking up the Bible, Ragonde stood before a window framed in sunlight and took her oath to tell the truth.

Shadows crept across the floor, for the truth took some time in the telling, and by the end Hugo and Bernadette had also been handed a Bible and made their oaths.

At last, Sir Francis gave a half-smile and caught Sir Gilebert's eye. 'You mentioned refreshments, sir. We shall have them now while I consider my judgement. Lady Ragonde, if you would be so good as to fetch the two children, I should like to meet them.'

Ragonde moved to the door. 'Of course.'

Hugo cleared his throat. 'Sir Francis, concerning the boy Dennis, I have a request to make. As you have been told, Dennis is the illegitimate son of my cousin Raoul of Sérillac.'

Sir Francis grunted. 'Sir Hugo, many would say you do the child no favours by keeping him here. The illegitimate son of a traitor is likely to have a miserable future.'

'My sister-in-law loves him.'

'Such affection is misguided,' Sir Francis said.

Bernadette stepped forward. 'Sir Francis, Dennis is a sweet child, you will see when you meet him. If Lord Aleran and Lady Ragonde agree to bring him up, perhaps there is a way his future might be safeguarded.' She paused. 'As far as I am aware Baron Raoul has no other issue. That would make Dennis heir to his father's land.'

'Not so, my lady.' Sir Francis frowned severely. 'In the first instance the child is, as I understand it, illegitimate. His rights are limited. And secondly, his father is guilty of treason. Generally, when a subject is found guilty of treason, all lands and property are forfeit. They return to the Crown.' Hugo shifted and Sir Francis looked enquiringly at him. 'Sir Hugo, you have something to add?'

'I do. Sir Francis, no law is set in stone. While you are coming to your ruling, I ask that you also consider whether the Fourcès estate might be placed in trust so that when Dennis comes of age, he may inherit it.'

'You wish to govern Fourcès on the boy's behalf?'

'I would be pleased to act as his guardian and Dennis will be brought up to appreciate the difference between right and wrong.'

'Thank you, Sir Hugo. I shall consider your request.'

Light footsteps and a flurry of childish giggles preceded the arrival of Laura and Dennis. The children were tearing along hand in hand with Ragonde and Jeanette hurrying at their heels.

Ragonde flung a despairing look at Sir Francis. 'My apologies, sir, they are very excited to see the heralds.'

Laura and Dennis rushed up to the heralds and stared solemnly at their richly emblazoned tunics. Pointing at a trumpet, Dennis turned to Ragonde. 'Mama, I should like to try a trumpet. May I? Please?'

Ragonde bit her lip. She looked mortified. 'I am sorry, sir.'

'No need to apologise, Lady Ragonde. I was a child once,' Sir Francis said. Bernadette could tell from the warmth in his tone that Dennis was not going to be made to suffer for his father's sins. Sir Francis had already made his decision. Dennis would be allowed to live with Ragonde and Aleran, and with Hugo as his guardian, the bastide town of Fourcès would eventually be his.

Dennis was jiggling with excitement. 'Mama, please?'

Epilogue

Nérac Castle—1343

Autumn was with them once more. In the field strips wheat was being harvested. Hazelnuts were ripening by the roadside. And why on earth wasn't Hugo back from patrol? Bernadette wondered as, hand on her belly, she hurried up the stairs to the solar. She had been in the kitchen checking that supper was going to be perfect when their visitors had arrived. A loud guffaw brought a smile to her lips. She would recognise her father's laugh anywhere.

At last, her family were here! The visit had been arranged in a flurry of letters between Nérac and Galard. Even Sybille, who usually moved heaven and earth to avoid long journeys, had promised to come. In her last letter, Allis had mentioned that she and Leon were bringing little Lucas. Hugo really should be here to greet them.

Bernadette was tired, yet she had never been happier. The months had passed in a satisfying frenzy of activity. With Ragonde and Lady Celeste's assistance, Nérac had been restored to its former glory. The last of the cobwebs had been whisked away; spiders had been evicted from dark corners.

Thanks to the services of Smudge and Slayer, two of the kittens that Dennis and Jeanette had found in the garden, the cellar was clear of mice and rats. With help from an army of servants, the results were astonishing. Tapestries hung on the walls. Floors gleamed.

She pushed open the solar door and her family leapt to their feet and surged towards her. Allis reached her first and flung her arms about her. 'Bernadette, you look marvellous.' She glanced at Bernadette's belly, which was so large it was impossible to ignore. 'Many, many congratulations. How do you feel?'

'Like a whale.'

Allis laughed. 'You have grown more than I expected, but you are beautiful.'

Eyes twinkling, Lord Michel elbowed Allis aside. 'Allis, allow me to greet the Countess, if you will.' With a courtly flourish, he caught Bernadette's hand and kissed it. 'My lady, you do look well.'

'Thank you, Papa.'

Her father subjected her to a thorough scrutiny. 'You have been overdoing it though, there are shadows under your eyes. Come, sit down. We can catch up with our news while you rest.'

Bernadette allowed her father to lead her to a chair

and sank on to a plump, embroidered cushion. 'I am a little weary,' she admitted, 'but I do not expect to be brought to bed until Michaelmas and that is a couple of weeks away.'

She was not about to admit that she had had strange tightenings in her belly all day. They were not painful, but she was at a loss to explain them, unless it was that she was still a little nervous about childbed. Most of her fears had gone, but not all. She would be glad when it was over.

At least she did not have to worry about the sex of her unborn child. Hugo had told her more than once that he would welcome a daughter as much as a son. Angel, he had said, all that matters is that you come through easily and that our babe is healthy.

Bernadette smiled at her sister's husband Leon, the only guest who was still on his feet. He was holding a young baby with a mop of dark hair and his mother's blue eyes. 'Leon, welcome.'

'Thank you, my lady. This young fellow is Lucas.'

Eagerly, Bernadette held out her arms. 'Will you permit me to hold him?'

Leon settled Lucas on her lap and her eyes misted as she gazed at her nephew. Leon gave her a concerned look. 'My lady, are you well?'

'Thank you, Leon, I am. It is just that I have wished to see you all...' her glance took in everyone '...for far too long.'

Nodding, Leon leaned forward and kissed her on

both cheeks. 'You have been equally missed, I assure you.'

Lucas waved a plump fist, caught the edge of her veil, and gave it an experimental tug. Her father cleared his throat. 'We brought your chattels with us—the bed and the rest of the furniture that form part of your dowry.'

'Thank you, Papa, Hugo will be delighted. The bed we are using is rather too short for a man of his stature.'

'I guessed as much. We saw Sir Gilebert downstairs, and I took the liberty of asking him to see that your bed was assembled in your chamber without delay.' He paused. 'By the by, how are Hugo's brother and sister-in-law?'

'They are both well. Once Hugo accepted that his brother would never recover enough to retain the title, he insisted they remained here. They have taken a set of apartments on the ground floor, to make it easier for Aleran.'

'Aleran is recovering then?'

'He is stronger every day.'

'And Laura and Dennis? I was surprised when you wrote to say that they had decided to keep them both.'

'Papa, Dennis may not be Aleran's son, but he is much loved.'

Her father grimaced. 'His prospects, as the son of Raoul Sérillac de Fourcès, a man executed for treason and sedition, are bound to be bleak.'

'No, Papa, on the contrary. Hugo has thought of a way of giving Dennis a bright future. Hugo has inherited Fourcès, and he has persuaded the King that when Dennis comes of age, it will be his.'

'Hugo is a good lad,' her father muttered. 'Not many men would be so generous.'

'Dennis is a sweet child. He and Laura get on well together. You will see.' Just then, another twinge rippled across Bernadette's belly. Inhaling slowly, she leaned back in her chair and allowed Lucas to play with her veil while it passed.

'This ceiling is most elegantly wrought,' her father remarked. The plasterwork above their heads looked like a diamond-shaped net, and each diamond contained a different motif—a rose, a rabbit, a fiery sun. Waiting for the tightness in her belly to ease, Bernadette listened with half an ear. She had been delighted when a sun had also emerged from beneath layers of grime on the hood of the fireplace—a dazzling gold disc dominating an azure field.

Her father pointed. 'I assume that sun represents the sun on the Nérac coat of arms.'

'It does.' Bernadette shuffled on her cushion and held back a grimace. Her back was really beginning to ache. And why was Allis frowning at her like that?

'Leon, be so good as to take Lucas,' Allis said. 'I believe Bernadette would like me to see her bedchamber.'

Lucas was lifted from her arms. 'Allis?' Bernadette's heart fluttered. Her hands, she noticed, had started to shake. 'Do you think it has begun?'

'I am not sure,' Allis said calmly. 'But there is nothing to be lost by going to your bedchamber. I will feel happier knowing your bed has been properly assembled and all is in readiness.'

'But, Allis, it is too soon,' Bernadette objected, hand on her belly. 'It is not yet Michaelmas. The cradle we were given at our wedding feast is still in the attic.'

'Babies choose their own time,' Allis said. 'I think we had best get that cradle down.' Gently, but firmly, Allis began leading her from the solar.

'Allis, dear?' Sybille called after them. When you need me, you must not hesitate to call for me.'

'Thank you, Sybille.'

'The baby cannot come yet,' Bernadette muttered, on a wave of panic. 'Not with Hugo still out on patrol. He promised he would be here. *He promised.*'

Gui and Pierre were hanging about by a water trough when Hugo rode in. As he dismounted, he saw new worry lines etched on Gui's face. Hugo tossed the reins to him. 'Something is troubling you, Gui?'

'No, my lord.' Gui hesitated. 'But we want you to know that everyone is praying for the Countess.'

Hugo turned to stone. 'They are praying for her? Why? What's happened?' It could not be the baby; the baby was due at Michaelmas.

'Lady Bernadette's travail is upon her, my lord,' Pierre said.

Seized with a terrible urgency, Hugo tossed his cloak at his squire and tore into the castle. Up the stairs, past the solar and along the corridor, going at such a pace his lungs were burning when he shot into the bedchamber.

Bernadette was propped up in bed, a bundle in her arms. Her cheeks were faintly flushed, and she was smiling. Smiling! Hugo stumbled towards her, vaguely conscious she was not alone, but he only had eyes for his wife. 'Angel.' He sank on to the side of the bed, unable to form any other word. 'Angel.'

Bernadette touched his cheek. 'I am sorry you were not here when he arrived, Hugo, but our son was impatient to get here.'

'Our son,' he managed to say, dazed, as behind him soft footsteps tiptoed towards the door. Allis, he rather thought, and Sybille. Thank God they had got to Nérac in time. The latch clicked shut behind them. 'It went well?'

'It was unbelievably intense,' Bernadette said. 'I expect that is why it happened so quickly. Here, look.' She adjusted the baby's wrappings and he found himself gazing in awe at a tiny, wrinkled face.

'He is asleep.' *Our son, we have a son.*

'He will waken soon, I am sure.' She paused. 'And perhaps by then we will have brought that cradle down from the attic.'

'I will see to that.' Later. Hugo's eyes burned. 'He is the most beautiful baby in the world. Angel, I am sorry I was not here. Were you afraid?'

She gave a soft laugh. 'A little, but there was not much time for fear. It certainly helped to have Allis and Sybille with me.' Her smile was warm. Sleepy. 'Put it this way, I no longer dread the thought of childbirth. To have a baby at the end of it—Hugo, it is such a miracle. You will be glad to hear that, God willing, I am happy give you more children, when I am recovered, of course.'

'Of course.' Settling himself firmly at her side, Hugo kissed her gently on the mouth and reached for his son. 'Here, let me hold him, you are half asleep.' When he had the baby safe in his arms, he took the first proper look at what they were lying on and frowned. 'Angel, this bed—'

'Is our old one from Galard.' She yawned. 'Papa brought all our chattels with him.'

Hugo grinned. 'Thank God for that. I am very pleased to see this bed.'

'You, my lord, are a rogue.' Bernadette gave a sleepy laugh and leaned her head against him. 'I rather thought you would be.'

* * * * *

COMING SOON!

We really hope you enjoyed reading this book. If you're looking for more romance be sure to head to the shops when new books are available on

Thursday 20th July

MILLS & BOON®

Coming next month

A LAIRD WITHOUT A PAST
Jeanine Englert

Where are my clothes? Why am I naked?

What was going on?

A dog barked, and Royce lowered into a battle stance putting out his hands to defend his body.

'Easy, boy. Easy,' he commanded.

The dog barked again and nudged his wet nose to Royce's hand. Royce opened his palm, and the dog slathered his hand with its tongue and released a playful yip. Royce exhaled, his shoulders relaxing. He pet the dog's wiry hair and took a halting breath as his heart tried to regain a normal rhythm.

A latch clanked behind him followed by the slow, creaky opening of a door, and Royce whirled around to defend himself, blinking rapidly to clear his vision but still seeing nothing.

'Who are you?' he ordered, his voice stern and commanding as he felt about for a weapon, any weapon. His hand closed around what felt like a vase, and he held it high in the air. 'And how dare you keep me prisoner here. Release me!'

'Sailor's fortune' a woman cried. 'I think my soul left my body; you gave me such a fright. You are no prisoner,' a woman stated plainly. 'By all that's holy, cover yourself. And put down the vase. It was one of my mother's favourites.'

Light footfalls sounded away from him, but Royce stood poised to strike. He stared out into the darkness confused. Where was he and what was happening? And why was some woman speaking to him as if she knew him.

The door squeaked as it closed followed by the dropping of a latch.

'Then why am I here?' he demanded, still gripping the vase, unwilling to set it aside for clothes. Staying alive trumped any sense of propriety. She might not be alone.

'I cannot say. You were face down in the sand being stripped of your worldly possessions when I discovered you.' A pot clanged on what sounded to be a stove. 'Care to put on some trews? They are dry now.'

'Are you alone?' he asked, shifting from one foot to another staring out into the black abyss.

'Aye,' she chuckled.

He relaxed his hold on the vase, felt for the mattress, and sat down fighting off the light-headedness that made him feel weak in the knees.

'Could I trouble you to light a candle if you do not plan to kill me? I cannot see a blasted thing, and I would very much like to put on those trews you mentioned.'

Continue reading
A LAIRD WITHOUT A PAST
Jeanine Englert

Available next month
www.millsandboon.co.uk

MILLS & BOON

THE HEART OF ROMANCE

A ROMANCE FOR EVERY READER

MODERN
Prepare to be swept off your feet by sophisticated, sexy and seductive heroes, in some of the world's most glamourous and romantic locations, where power and passion collide.

HISTORICAL
Escape with historical heroes from time gone by. Whether your passion is for wicked Regency Rakes, muscled Vikings or rugged Highlanders, awaken the romance of the past.

MEDICAL
Set your pulse racing with dedicated, delectable doctors in the high-pressure world of medicine, where emotions run high and passion, comfort and love are the best medicine.

True Love
Celebrate true love with tender stories of heartfelt romance, from the rush of falling in love to the joy a new baby can bring, and a focus on the emotional heart of a relationship.

Desire
Indulge in secrets and scandal, intense drama and sizzling hot action with heroes who have it all: wealth, status, good looks…everything but the right woman.

HEROES
The excitement of a gripping thriller, with intense romance at its heart. Resourceful, true-to-life women and strong, fearless men face danger and desire - a killer combination!

To see which titles are coming soon, please visit

millsandboon.co.uk/nextmonth